A resourceful beauty's determination
to locate the true father
of a poor foundling sets off
a society scandal—and ignites a fire
in handsome Reggie Carmarthen's
world-weary, aristocratic heart,
in **Stephanie Laurens**'s unforgettable . . .

Lost and Found

Captivated by the fetching,
marriage-wary noblewoman
he finds concealed in his shrubbery,
Harry Chamberlain, the roguish
Earl of Granville, agrees to help the
delightful lady escape . . . while hatching
a plan to woo and win her himself,
in **Christina Dodd**'s smoldering . . .

The Third Suitor

A wounded hero, James Reyburn
has no expectations of romance—
until a storm-tossed beauty
with a secret blows into his life
in **Elizabeth Boyle**'s enchanting . . .

The Matchmaker's Bargain

STEPHANIE LAURENS

CHRISTINA DODD

ELIZABETH BOYLE

Hero, Come Back

AVON BOOKS

An Imprint of HarperCollins*Publishers*

AVON BOOKS
An Imprint of HarperCollins*Publishers*
10 East 53rd Street
New York, New York 10022-5299

ISBN: 0-7394-5436-6

Contents

Lost and Found
Stephanie Laurens

One

London
September 1834

They were twits—foolish, fashionable, and frivolous.

Reggie Carmarthen stood in Hyde Park beyond the end of Rotten Row, and studied the tonnish females currently gathered about the Avenue with a distinctly jaundiced eye. Especially the younger ladies, those desirous of finding a husband.

Their shrill laughter reached him. The ton was drifting back to the capital for the September and October round of balls and parties. In and about their mamas' coaches lined up along the carriage-way, the unmarried young ladies chatted avidly, exchanging the latest news, every one of them hoping, soon, to feature in the latest story. Sun glanced off artfully arranged curls or was deflected by fringed parasols. The breeze flirted with full skirts, teasing the myriad ruffles currently in vogue.

Fashions had changed over the last ten years, but little else had—he felt not the slightest wish to marry any one of the young things parading in the morning sunshine.

With an inward humph, he swung away and determinedly strolled west across the lawns, leaving the fashionable horde behind.

Despite his antipathy, he had to think of marrying. He was thirty-two. His mother had dropped hints, increasingly pointed ones, over the past decade, but she knew she could push him only so far—after a few failed attempts, she'd refrained from pressing specific young ladies on him. This morning, however, the dam of her patience had broken, ruptured by the news of his great-uncle's failing health.

His great-uncle was the Earl of Carlisle; his father, Herbert Carmarthen, presently Viscount Northcote, was the earl's heir. Which meant he, Reggie, would, on his uncle's death and his father's accession to the earldom, step up to his father's present title.

Those facts were widely known, yet waking one morning to find himself Northcote was guaranteed, as his mother had waspishly informed him that morning, to focus the attention of every last matchmaking mama on him.

He could either exercise his prerogative and select a wife forthwith, or be inundated with candidates.

Reaching the carriageway that separated Hyde Park from Kensington Gardens, he paused. The looming threat filled his mind. Crossing the gravel, he walked into the heavily shaded walks of the gardens; in the less fashionable area there were only a few nursemaids and matrons quietly strolling.

The idea of marriage had gradually been gaining ground in his conscious mind. Visits, summer and winter, to old friends like the Fulbridges and the Ashfords were largely to blame—impossible not to notice the satisfaction, the stability, the strength that successful marriage wrought. The Cynster twins, now Amanda Fulbridge and Amelia Ashford, had been his closest friends from childhood and had remained so through the years; the Cynster family in all its various branches numbered among his parents's closest acquaintances. If ever there was a case to be made for marriage, the Cynsters as a group exemplified all that was best, all that could be achieved in that sphere.

Other friends, too, had succumbed; most were quite contented now, even if that had not been their initial expectation. A few male friends remained bachelors, yet the companionship and activites they shared no longer satisfied as once they had.

Marriage.

His mother was right—it was time he took the plunge. And far better to make the choice himself rather than have it thrust upon him.

He was naturally inclined to laissez-faire—to leaving well enough alone—yet in this case letting matters slide was not an option; to simply stand waiting and let the matchmaking mamas have at him would be the action of a lunatic.

He had to make up his mind and act swiftly.

So whom should he marry? In which direction should he look?

What he had to offer was easily catalogued—a family ranked within the haut ton, sufficient wealth to make actual amounts of no account, and ultimately the earldom and all that meant. He possessed an even temperament, was not given to excess in any sphere, was experienced and assured in all tonnish matters, and was handsome enough—admittedly not the sort who drew eyes or stood out in a crowd, yet the ladies with whom he'd shared liaisons over the years had never complained.

His lips twisted wryly. He suspected his quiet, unassuming handsomeness was viewed as less threatening by many ladies, in some cases as less in competition with their own beauty. Regardless, he was content with his appearance, confident in it.

So what of the lady he would wed? An infinitely more difficult question. He hadn't met her, or any like her, yet. He felt not the slightest connection—physical, intellectual, or emotional—with the young things paraded by their mamas through the ballrooms, the silly, giggling horde from which society would expect him to make his choice.

He wanted . . . someone different. Not, as some might suppose, a lady like Amanda or Amelia. Some of their traits he appreciated, like their honesty and courage, their intelligence, their understanding of their world; others, like their wildness, their willfulness, underpinned by their inherent Cynster strength, he could do without—such traits were too powerfully disruptive.

He wanted . . . a lady with whom he could converse sensibly, who shared his views and his liking for a peaceful existence, a lady with whom he could share a pleasant life . . .

Voices reached him. A gentleman's, tones harsh, denying; a lady's, soft and urgent.

The sounds jerked him back to the here and now; he realized his feet had led him down one of the garden's winding paths. The voices came from just ahead, the speakers screened by the next bend.

His first impulse was to retreat undetected, but then the lady spoke again. Memory pricked— instinct came to the fore.

Apparently nonchalantly, he strolled on.

Jaw stubbornly set, Anne Ashford kept her gaze fixed on Lord Elderby's face.

"What you are suggesting is preposterous!" Elderby shifted his cane to his other hand and frowned at the young boy Anne held firmly by the hand.

She could feel Benjy quiver, but he didn't cower as any child might if faced by Elderby's black scowl; she wondered if Benjy recognized the face he would see if he frowned into any reflecting surface.

"The truth is not preposterous at all, my lord. The evidence is clearly before you." She resisted the urge to wave at Benjy; the resemblance between the nine-year-old foundling and his lordship was too marked to require further comment. She lifted her chin. "I'm sure if you consider the matter you will see there is only one reasonable course of action."

Elderby shifted his dark gaze to her face; she thought he paled.

"My dear Miss Ashford." For all he was shaken, he spoke incisively. "You have patently no idea what such a revelation might mean, or in what matter of subject you are meddling."

Tall, thin, well-dressed, he cut a figure of some distinction.

"On the contrary, my lord, we move in the same circles, as you are well aware. I know precisely what the evidence before us demonstrates." Greatly daring, she added, "What I have yet to hear is what you, and your family, propose to do about it."

Elderby very nearly goggled. It was a moment before he could speak; when he did, his voice was low. "Are you threatening—"

"My lord!" Anne opened her eyes wide. "I'm shocked at the notion you could in any way connect the concept of threat with this subject."

Elderby blinked; she'd left him very few avenues of escape.

After a moment, he compressed his lips, then said, "This has come as a shock. You will have to let me consider—"

He broke off and looked past her. Gravel scrunched behind her; instantly Elderby glanced down at Benjy.

She drew Benjy closer.

A pleasant voice said, "Good afternoon, Miss Ashford. Elderby."

She turned as Reggie Carmarthen joined them, nodding urbanely to Elderby. With his customary lazy, good-humored grace, Reggie reached for her hand; she'd given it to him before she'd thought. He met her eyes with an easy smile, shook her hand, but didn't release it. Calmly he set it on his sleeve, as if he were her cavalier and she'd been waiting for him to join her.

"Odd place to stroll, although it is quiet, I grant you. Thought I saw your mama's carriage—we should head back before she gets impatient."

That was a lie; she hadn't come with her mother. Reggie smiled innocuously at Elderby; he couldn't see Benjy, on her other side, screened by her wide skirts.

Elderby threw her a dark yet uncertain look, then bowed stiffly. "If you'll excuse me, Miss Ashford." He hesitated, then added, "I'll be in touch in due course."

It was, realistically, the best she could hope for; suppressing her mental curses at Reggie's interruption, she inclined her head. "Indeed, my lord. We'll look forward to hearing from you shortly."

With a last glance at Benjy, Elderby nodded curtly to Reggie, set his hat on his head, and strode away.

Reggie watched Elderby go, then let his expression of amiable idiocy fade. He turned to Anne. "What the devil was that about?"

The look she threw him was complex; she was irritated with him for interrupting, but there was stubbornness and a certain assessment in her gaze. She hesitated, then drew the young lad who'd been standing on her other side forward. "Allow me to present Benjamin. Benjy, this is Mr. Carmarthen."

The boy glanced at her, then at him, then bowed, a trifle awkwardly. "Good afternoon, sir."

Reggie blinked. Anne had not supplied the boy's

surname—hardly necessary. The striking features borne by all male Caverlocks, currently numbering the old Duke of Portsmouth, his heir, Hugh, Marquess of Elderby, and his second son Lord Thomas Caverlock, a peer of Reggie's, looked up at him as the boy straightened.

He held out his hand, and solemnly shook Benjamin's. "Pleased to make your acquaintance."

What the hell was going on?

Releasing Benjamin, Reggie looked at Anne. He'd recognized her soft voice, and all notion of politely retreating had vanished. Anne was Amelia's sister-in-law, Luc Ashford's second sister, known to all family and close friends as highly nervous in crowds.

They hadn't met for some years; he suspected she avoided tonnish gatherings. Rapid calculation revealed she must be twenty-six. She seemed . . . perhaps an inch taller, more assured, more definite, certainly more striking than he recalled, but then she wasn't shrinking against any wall at the moment. She was elegantly turned out in a dark green walking dress. Her expression was open, decided, her face framed by lustrous brown hair caught up in a topknot, then allowed to cascade about her head in lush waves. Her eyes were light brown, the color of caramel, large and set under delicately arched brows. Her lips were blush rose, sensuously curved, decidedly vulnerable.

Intensely feminine.

As were the curves of breast and waist revealed by the tightly fitting bodice . . .

Jerking his mind from the unexpected track, he frowned. "Now cut line—what is this about?"

A frown lit her eyes, a warning one. "I'll explain once we've returned Benjy to the House." Retaking Benjy's hand, she turned back along the path.

Reggie pivoted and fell in beside her. "Which house? Is Luc in town?"

"No. Not Calverton House." Anne hesitated, then added, more softly, "The Foundling House."

Pieces of the puzzle fell, jigsawlike, into place, but the picture in his mind was incomplete. His long strides relaxed, he retook her arm, wound it with his, forcing her to slow. "Much better to stroll without a care, rather than rush off so purposefully. No need for the ignorant to wonder what your purpose is."

The look she cast him was, again, assessing, but she obediently slowed.

"This House—I vaguely recall hearing that you and your sisters had become involved in some charity of that sort."

Anne nodded, fighting to quell the peculiar skittishness dancing along her nerves. This was Reggie; she'd known him for years. She couldn't understand why her senses were leaping, let alone explain the fact it wasn't in fear. She drew breath, aware of a tightness in her chest. "Portia and Penelope became involved first, when it was merely an idea. You know what they're like."

"Two more determined and opinionated young ladies it would be difficult to find."

"Yes, well, they joined with three other ladies and established the Foundling House for training some of the foundlings who pass through the Foundling Hospital in Bloomsbury. Some of them are quite presentable." She paused, then added, "Like Benjy."

She sensed Reggie's glance but didn't meet it; she was acutely conscious of him as he paced beside her. "We train as many as we can for work as maids, footmen, and so on. It gives them a means to earn their way."

"I see."

Reggie glanced at Benjy, striding manfully along on her other side, but he asked no more.

They reached the edge of the park. Reggie hailed a hackney, handed her up, then waved Benjy in. Reggie followed and sat opposite her. To her surprise, he engaged Benjy, drawing the boy out about his life at the Foundling House.

Gaining Benjy's trust.

She realized that when, without any prompting, Benjy offered, " 'Course, afore—*before* that, I lived with my mum. Up Clerkenwell way. But she died." A shadow passed over his young face.

"And was that when you came to the hospital?"

Benjy shook his head. "There were others in the street—old Mrs. Nichols, and the Patricks, and Mrs. Kieghly—they looked after me for a while. But then Mrs. Nichols died, and the Patricks moved north. Seemed best, they said, for me to go to the hospital then."

Anne took Benjy's hand, smiled when he looked up at her. "Benjy's a star pupil of Penelope's. He's been at the Foundling House for a year now."

While they'd dithered and wondered, until age had stripped enough from Benjy's face to establish the Caverlock features beyond doubt.

Benjy looked at Reggie. "It's good there. Better'n a lot of other places I might have ended at."

Reggie smiled easily and sat back, apparently amiably content; Anne wasn't so gullible as to believe it. She caught his eye, glimpsed the underlying seriousness behind his easygoing, almost foppishly unthreatening mask. A mask that, with the years, sat increasingly ill; she was perfectly aware Reggie was no fool, but often hid his perceptiveness—his knowledge of the world, of the ton and its intrigues—behind an inconsequential facade.

She'd first become aware of him as more than a mere acquaintance when she and her older sister, Emily, had had their Season. Reggie had been forever in Amanda and Amelia's train, and the twins had been great friends, supporting her and Emily. So they'd met Reggie often; he'd always seemed slighter, shorter than her brother Luc, much less overwhelmingly male. Now, however . . .

She glanced across the carriage, masking the action as an effect of the swaying.

Reggie was still a few inches shorter than Luc, but then her brother was over six feet tall. Any slightness, however, had fled with the years; Reggie's shoulders were broad, his chest muscled and wide—there was no extraneous padding in his coat. He was fashionably but quietly dressed, not to stand out but to fit into the scene, style, fabric, and color carefully chosen to project an image of simple elegance, the hallmark of a true gentleman. His hair was pale brown, fashionably cut to frame his head; he wore no hat, but carried a cane, his long fingers curled about the ornate silver head.

His face—that was the physical aspect hardest to define. Chameleonlike, he could appear quite insignificant, utterly bland, and of no account, yet when he dropped all pretense, there was a clearness in his gaze and a firmness about his lips and chin that spoke of quiet strength, common sense, and an unwavering hold on his world.

The carriage slowed. She looked out of the window; the railings circling the yard of the Foundling House came into view. Given what she'd undertaken, what she'd started through her meeting with Elderby, Reggie might just be the godsend she needed.

Leaving Reggie outside the main office, Anne returned Benjy to the matron-in-charge, Mrs. Keggs, then, once Benjy had hurried out to join the other boys, remained to tell Mrs. Keggs of the outcome of their mission.

"His lordship should be properly 'umbled, and do the right thing by the lad." Mrs. Keggs fluffed like an agitated hen. "He's a good lad, he is—no reason he couldn't hold his head high, not even in his lordship's circles."

"Indeed—we must hope his lordship sees the light. But if he doesn't, we'll simply persevere. I chose to approach Lord Elderby first, but there are other members of the family I could contact, and will if need be."

With an encouraging smile, she left Mrs. Keggs and returned to the office. From the bench outside, his legs stretched out, booted ankles crossed, Reggie watched as she went inside. The look in his eyes stayed in her mind; in his chameleonlike way, he could be seriously helpful should she enlist his aid.

As quickly as she could, she dealt with the various matters awaiting her attention in her capacity as the House's administrator in charge of the children's welfare. Penelope was in charge of their education; Portia handled the fund-raising and public awareness. Anne's sole concern was the children themselves, their well-being, their happiness, their futures.

She was perusing an account for candles when a large shadow blocked the doorway. Looking up, she saw Reggie; he caught her eye and raised a brow.

Color rose in her cheeks; she gestured to the small pile of accounts before her. "I really must deal with these."

His eyes held hers, then he nodded. "I'll wait."

He drew back; she imagined him heading back to the hard bench. She got the distinct impression he'd thought she was trying to evade him—make him wait until he grew bored, gave up all thought of interfering, and left. Lips lifting, she turned back to the bills.

Fifteen minutes later, she rose, bade the secretary good bye, and went out. Reggie uncurled his legs and stood as she approached; falling in beside her, he closed his hand about her elbow and escorted her down the steps. As if he didn't intend to let her go until he learned all he wished. Hailing a hackney, he assisted her into it, then followed and closed the door.

"Now!" He frowned at her. "What the devil did you think to achieve by shocking Elderby into incoherence by confronting him with—"

He broke off. She continued, "With Benjamin, a close relative?"

Lips thin, Reggie nodded. "Indeed."

She thought back. "He was truly shocked, wasn't he? He didn't know."

"He nearly had heart failure. And yes, I agree—he didn't know the boy existed. He was shocked by an unknown, not surprised and angry that something he knew about had surfaced."

"Exactly!" Pleased to have her reading of Elderby's reaction confirmed, she eagerly continued, "So if Benjy is not Elderby's son, then . . ."

To her surprise, Reggie frowned. He studied her eyes, then stated, "If you're asking me, I wouldn't like to guess."

It was her turn to frown. "But that only leaves Thomas, doesn't it? And given his reputation, it hardly seems a long bow to draw—"

"Before you get too far down that road, there're a few points you should consider. Yes, Thomas could be Benjamin's father, but if so, the liaison happened when Thomas was in his early twenties and hardly difficult to approach. The boy says he was living with his mother in Clerkenwell—had she told Thomas? If so, rake or not, I find it hard to believe Thomas would not have done something—it's not as if these things are not commonplace enough. The Caverlock estates are scattered over half the country; easy enough to send the boy and his mother somewhere to live in reasonable safety."

"That's assuming Thomas thinks as you do."

Reggie studied her, then replied, "Thomas and I are not that different."

She blinked. Lord Thomas Caverlock was a gazetted rake.

"Aside from anything else," Reggie went on, "there's the undeniable fact you illustrated this afternoon. Caverlocks breed true. Everyone knows that. Forehead, eyebrows, nose, mouth, and chin—they're all cast from the same mold. Thomas, and Hugh, too, if they'd known of a boy child, would know there was no hope of denying paternity."

Anne digested that; as the carriage turned into Mount Street, she asked, "There aren't any other branches of the family, are there?"

"No. Just the ducal line."

She drew in a breath, focused on Reggie. "So what do you advise? I don't intend to let the matter rest."

The look he bent on her stated he was perfectly aware of that last. "Give Elderby a chance to consider, to take stock and determine the truth. He's a dry stick, but he'll do it."

"The truth?"

"Which one of the three of them is Benjamin's sire."

"Three?"

The carriage rocked to a halt outside Calverton House; Reggie reached for the door. "You've forgotten old Portsmouth. There's a decent possibility Benjamin's father wears the purple."

She honestly hadn't considered that; it cast the potential for scandal should the Caverlocks resist in an even stronger light.

Three nights later, Anne stood in the receiving line wending up Lady Hendrick's stairs, the possible breadth of the secret she herself had let out of its box very much in her mind.

Hugh, Lord Elderby, was married and had been for over ten years. She placed him in his late thirties. His wife, Imogen, was a woman of few smiles, and those that dawned were rather sour. Reggie had called Hugh a dry stick, but Imogen was drier, and even more sticklike. Anne doubted the child was Hugh's, although it was possible he'd had a liaison and had never been told of Benjy's birth, but regardless of which of the three Caverlock males proved to be Benjy's father, Imogen was not going to be pleased.

At her mother's heels, Anne reached their hostess and exchanged greetings, determinedly ignoring the old familiar panic welling inside. Lady Hendrick was delighted to see her; she'd eschewed large parties and balls for some years, seeing no need to feed the silly nervousness she'd never grown out of.

Tonight, however, would be different; she wasn't here to look for a husband, to allow herself to be weighed and considered. She was here for a purpose; she had a goal to pursue. She'd dressed for the task in a gown of mulberry silk that she knew became her, as did the latest fashion of fitted waists and skirts held wide with multiple petticoats.

Leaving Lady Hendrick, she paused at the entrance to the ballroom, drew in a deep breath, lifted her head—and let her gaze take in the sea of people, let her ears hear the cacophony of voices.

To her surprise, neither sight nor sound evoked as much fear as she'd expected. As much trepidation as in the past.

Somewhat reassured, she followed her mother into the throng.

From the shadows of an archway where he stood chatting with friends, Reggie watched Anne glide after her mother, Minerva, the Dowager Lady Calverton, to a chaise by the wall. He hesitated, then, with an easy word, excused himself and moved into the crowd.

For the past two days, he'd been watching, wondering . . . it had surprised him how fixed his mind had become on Anne Ashford and her endeavors. Especially on her attempt to jog the collective Caverlock conscience.

Invited as he was to every major ball and party, it had been easy to guess which events Hugh, Imogen, and Thomas would attend. Anne would not attend any such affair by choice; if she hadn't appeared, he would have concluded that Hugh had acted swiftly and the family had assured Benjamin's future in some acceptable way.

He now knew that hadn't happened. Yet. He had a deeper appreciation than she of the difficulties Hugh would face in raising the matter and seeing it appropriately dealt with. However, he was also acquainted with the Ashford temperament—none of them was patient.

What scheme Anne was hatching he didn't know—he just knew there would be one.

Reaching the chaise, he bowed to Minerva; she

was one of his mother's closest friends. Lady Far-well and Mrs. Pickering sat beside her; while uttering the usual greetings and platitudes, he wondered what Minerva made of her daughter's presence. She would know there had to be a reason, yet she was probably glad of any circumstance that brought Anne out, into the ton.

Eventually drawing back from the older ladies, he turned to Anne, standing beside the chaise. Her curtsy, his bow dispensed with, he offered his arm. "Would you care to stroll?"

Her smile was quick, illuminating her face. "Please."

Minerva inclined her head graciously as he met her eye. Anne's hand on his sleeve, he steered her into the crowd; it quickly closed about them. Leaning closer, he inquired, "Just what are you planning?"

She looked up, searched his eyes.

He felt his expression harden. "You needn't imagine I'll swallow any tale that you were suddenly visited by an unquenchable urge to reacquaint yourself with the gadding throng. Given you're here, you're here for a reason." He held her gaze. "What?"

Her lips thinned, but her decision to include him in her confidence flowed across her eyes. The sight was unexpectedly satisfying.

"Lord Elderby hasn't contacted us. Doubtless he's imagining the matter will simply disappear if he ignores it." She looked ahead, head rising, and started to scan the faces. "I decided it was time to speak to at least one other member of the family. Both Thomas and Imogen will most likely be here."

Reggie drew in a breath—through his teeth. His features had set, but he was too wise in the ways of determined women to simply say no. He clung to impassivity. "Imogen should be last on your list. While she would most likely make no bones about a mistake of Thomas's, if Benjamin is Hugh's, or worse, Portsmouth's, then she might well see him as a threat. Her eldest son must be only a few months younger than Benjamin."

Anne frowned, but after a moment nodded. "It'll have to be Lord Thomas, then."

If he'd mentally goggled at the notion of her bearding Elderby with the existence of a family by-blow, he reeled at the thought of her approaching Lord Thomas Caverlock with the same news. "No!"

She turned her head and stared at him. "No? What do you mean—no? Of course I'm going to speak to him—"

"No. You're not." Her hand slid from his sleeve; Reggie gripped her elbow and had no intention of letting go. "You are not going to march up to a rake like Caverlock and blithely inform him you happen to have stumbled on a child of either his, his brother's, or his father's that the family has apparently misplaced, and demand he take responsibility."

"Why not?" Anne drew herself up. "I managed perfectly well with Elderby."

"That was different! This is not the time or place—"

"Are you suggesting I make an appointment to meet with Lord Thomas privately?"

"Of course not!" He glared at her.

She glared back. "I've come here tonight for the sole purpose of speaking with either Imogen or Thomas. I am not going to let the Caverlocks simply forget about Benjy. You have no idea how many other children are in similar straits—forgotten, when the families are more than wealthy enough to provide for them."

She held his gaze fiercely—and fearlessly; it was the first time he'd ever seen her so. So animated, so alive. It momentarily stunned him.

"I am not going to let Benjy down!"

Her eyes flashed, then she twisted her elbow free of his grip and sailed into the crowd.

Inwardly grim, outwardly impassive—still a trifle stunned—Reggie fought a sudden impulse to seize her anew, haul her out of the ballroom and . . .

He shook aside the dizzying compulsion, drew a deep breath, and stepped out in her wake—

"Mr. Carmarthen! *Such* a happy chance!"

Halting precipitously, he focused on the stout matron who'd sidestepped directly into his path. "Er . . ." Who the devil was she? Then he recalled, and bowed perfunctorily. "Lady Hexham. A pleasure." Even as he said it, he lifted his head and scanned the shifting throng. He could no longer see Anne.

"And this is Melissa, my daughter. I daresay you remember her."

He bowed, shook the young lady's hand, and murmured the right things. He'd seen Thomas earlier and knew where he'd be—would Anne guess and make for the card room?

"I've just returned from the north—such a full summer we've had! But we heard the news about Carlisle—have there been any further developments?"

The question recalled Reggie to reality with a thump. He stared into Lady Hexham's hopeful face. "I don't believe so."

Dear God! While he extricated himself with what grace he could muster, his mind raced. Lady Hexham enjoyed a good gossip; the news of his family's pending change in state would soon be rife.

And if the look in Lady Hexham's eyes—let alone Melissa's—was anything to judge by, he was going to be in deep trouble.

Hounded. Hunted.

With a charming smile, he left her ladyship; immediately he turned his back, he replaced the smile with an aggravated frown. Never mind his potential pursuers, where the hell was Anne?

"I would be very much obliged if you could spare me a few minutes of your time, my lord." Anne smiled evenly at Lord Thomas Caverlock. "In private."

Thomas, a handsome devil of a rake who showed no sign of succumbing to any of the highly respectable lures constantly thrown his way, looked down at her, an unreadable expression in his changeable blue-gray eyes. "What a very . . . tantalizing request, my dear."

He studied her face for an instant longer, then

glanced around. The card room was full, the tables host to a goodly throng, both male and female, most engrossed with the play. "Come." He offered his arm. "Let's stroll through the ballroom and see if we can find a quiet corner."

Anne inclined her head and set her fingers on his sleeve. Despite her brave words, she was relieved he'd fixed on a corner of the ballroom, and not on some more deserted spot.

As they walked through the crowd, Thomas quizzed her—on her penchant for avoiding the ton, on her thoughts on society, on her family. Not once did he touch on her reason for seeking him out. Anne parried his queries easily enough, but wondered . . .

Abruptly Thomas changed tack and steered her through an archway into the corridor beyond. Her suspicions leapt to life, but before she could collect herself enough to protest, he threw open another door, and she found herself deftly swept into a small parlor.

She had to scuttle quickly forward or Thomas would have been on her heels—far too close. The door clicked shut in the instant she realized the parlor was quite deserted. It had been years since she'd graced tonnish entertainments—years since she'd worried about such things as compromising situations.

With a jolt of unwelcome surprise, she realized she was in one.

Lips parting in complaint, she swung to face Thomas—

Only to find him much closer than she'd expected.

His arm locked about her waist; smoothly he drew her to him.

It wasn't the gentle laughter in his eyes, but the intent she sensed behind it—an intent she'd never before been the focus of but recognized instinctively—that frightened her; she braced her hands on his chest and pushed back. "My lord—Thomas! Release me at once!"

He chuckled and drew her closer.

She tried to struggle, but his arms were fully around her. "No! You don't understand!"

"Oh, but I do, sweet Anne—most assuredly I do. You've hidden yourself away for years, but now you've decided to enjoy the fruits of life, and I'm flattered, believe me, quite flattered, that you've chosen me—"

"I *haven't*!" Anne kept her voice down with an effort, assisted by the fact that Thomas had at least stopped drawing her closer. "Good heavens! As if I would . . . I mean—" She broke off, painfully aware his misunderstanding was at least partly her fault. "I wanted to *talk* to you. To tell you something!"

The laughter in Thomas's eyes faded, to be replaced by wariness. "What?"

He didn't release her; he was still too close—she could barely breathe. It wasn't fear she felt—she wasn't a ninny; she knew Thomas wouldn't force her—but the feeling of being restrained wasn't pleasant; if she thought about it too much, she might swoon. "Let me go, and I'll tell you."

Thomas's eyes narrowed.

From the door came a sigh. "Let her go, Thomas."

His arms still around her, Thomas turned, allowing Anne to peer past his shoulder.

Reggie stood inside the room, leaning back, nonchalantly graceful, his shoulders against the closed door.

Neither of them had heard him come in.

Reggie's gaze, exceedingly level, was fixed on Thomas. Thomas met it. For one instant, Anne could have sworn some intrinsically masculine communication took place, then Thomas's arms slowly fell from her, and he took a step back, putting an acceptable distance between them.

He frowned, first at Reggie, then, more definitely, at her. "What's going on?"

She straightened, clasping her hands before her, drawing in a deep breath. "I—"

"If you have the slightest sense of self-preservation, you will keep your lips shut."

The force behind the words made her start; she stared, utterly astounded, at Reggie. He'd spoken in his usual even tone, yet the authority beneath it—even more the fury in his eyes—shocked her into silence.

He noted it; apparently satisfied, he looked at Thomas.

"Have you spoken to Hugh recently?"

"Hugh?" Increasingly confused, Thomas shook his head. "He called last afternoon but missed me. He left a message but I haven't found the time—"

"Find the time," Reggie said. "There's something you need to know, and you'd best hear it from him."

Thomas frowned. "Imogen's here—"

"No. Imogen may not be in Hugh's confidence—

not in this." Reggie pulled out his watch, glanced at it. "Daresay Hugh'll be at White's by now." He looked at Thomas. "Don't you think?"

Thomas nodded. "Most likely."

"Well, then." Tucking his watch back in his pocket, Reggie stepped away from the door, opening and holding it wide.

Thomas considered him. "You won't tell me?"

Reggie met his gaze, shook his head. "Family matter. Less said about it by anyone else, the better."

Thomas studied his eyes, then raised his brows. "Very well." He stepped toward the door. "I'll hie myself to White's, then." Swinging around, he swept Anne a bow. "Good evening, Miss Ashford." He straightened; his gaze lingered— unholy appreciation lit his eyes. "Until next time, sweet Anne."

With a devilish smile, he nodded to Reggie and walked from the room.

Reggie very carefully shut the door, grasping the moment to strengthen his hold on his temper. He hadn't even known he possessed one—not of this type, not of this magnitude; subduing it, wrestling it back under control, wasn't a simple matter.

Turning from the door, he looked at Anne, standing, hands still clapsed before her, staring at him. He couldn't truly see anything else in the room. He started toward her. "I believe I told you not to attempt to explain this matter to Thomas?"

He kept his voice level, even, soft; it still brought her chin up.

"It was necessary—"

"No. It wasn't." He was hanging on to his temper by a thread—an increasingly frayed one. "As you just learned, Hugh has been trying to contact Thomas—it's unlikely to be about any other subject. Neither Thomas nor Hugh will think there's any urgency about this matter—Benjamin is presently quite *safe*."

He stepped nearer; his temper infused his last word with enough emphasis to make it quiver.

Her eyes flew wide; she took a step back—as if finally understanding that she wasn't as lucky as Benjamin. "I . . ." Her eyes searched his, then she blinked, drew herself up—and met his gaze defiantly. "I have absolutely no idea why you consider yourself my keeper in this—"

"Just be thankful I do." He stepped forward on the word, and she backed again.

Into a sidetable; without looking, Anne stepped around it. "That's ridiculous. No one would hold you responsible—"

"*I* would. I do!"

He stepped forward again; an air of aggression—not the typical male sort she'd been accustomed to seeing from her earliest years in her brothers, but something finer, more honed—infinitely more dangerous—seemed to shimmer about him. She couldn't stop herself taking another step back.

"But nothing happened! Everything's perfectly all right—"

"No. It isn't."

Stepping back again, she locked her eyes on his. "Thomas now knows—and Hugh hasn't forgotten, so—"

"All is well on the Benjy front. Quite."

On the last, ferociously clipped word, Reggie stepped forward again—and her back hit the wall. She didn't dare blink. He had to be able to see her reaction, yet he took still another step. Deliberately crowding her, leaving her not an inch to breathe.

She'd expected panic to overwhelm her, but it wasn't fear that raced down her veins. She'd never felt excitement, expectation—exhilaration—to match this.

His eyes, furious, cloudy, roiling with anger, held her gaze mercilessly. "All, however," he enunciated softly, "is not right—nowhere near right—on the *Reggie* front."

Raising his hands, he slapped them, palms flat, on the panels on either side of her head—and leaned nearer yet. He was very close. The temptation to drop her gaze to his lips—to lick her own—grew.

She fought to hold his gaze. Managed to find breath enough to ask, "Why are you so angry?"

His eyes searched hers; she saw something shift behind the turmoil, then his features hardened. "Be damned if I know."

The words reached her ears as he bent his head, and his lips found hers.

Not gently. Yet neither was he driven by anger—even in that first instant, she understood that. It was another passion that drove him; she shivered at the first contact, at the realization, one too delicious to resist.

He seemed to know, to sense her recognition; his lips firmed, demanded—she surrendered on a sigh, parting her lips, welcoming him in.

Glorying when he surged in, slow, deep, exploring. Branding, inciting.

She'd been kissed before, but never like this—
never had any man wanted her like this. With a
clear, unbridled passion, one so lacking in guile,
in any attempt at concealment, that it was almost
innocent.

Infinitely more powerful.

Her hands rose of their own volition and rested
on his chest. She felt the heavy thud of his heart
against her palm. She kissed him back, felt his
breath catch—felt his chest swell as he drew
breath, then took her mouth again.

She gave it gladly, pushed her hands up and
twined them about his neck, and lifted away from
the wall. He shifted, easing upright; his arms slid
around her, then closed, steadily, gradually, until
he had molded her to him, until she'd pressed as
tightly to him as she could.

The heat was intoxicating, pouring through her,
from his lips, his mouth, from his body enfolding
hers. She wanted to get nearer still, wanted—very
definitely—more.

He drew back for a moment, releasing her lips,
albeit with obvious reluctance. She lifted her lids,
suddenly heavy, and met his gaze. They were
both breathing rapidly, both heated—both con-
sumed by what, looking into his eyes, she recognized as mutual desire. One part of her mind
mentally blinked in amazement; most of it sang
with hunger. As for her body, it was quivering
with a need she had never felt before, but saw absolutely no reason to deny.

Something of that decision must have shown in

her face. His features were set, unreadable, but his eyes saw; desire flashed, welled. He lowered his head once more; her lips throbbed. His lips were barely an inch from hers—a mere breath—when he hesitated. She grasped the moment, made the decision. Tightening her arms, lifting her head, she sealed their fates.

Reggie drew her deeper into his arms as their lips fused, as she gave herself without reserve, as she tempted him to plunder, her mouth, and her.

Her message was very clear. He didn't even need to think to know he was the first man she'd ever wanted like this, the first man she'd invited even this far. The knowledge sang through his bones, stoked a desire that had already grown far beyond his previous experience.

He wanted her now, with an urgency that was driven by so much more than mere lust, so much more than physical desire. The feel of her, soft, supple, and slender in his arms, pliant under his hands, set his pulse racing. He was giddy, deliciously so, his body aching with a need made all the more potent by knowing it would not have to go unslaked.

Without breaking the kiss, he lifted her, swept her up in his arms, and carried her to the sofa. He'd locked the door after Thomas, more from instinct than design. Thank God for instinct—he didn't think he could leave her now to go even that far. The taste of her was like a drug, one he craved more with every breath, every kiss.

He sat on the sofa, tumbled her down, leaned over her. She murmured encouragingly, arching closer, as urgent as he. He pressed her back, laid a hand on her breast—instantly, she stilled. Not in fear but in concentration; he could sense it through their kiss, feel her attention tracking every movement of his fingers as he learned her shape, stroked her softness until it firmed.

She very quickly wanted more; when he laid her breasts bare, she sighed with pleasure, then gasped when he set his hand, skin to skin, to one soft mound. The peak was already tight; he rubbed it to aching hardness while with her mouth she pleaded eloquently—for what, he was perfectly well aware she didn't know.

It was that knowledge that made him draw back, that drew a line over which his honor would not allow him to step.

His blood thundered in his ears when he eased free of the kiss, drew his lips from hers, raised his head. His hand was still at her breast, his touch possessive, his thumb circling the pebbled nipple.

A moment passed before she drew in a shuddering breath, opened her eyes, and stared into his.

There was no hesitation in her gaze, nothing but a roiling storm of passions and emotions, a mirror to his own. She drew in a deep breath; the movement pressed her breast more firmly to his palm. She glanced down, then back at his face. Raised her brows, tilted her head slightly in question.

His features were locked; he knew precisely what she was asking, what, indeed, she was suggesting—her eyes made no pretense, considered no excuse.

Drawing breath was difficult. "Not yet."

Holding her gaze, he bent his head and touched

his lips to her breast, kissed the aching peak infinitely delicately.

He felt the shudder that racked her, felt his
body harden—knew she felt it, too.

Their gazes locked, held, then her lids fell on a
soft sigh.

On the subject of desire, they understood each
other perfectly.

Two

Be damned if I know.

He'd lied, of course. He did know. Had known, even then.

It seemed he was indeed damned.

Oddly, he didn't feel the least bothered. The only impulse riding him now was one of impatience.

Over breakfast, he relived the previous evening's interlude. He'd been tempted to take her then and there—to make her his beyond all question—regardless of any notions of propriety. She'd been willing, he even more so. And he'd been perfectly willing to marry her thereafter.

What had held him back, drawn him back from the brink, was the knowledge she was so much an innocent, so naive in that sphere, that passion might have swept her away before she'd realized the true nature of what it was that so surprisingly lay between them.

Where it had come from, when it had grown, he had no idea. It simply was; somehow life had shaped them like lock and key.

A memory, a long-ago conversation, resurfaced in his mind. He, Luc Ashford, and Martin Fulbridge had been lolling late one night in some library, alone and well supplied with good brandy. Somehow, the subject of when the other two had recognized their state—the state that had impelled them to marriage—had arisen. Martin had said the realization had dawned slowly, over some weeks, until it had been impossible to ignore, but then Martin had not previously known Amanda. Luc, however, had known Amelia for much the same length of time Reggie had known Anne, and in the same vein of familial friendship; Luc had confessed he'd suddenly—in a flash of understanding—simply known.

Just as Reggie, now, simply knew. It was not a matter of a question and an answer, of an answer that was logically the best fit, but of a reality that needed no further justification. It simply was.

Sitting back, he sipped his coffee and glanced consideringly about the room. The small house in Curzon Street was a perfectly acceptable address to which to bring a new wife. His affairs were in order—there was no impediment to moving quickly in the direction his impatience was pushing him.

He wondered how Luc, Anne's guardian, would react to his request; lips lifting, he had to admit he was looking forward to finding out.

But first . . .

He'd thought, last night, that Anne had understood. That, despite being as surprised as he, she'd recognized what had flared between them for what it was. Yet on the subject of the relationships that might exist between male and female within the ton, he knew she was inexperienced and naive. Even recognizing what was between them, she still might not see what was in his mind.

Might not be prepared to agree.

He knew far too much of women, tonnish ladies especially, to take her acceptance for granted. Best to tread warily, at least until he'd confirmed her views, her understanding.

Confirmed she returned his regard.

Impatience sank its spurs deep. She was twenty-six, no giddy young girl; he was thirty-two—they were both too old to have any interest in games. Too old not to seize the unexpected opportunity. Too old to dither and waste time.

Jaw firming, he set down his cup, rose, settled his coat, straightened his sleeves, and headed for the door.

He'd hoped to find her at home, but on answering his knock, Leighton, the young butler at Calverton House, his own surprise showing, informed him Miss Anne had left with Lady Calverton on her round of morning calls.

"Did her ladyship intend to call at Elderby House?" Reggie asked, as if intending to do so himself and wondering if their paths would cross there.

"Lady Elderby wasn't on her ladyship's list, sir. Would you care to leave a message?"

Reggie favored him with a mild smile. "No, no." His smile hardened as he turned away. "No doubt I'll catch up with them in the park."

He did; as he'd foreseen, Anne was more interested in spotting Imogen Caverlock than in the sprigs of the ton whose eyes she'd caught.

Presuming on their familial acquaintance, he marched boldly up to the Calverton landau the instant it halted on the verge. After exchanging greetings with her mother, who was intrigued but too shrewd to let it show by word or deed, he turned to Anne.

And realized in the instant their eyes touched that she'd tensed, waiting—not quite panicking—wondering what he would say, what he was thinking—how he saw their last meeting, and all it had encompassed.

Impossible to tell her there, with half the ton looking on.

He smiled, genuinely, with warmth and sincerity a degree beyond all he'd ever felt before. "I wondered if you'd care to stroll . . . ?"

Her features softened, lips lifting in a fleeting but still nervous smile. "Thank you. That would be pleasant."

He handed her down; with a nod to Lady Calverton and a promise to return Anne in half an hour, he set her hand on his sleeve and turned her toward the lawn.

He felt her quiver—just for an instant—then her head rose. "Actually"—her voice quavered; she cast him a swift glance, then looked along the row of carriages lining the drive—"I was hoping to see if Imogen was here."

That fleeting glimpse of wide brown eyes was enough to warn him—while she recognized that what had passed between them the previous evening required something be said, it was not a subject she felt at all confident of broaching in their present surrounds.

He debated for only an instant before reining in his impatience. "I assumed as much."

His disapproval rang in his tone; Anne was simply glad he was agreeable to being distracted.

"You absolutely cannot speak to Imogen on this matter."

She glanced at him, her nervousness rapidly retreating. "I wasn't going to say anything about Benjy! I just thought that if she was here, I could simply pass the time—we have been introduced—and just"—she gestured—"*see* if she knew."

Most men would have frowned and asked how; Reggie frowned, but the acceptance in his eyes, the reluctant twist to his lips, said he understood.

She pressed her advantage. "If she knows, she'll be concerned and distracted—it'll show."

"Very well." Inwardly grim, Reggie glanced along the row of carriages. "Let's see if we can find her."

They strolled along the verge, stopping here and there as ladies called greetings. He would have infinitely preferred putting a greater distance between himself and the fond mamas, but if Imogen were there and they wished to approach under the guise of mere socializing, they had to set the stage.

Despite her shyness, Anne determindedly did

her part; only he could tell how much she steeled herself, how her fingers tightened on his arm when they approached groups of people she only distantly knew. He watched, supported her, ready to step in and deflect any comment likely to fluster her—and grudgingly approved, felt reluctant appreciation of her courage and commitment to Benjy's cause.

Unfortunately, news of his great-uncle's health had started to circulate through the ton; some ladies pressed him for news, others made arch comments on his pending title.

Anne looked at him, confusion in her eyes; she hadn't heard the rumors. He grasped a moment as they strolled between carriages to explain.

"Oh." She blinked. "I see."

The sudden withdrawal he sensed in her had him inwardly swearing.

"No. You don't." He heard the words, clipped and precise, and met her startled glance. Felt his features harden. "But I can't explain here."

He looked along the carriages. Inwardly scowled. "I don't think Imogen's here."

"She usually is—that suggests some more important matter has claimed her attention."

Rising confidence infused Anne's voice; he bit back the observation that there was no reason Hugh would necessarily tell his wife about Benjy. Arguing over the confidences shared between husband and wife did not seem wise, given their present state.

He wanted to speak about that, about them, about the future, but no opportunity arose. The park was not the place for such a discussion, especially as his socially attuned antennae reported that, alerted by the news, the matrons and grandes dames were watching them strolling together, the ease between them, the lack of social constraint, very apparent. Their relative age set them apart, excused them, but also focused more eyes upon them.

He steered her back toward the Calverton carriage, determined to engineer a suitably private meeting. There was no reason for equivocation, not between them. "I assume you intend monitoring the Caverlocks' reactions, at least as far as they allow them to show."

She nodded, determination lighting her face. "They'll be attending Lady Hammond's soirée this evening."

He might as well be hanged for a wolf as for a lamb. "If your mother's agreeable, I'll escort you there."

She halted; gaze direct, she met his eyes. He didn't try to conceal any of what he felt, neither the aggravation at the wasted day, nor his intention.

Her eyes searched his, then she smiled, tightened her fingers briefly on his sleeve, and turned toward the carriage. "I'm sure Mama will be delighted to accept your escort."

That much of his plan went well—when applied to, Minerva was indeed willing to have him escort them that evening. Her dark eyes met his, but she merely smiled and refrained from comment, much to his relief.

Subsequently, however, nothing went quite as he wished.

Lady Hammond's soirée proved too crowded to indulge in anything beyond the social norm; Hammond House was sadly lacking in amenities—at least the sort of amenities that might have helped. He was reduced to doing the pretty for the entire evening. The only mitigating circumstance was that Anne remained by his side throughout, and nothing—no word, no glance, no touch—in any way suggested she regretted the previous evening's interlude in Lady Hendrick's parlor.

Quite the opposite, which only lent yet another layer of tension to the evening.

Added to that, none of the Caverlocks appeared, which fact exercised Anne greatly.

Nerves he hadn't known he possessed rubbed raw, he set out early the following morning, too early for the social round, determined to catch Anne at home and speak privately with her—put what lay between them into words, and take the next step—only to discover she'd already left for the Foundling House.

He followed her there—as long as the room had a door he didn't care where it was—only to be totally distracted; he spent the entire day learning things about her—and himself—that, while decidedly relevant, only built the pressure within him, and her, until the need to speak filled their eyes, colored their words, infused every touch.

And still they had no opportunity, no chance to be alone and broach that one, urgent topic.

Now, later that evening, standing by the side of the Grismeades' ballroom, he watched Anne whirl down a country dance. Even from this distance, he knew she was slightly flustered, although she knew her partner, Gordon Canterbury, quite well. She didn't like being physically close to other men, yet conversely, with Reggie, she took his arm with relief, stepping as close as propriety allowed. And when they waltzed, she came into his arms with an alacrity she didn't try to hide; her senses might leap, but they did so with pleasure, with anticipation and delight.

The noise about him faded; a vision swam before his eyes—the first sight he'd had of Anne that morning at the Foundling House. She'd been seated on a stool reading a story to a score of children gathered about. Her attention had been complete, as had been theirs.

And his.

Then she'd looked up, seen him—and smiled.

And promptly conscripted him into helping with the older boys.

Later, he'd looked across the yard and seen her with two toddlers in her arms, one balanced on each hip. By then, her pins had come loose, or been pulled loose by chubby hands; she'd been flushed and radiant.

The sudden surge of remembered feeling jerked him back to the present, but left him slightly giddy. He dragged in a breath, then uttered a prayer of thanks as the music ended.

Enough was enough.

Concealing grim resolution behind his usual affable mask, he crossed the floor to rescue Anne. She looked about, searching for him, then saw him and smiled. When he joined her, she slid her hand onto his arm.

Gordon Canterbury blinked, but was too polite to comment.

The end of the ball was nigh; once again, the Caverlocks had been noticeable by their absence. Reggie steered Anne toward the chaise where Minerva sat.

"I'm not sure what to make of it," Anne murmured. "Harriet Grismeade said Imogen had intended to come but sent word yesterday that she was indisposed." She glanced briefly at Reggie. "She hasn't been about for the past two days."

Reggie didn't truly care about Imogen. "Perhaps she caught a chill."

Anne caught the edge to his tone; startled, she glanced at him.

He captured her gaze. "Tomorrow morning." Once assured he had her complete attention, he stated, "I'll call to speak with you at noon."

"Noon?"

"Yes. Be there."

She searched his eyes, then, a touch of nervousness returning, nodded. "Very well. I'll be in."

"Good morning."

Anne's soft voice reached him; he turned as she shut the parlor door.

A morning gown of pale green emphasized her delicacy, turning her hair a deeper chestnut in contrast. The wide skirts shushed as she came toward him, searching his face, her expression guarded; he kept his features impassive, searching her eyes in return.

He saw a frown grow, inwardly frowned in response.

She halted with a yard between them, drew herself up, clasped her hands before her. "If you've come to lecture me on watching the Caverlocks . . ."

Her uncertainty reached him; irritation surged anew. He felt his lips thin. Caverlocks, be damned! "You don't need—" He saw her draw back, steel herself; he broke off, hauled in a quick breath, held it for a fraught second, then let it out with the words, "That wasn't what I wanted to speak with you about."

Her eyes widened. "Oh." Her defensiveness abruptly eased, replaced with a finer tension. After a moment, she prompted, as always gentle, "What, then?"

He felt his jaw set, fought to overcome the instinct not to reveal himself in anything so definite as words—even now not to make himself vulnerable to the hurt she could deal him if he'd misjudged her.

Yet he hadn't misjudged—either her or him; he could see it in her eyes, watching him, as wary and as hesitant as he felt, every bit as unsure, wondering if it was possible to hope.

"At Lady Hendrick's. In the parlor." He ran out of words. How the devil was he to phrase it?

A blush rose to her cheeks; she was struggling to follow his direction. Her blush grew brighter; her gaze fell. "I . . . apologize if I was too forward—"

"No." He stepped closer, ran a finger down her cheek. *"Don't* apologize. If anyone should it should be me—" He broke off as she looked up, was lost for a moment in her eyes, then continued,

"But I have no intention of doing so. If I hadn't— if we hadn't—I might never have known. Never realized."

Her gaze was locked with his. "Realized what?"

She—her wide eyes, the softness in her face, the delicate curve of her lips, the rich fall of her hair, the light perfume—some combination of apple blossom and honeysuckle—that rose from her skin, that skin itself, pure and pale, the promise of womanly warmth that, standing so close with her skirts brushing his boots, reached for him and wrapped him about—all that gave him the courage to take her hand, raise it to his lips, say, "That if we wish—if you agree—we could share our lives in great happiness."

She blinked; like veils falling, her shields came down and he could see the wonder in her eyes. "You felt it, too. I thought perhaps it was just me, or that I was reading too much into the moment—"

"No. It was as . . ." He couldn't stop his lips from twisting wryly. "Powerful as you thought. And as surprising."

An answering smile curved her lips. "I hadn't thought of you before—you hadn't thought of me, either."

"No." He frowned at her, the her he could now see. "I can't understand why."

"Does it matter?"

He looked into her eyes, lit with a warm eagerness that was all he could ask, all he'd hoped for. "No. Not at all."

His arm slid around her; he drew her to him,

and she came without hesitation. He lowered his head; their lips, eager to recapture the sweetness, touched, brushed—

They both heard voices, then footsteps hurrying along the corridor outside.

Reggie released her; quelling an uncharacteristically violent flash of temper, Anne stepped back and swung to face the door.

Her heart was thudding, her lips throbbed.

It took effort not to glare at Leighton when he entered.

"Excuse me, sir, Miss Anne, but there's an urgent message come for you, miss." He proffered a salver on which lay a folded note.

Anne took it. "Who brought it?"

"A boy. He said the ladies at the house were in quite a state."

She unfolded the note, briefly scanned its contents. "Good heavens!" She heard the faintness in her voice, felt the clutch of sudden fear, felt the blood drain from her face.

Reggie's fingers closed about her elbow; he was there, beside her, strong, supportive. "What is it?"

"Benjy. He's been stolen away." She could barely take it in.

She offered Reggie the note, and he took it. She looked at Leighton, waiting for her orders.

"The carriage—no, that'll take too long. Find a hackney, and get my maid to bring my coat and bonnet, please."

"I drove here—my curricle's in the street. I'll drive you." Reggie lifted his head and looked at Leighton. "Get the coat and bonnet—we'll be waiting in the hall."

* * *

Reggie drove like a madman to the Foundling House.

The first thing Anne noticed as Reggie drew up was the absence of children in the yards to either side. At this time of day, the yards should be overflowing with children, laughing and playing.

Now they lay deserted.

Inside was equally strange; a sense of suppressed panic reigned. Various women whose job it was to oversee the children hurried back and forth, footsteps echoing down the corridors. There was no sign of their charges.

Anne went straight to the office and found Mrs. Keggs, pale and gaunt, collapsed in a chair.

"Such a terrible thing, miss! That poor wee mite—whisked away he was by some gentleman! Some evil cur."

Anne dropped her bonnet on her desk. "Indeed—now it's up to us to get him back." Pulling up another chair, she sat and took the older woman's hands in hers. At the edge of her vision, she could see Reggie blocking the doorway; the intensity of his gaze, fixed on her, kept her panic at bay. "Now tell us exactly what happened."

Mrs. Keggs gathered herself. "We only knew he was gone when we sat them down for lunch— he'd been playing with the others in the yards. According to what Robbie Jenkins and Petey Smythe told us, he must have been taken about an hour or so before that, as soon as they'd been let out after their morning lesson. Seems a black carriage was drawn up a little way along the street. When the boys raced down to the fence to climb it—you know how they do—the carriage rolled closer."

She drew in a breath. "According to Robbie and Petey, the carriage door opened, and a gentleman called Benjy by name—called him Benjamin. Beckoned him to come closer. Benjy went. He climbed over and down to the pavement, but he hung back at first. He and the gentleman in the carriage talked—Petey thought the man said something about Benjy's mother. Then the man beckoned again, and Benjy went and climbed in. The door shut, and the carriage rolled off." She sniffed. "Robbie and Petey thought Benjy went off for a lark so they weren't going to tell tales. We had to drag that much out of them, but they're worried, now, so I daresay it's the truth."

"What did the gentleman look like?" Reggie asked.

Mrs. Keggs seemed to notice him for the first time. She shook her head. "The boys didn't see him, only his hand—gloved—beckoning. They were too far back and the shadows of the carriage hid him."

"Did they notice anything about the carriage?"

"Just that it was black."

Anne exchanged a look with Reggie. A black carriage in London was one straw in a haystack. Trying to exude a confidence she didn't feel, she stood. "For now, don't worry—it's possible the gentleman I spoke to recently might know something of this. I intend to find out. But for now, we need to get the rest of the children back into their normal routine. I don't think it's likely any of them are at risk. It was Benjy the man wanted."

Mrs. Keggs looked at her, following her argument, then her expression cleared. "Aye—you're right. I hadn't thought of it like that." She heaved herself up. "I'll get everything here back on track, but you'll let us know . . . ?"

"Of course." Anne whisked up her bonnet and started for the door. "The instant I find him, I'll send word."

Reggie followed her onto the street. She reached his curricle, then stopped and whirled to face him. "I'm sorry—I just assumed. I can take a hackney, of course."

"Don't be silly. Get in."

He handed her up, then followed and took the reins. Without asking where she wanted to go, he set the horses trotting. "You can't seriously believe Elderby stole Benjy away."

She pressed her lips together, then replied, her gaze on the street ahead, "If not Elderby, then Lord Thomas. I didn't tell anyone else, and I seriously doubt they've made the information public."

"True, but—"

"Benjy wasn't a threat to anyone else."

After a moment, Reggie said, "We don't know that he was a threat to Elderby or Thomas either."

She drew a breath, held it, then inclined her head. "Yet surely it's too much of a coincidence that after being at the House for a year, some gentleman turns up to find Benjy just days after I told the Caverlocks of his existence."

Reggie heard the fear and self-blame in her voice. He glanced sharply at her. "You didn't do anything wrong." He could see only her profile; its bleakness didn't change. "We'll find him, I promise."

She did look at him then, met his gaze, saw the concern in his eyes. The line of her lips eased; she laid her hand on his arm and squeezed gently.

Then she faced forward.

He drove on.

Thomas's house in Duke Street was closest; Anne insisted they stop there first. Reggie drew up before the house and turned to her. An urchin materialized, offering to hold his horses; by the time he'd negotiated and handed over the reins, Anne, in a fever of impatience, had jumped down and started up the steps.

With a muttered curse, he leapt down and strode after her. He caught up with her—caught her arm—just as she was reaching for the knocker.

She swung to face him.

"Let me handle it." He glared down at her.

She glared back. "Benjy is my responsibility. I want to hear what Thomas has to say."

"Damn it—I'll wager Thomas isn't even out of bed yet!"

She narrowed her eyes at him. "It's after one o'clock. He must be awake."

With an effort, Reggie swallowed his retort. Thomas might well be awake, but he still wouldn't have left his bed. He glanced at the curricle; in truth, he couldn't leave Anne alone outside. "Very well. But let me do the talking."

He thought she humphed, but as she lifted her head and swung to the door, he took that as assent.

The man who answered their knock looked doubtful—as well he might—when faced with their request to speak with his lordship. Reggie swept his stammering excuses aside, swept Anne over the threshold, and summarily sent the man for his master, stressing the urgency of their case.

He ushered Anne into the parlor. They were standing on either side of the small hearth when the door opened and Thomas walked in.

One look at his face, one glance at the multi-hued silk dressing gown swathing his long figure, and it was clear Reggie had been right. Thomas had been in bed.

He wasn't, however, sleepy; his gaze sharpened as he looked from one to the other, then he closed the door.

"What is it?"

"I assume," Reggie said, before Anne could open her mouth, "that Hugh told you what Miss Ashford made known to him recently."

His black brows drawing down, Thomas nodded, his expression impassive, his eyes guarded.

He said nothing; Reggie continued, his tone at its blandest, "I take it you have no . . . personal interest in the matter?"

Thomas blinked, glanced at Anne, then colored faintly. He looked again at Reggie, and raised his brows.

"I'm assisting Miss Ashford with certain inquiries we unfortunately have to make."

Thomas considered, then looked at Anne. "Hugh told me you'd discovered another

Caverlock—a boy. He said the lad was nine years old. Is that correct?"

Anne nodded. "He turned nine last month. He's sure of his birthday, and it matches that on the parish records. And before you ask, the name the mother gave appears to be a fabrication, and there was no father listed."

Thomas shrugged. "The mother's name would mean nothing to me anyway. If that's his age, then I can be absolutely certain he's not my son."

Anne's eyes narrowed. "How can you be so sure?"

Reggie rolled his eyes. Thomas frowned at her, but answered, somewhat waspishly, "Because I know which lady I was consorting with at the time, and she did not fall pregnant."

"How can you know? Maybe she spent some time in the country once your liaison ended?"

Thomas inclined his head. "Indeed, she did, but even then, I can be sure, because I seriously doubt she could have concealed such a state from her husband."

Anne blinked. "Oh."

"Indeed." Thomas waved them to the two arm-chairs and drew a chair from the small table for himself. "And the boy's not Hugh's, either," he added as they sat.

This time, Anne was more circumspect. "Why do you say that?"

A glimmer of a smile played about Thomas's lips. "Because, strange though it may seem, Hugh is thoroughly devoted to Imogen. Yes, she's a stickler and sometimes so stiff-backed you expect her to break rather than bend, but..." He shrugged. "I'd be happy to swear an oath that the boy's not Hugh's either."

Reggie pulled a face. "That leaves . . ."

"Precisely." Thomas grimaced, too. "And that's what's been causing the delay. Hugh, naturally enough, wanted to know if I knew anything to explain this boy's existence before he girded his loins and broke the news to the pater."

Thomas looked at Anne. "It's really not that easy to find the words in which to put it to one's father that he did not do the right thing."

"He may not have known about the boy," Reggie put in.

Thomas looked at him, rather bleakly. "He would never accept such an excuse from either Hugh or me; I rather doubt he'll expect us to accept it of him."

Reggie held his gaze, then nodded. Seeing Anne's lips part, he quickly asked, "I take it you've been upstairs all morning?"

Thomas blinked. "As it happens, yes. Why?"

"Some gentleman lured Benjamin, the boy, into his carriage this morning. He's disappeared."

Thomas's shock was transparently genuine. He glanced from Reggie to Anne. "You've *lost* him?"

Anne blushed. "Yes. But it has to be someone associated with your family who took him—no one else among the ton knows of his existence."

Thomas's gaze grew distant; he frowned. "Perhaps Hugh wanted to speak with him..." Abruptly he shook his head. He rose. "Allow me to sort things out here, then I'll meet you in

Charles Street." He glanced at the clock. "With luck, Hugh will still be at home."

Reggie nodded, and briskly ushered Anne out before she could think of anything more to say. He handed her into the curricle; as he sat beside her, she humphed. "If Hugh has taken Benjy, of course he'll be at home."

Reggie said nothing. A frown in his eyes, he turned his horses and set off for Hugh's house.

The butler showed them into the morning room. "I will inquire if his lordship is at home."

Anne glared at the door as it shut. "Hugh better not try to deny us."

Reggie noted the belligerence that sat so ill on her gentle face; he hid a smile. "He won't—your name will be enough to get him down here."

It was, but to their surprise it was Imogen who came through the door first. A tall, thin woman, pale, brown-haired, with fine ascetic features rather too severe to be fashionable, she carried herself well, but somewhat rigidly. Hugh followed her, grave, concerned—and not just for them, or what they might say. His gaze followed Imogen as she swept across the room.

"Good morning, Miss Ashford. Mr. Carmarthen." Imogen shook hands, then gestured them to seats. Immediately they'd all sat, she leaned forward. "I assume this concerns Benjamin Caverlock?"

Unless she was the greatest actress since Sarah Siddons, her concern was genuine—transparently so.

Anne slanted Reggie a quick look, then nodded. "I'm afraid he's been kidnapped."

"Kidnapped!" Hugh stared at them.

Imogen blanched and sat back, her hand rising to her throat. "Oh, dear!" Her eyes fluttered closed, then she drew a deep breath, opened them again, and fixed Reggie with a commanding look. "But that's not the end of it—I take it there's been a ransom note?"

Reggie met her gaze, then looked at Hugh. "No. That wasn't how it was." He explained, concisely. "The other boys are quite sure the gentleman called for Benjamin. He was looking specifically for him." He gave Hugh, shocked and bewildered, a moment to gather his wits. "We've just come from Thomas—he knows nothing about this. Do you?"

Hugh looked at him, then paled. "Good God, *no*! If I'd any idea . . ." The horror in his face was impossible to mistake. "I can't think . . ."

He looked at Anne. "I'm so sorry. The delay . . ." He broke off and ran a hand through his dark hair, disarranging the heavy locks. "After checking with Thomas, it became clear I'd have to broach the subject with my father. I've been struggling to write to him—it's not that simple a thing to put into words. You would likely not understand, but the pater isn't the most . . . well, temperate being, and—"

"My dear, hush." Imogen put a hand on his arm. His words dying, he looked at her. She smiled, a little ruefully. "I knew you'd find it difficult, but truly, old Portsmouth might be an ogre and as grizzly as they come, but he's an honorable man." She looked at Reggie and Anne. "I wrote to him and told him of the boy as soon as Hugh confirmed he wasn't Thomas's son." Her lips pinched slightly. "Regardless of how I view Thomas's chosen lifestyle, I would trust him—or indeed any Caverlock—on such a matter. Portsmouth had to know"—again her smile softened her face—"and I knew both Hugh and Thomas would shrink from telling him. So I did—just the bare facts." She straightened her shoulders. "As the mother of his grandson, I do have certain privileges."

"When did you send the letter?" Reggie asked.

"The day before yesterday." Imogen stared back at him; they all started doing estimates in their heads.

"Where is the duke's residence?" Anne asked.

"Surrey." Imogen blinked. "Near Caterham . . ."

"He could have driven up and—" Reggie broke off, frowning. "The boys said a black coach—I'm sure they meant a town coach. If it had been a traveling carriage with four horses, they would have mentioned it."

Hugh shook his head. "Portsmouth House. In Park Lane. He would have stopped there and changed carriages." Abruptly he stood. "I'll send a footman to ask. It's just around the corner."

They all waited in a mounting fever of impatience. Imogen offered refreshments, and they accepted, but none of them paid any of it the slightest heed.

The footman returned in ten minutes, out of breath from running but quick to say, "His Grace stopped by this morning. Esher was right surprised. No warning at all. His Grace had out the town coach, the one with no crest, but had his own coachman drive. They came back an hour or so later, and drove straight into the stable yard. The grooms said as His Grace had a young lad with him." The footman suddenly looked highly self-conscious.

"Indeed," Imogen declared. "A distant cousin."

The footman looked relieved. "Just so, ma'am. Did seem he was one of the family. His Grace and the boy got into the coach and off they went. Didn't say nothing to Esher—just sent the groom in to say he'd gone home to Surrey again."

Hugh dismissed the footman.

Reggie rose, as did Anne. "Surrey, near Cater-ham."

Hugh exchanged a concerned look with Imogen. "I can't imagine why . . ."

"Nor I." Imogen rose. "But I'll get things in order here, then we better start down. Will you order the carriage?"

Hugh nodded. "I've got Phillips, my agent, waiting in my study. We'll leave as soon as I'm finished with him."

"We'll go straight down." Reggie moved to open the door. "Benjy will be worried being with strangers."

Hugh nodded again, then drew in a deep breath. "My father. He can sometimes be some-what irascible, but . . ."

"If he roars," Imogen said, sweeping out into the hall, "just ignore him and wait until he stops." She nodded to Reggie, and exchanged a deeper, more meaningful nod with Anne. "We'll follow you down as soon as we may."

On the pavement, Reggie stopped and turned

to Anne. "Will you let me take you home?"

She stared at him. "*No!* I'm going with you."

He swallowed a sigh. "We don't know what we'll find when we reach Caverlock Hall."

"Whatever we find, we need to bring Benjy back, and he'll most likely be frightened. Regardless of his training, he hasn't had any exposure to ducal houses, let alone crusty old dukes. But he knows me, and besides, he's legally in the care of the Foundling House. You'll need a representative to take him back if His Grace turns difficult." Her jaw set; she met his gaze defiantly. "I'm coming with you."

He read the message in her eyes; there was nothing for it but to nod and acquiesce. "All right. But when we get there, you will bite your tongue and let me do the talking."

She humphed—that seemed to be her way of signifying grudging assent; before he could help her, she clambered up into the curricle.

The day was fine, cool with no rain although clouds were gathering in the east. Anne was glad she'd thought to don her new pelisse; its warmth kept her from shivering as the wind of their passing swept through her. Reggie kept the horses well up to their bits and they rushed and rattled south past Battersea and Croydon, then on down the Brighton Road before veering east for Caterham.

Caverlock Hall wasn't hard to find; the innkeeper at the Caterham Arms directed them to where the drive joined the road through the village just past the last houses. Reggie turned his horses in between the tall gateposts, then set them trotting down a long avenue lined with old oaks.

It was late afternoon and the shadows were lengthening, the sun slanting beneath the clouds that had swept across the sky. With the prospect of seeing Benjy again, of perhaps having to do battle with an irate and grumpy old autocrat accustomed to absolute command in order to win the boy free, nearing with every clop of hooves, it was time to think of strategy.

Anne glanced at Reggie. "His Grace won't be expecting us. We don't know what he intends by Benjy—we shouldn't give him time to hide him away."

His gaze on his horses, Reggie nodded, frowning, then he shot her a glance. "Ducal butlers being what they are, I seriously doubt we'll be able to bully the man into letting us see His Grace unannounced."

She said nothing, simply waited.

The drive ended and the house—a long, low, early Georgian mansion set neatly into a landscape of lawns and parkland—appeared before them.

Reggie grimaced; he steered the horses toward the front steps. "Let me do all the talking, behave accordingly—all smiles and charm—and—" He broke off and glanced at her feet; she hadn't expected to go wandering and still had on the shoes she normally wore in the house in the morning. "Good—when I move, stick with me, by my side, but walk as silently as you can."

There wasn't time to say more; a stable boy came running around the side of the house, alerted by the crunching gravel. He deftly caught the horses' heads, then the reins as Reggie tossed them to him.

Helping Anne down, Reggie murmured, "Remember," then the huge front door swung wide and a very correct butler loomed large.

"Yes?"

It happened in the blink of an eye; Reggie's amiable, affable, completely unthreatening mask slid into place, admirably concealing any hint of purpose, any sense that he was there with any goal whatever in mind.

"Ah! Good afternoon. Is His Grace about?" Reggie set Anne's hand on his arm and conducted her up the steps, airily chattering. "We've just been wandering the countryside—it's been such a pleasant day. Met His Grace at m'parents—a dinner, you know—some time ago. The pater heard I was headed this way and asked me to call in and remember him to His Grace."

They reached the porch, and the butler stood back to allow them to enter. Anne beamed at him and swept in. Reggie followed, still declaiming, "Quite wonderful, these old places. Gather m'father thought there might be something of news His Grace might wish me to bear home again."

The butler bowed low. "Indeed, sir. And the name?"

Reggie smiled idiotically. "Oh, didn't I say? It's Carmarthen. Well, that's my name, but the pater's Northcote, don't you know."

Anne smiled sweetly. To give the butler his due, he merely bowed again.

"I shall inquire if His Grace is available, sir. If you and Miss . . . ?"

"Ashford," Reggie supplied.

"If you will wait in the withdrawing room I will inquire of His Grace."

The butler showed them into the drawing room, then shut the door. Reggie immediately halted. "No footmen in the hall, thank heavens!"

Gripping Anne's arm, he swung back to the door. "Stay close." With that whispered injunction, he eased the door open again.

The butler was just disappearing into the mouth of a corridor leading from the main hall.

Reggie whipped out of the drawing room, anchored Anne's hand on his sleeve, then stepped out, strolling quickly and all but silently in the butler's wake. Any footman who chanced to see them would assume they'd been summoned to His Grace's presence.

They hung back far enough for the butler to remain unaware of them; accustomed to guests of quality and their rigid adherence to accepted rules, it would never occur to him that they might flout them and follow.

The butler went to a door, opened it, and entered.

Reggie halted just before the doorway; they listened.

"Your Grace, there are two persons—"

Reggie's mask slid away; jaw firming, he stepped into the doorway, then strode into the large room beyond.

The butler, facing the area before a huge fire-place in which a healthy blaze crackled and roared, did not immediately see them.

His Grace of Portsmouth, a massive figure with a wild mane of startlingly white hair and a heavy face that despite the lines of age still bore the un-mistakable Caverlock features, seated in a large wing chair to one side of the hearth, did.

As did the two boys, slumped like tired pup-pies on the rug before the fire; they'd been poring over a large book, turning the heavy pages, but had looked up at the butler's words.

Their faces were so alike—nearly identical; their coloring was stunningly similar.

One face remained merely curious, wide, dark eyes fixed on them.

The other face—Benjy's face—lit with a smile. "Miss Ashford!"

He scrambled to his feet as the butler swung around with an audible gasp. The butler took a step toward them, raising his arms as if to shoo them back, but Benjy held out a hand. "No, Cooper. They're my *friends*."

Benjy stepped forward, his delight dissolving into uncertainty, his gaze fixing on Anne's face. "I know it wasn't right to go off like that." He glanced sideways at Portsmouth. "I did say as you'd be worried, but you see he's my granddad, and he said as I should come and live here with Neville, and learn to be a Caverlock. That's my surname, he says. He did say we'd send a message . . ."

He stopped, clearly fighting the urge to look to his newfound grandsire for assistance; he swal-lowed and fixed Anne with a beseeching look. "Is that all right then? Can I come here and live with my grandfather?"

Anne had kept her face blank, unwilling to react until she knew and understood. Now she relaxed, and beamed, smiling so hard it hurt. "Of course, you can, Benjy—*of course.*"

Three

"Not every day a man discovers a grandson he didn't know he had." Portsmouth lowered himself into one of the armchairs in the drawing room to which, at his direction, they'd all retired once the furor attendant upon first Imogen and Hugh, then Thomas, all arriving in a lather, had died down.

Sizing up matters in a glance, His Grace had decreed that Benjy and Neville, Hugh and Imogen's son, should retire to the schoolroom and tidy themselves before joining their elders for dinner—a special dispensation they were keen not to jeopardize, ensuring their eager obedience.

"No need for them to hear it all—we can tell Benjy what he should know when the time comes."

With that, His Grace had led them all here; he

waited until they'd all sat—Imogen and Anne on the sofa, Reggie beside Anne, Hugh and Thomas on chairs they drew up—before letting his gaze come to rest on Anne.

"I must thank you, my dear, for having the backbone to bring this matter to the family's attention. Many would have quailed at the thought and found reasons enough to let such a most likely unwelcome piece of news fade from their minds. We are indebted to you." Gravely, he inclined his head.

Anne blushed. "We strive to do the best we can for the children in our care."

Portsmouth inclined his head again in acknowledgment; his gaze shifted to Imogen. A lilting smile touched his lips. "And you, my dear. I'm obliged that you credited me with enough sense to be able to deal with the news without any roundaboutation." His gaze flicked to his sons, but his expression remained benign. "God knows how long it would have taken Hugh to find the right words."

Hugh blushed, but shook his head. "All very well, but I'm still confused."

"And me," Thomas echoed.

When the duke's gaze swung to Reggie, he assumed his blandest expression. "I take it Benjy really is your grandson?"

Portsmouth smiled, a trifle sadly. "Indeed, he is."

"But"—Hugh's brow was creased in perplexity—"who *is* his father?"

Portsmouth grimaced. "As to that, I can't say. Never did know, which was half the problem."

He waited for his sons' expressions to clear; when they didn't, he snorted. "For heaven's sake—he's your sister's boy."

"*Angela's?*" Hugh looked stunned.

"But . . ." Thomas blinked. "Good God. *That* was why she ran away?"

"Angela? But—" Now it was Imogen who was confused. She looked at Hugh. "I thought she married an American and sailed to America?"

Portsmouth grunted, his expression serious and sorrowful. "I'm sorry, my dear. That was a fiction we concocted at the time, for the family's sake." He looked at Reggie, then Anne. "Miss Ashford, I feel you deserve to hear the truth, and indeed, you may need to know. I'm not sure how these things operate, but I assume Benjy is presently legally in your care?"

Anne nodded. "In the care of the Foundling House, which I represent."

Portsmouth nodded. "Exactly so." He hesitated, then said, "I trust you will treat what I tell you with the utmost confidence. There is no one the truth can help, and Benjy's future will be much less problematical if it remains buried as it has for the past ten years."

Both Reggie and Anne murmured assurances.

Nodding in acceptance, Portsmouth drew a deep breath. "My daughter, Angela—she was older than Hugh here . . ."

Step by steady step, he told the story of a strong and determined young woman who had refused to marry any of the eager young gentlemen who had vied for her hand.

"She always said they were only after her for the money and the connection—the name."

She'd clung to her refusal, and then quite unexpectedly fallen in love with some man in station far beneath her.

"Never told us who he was, not a hint." Portsmouth sighed, looking back on the past. "She was afraid of what I'd do."

After a moment, he went on, relating how his daughter had simply vanished one night, leaving a note saying she had gone off to live her life as she wished, warning them not to try following her.

They'd tried, but she'd disappeared into the teeming streets of London, and no word of her did they find.

"We put out the story of the trip to America and the shipboard romance—it wasn't unusual. Families like ours often sent our less-obedient young ladies off for a sojourn in Boston. We kept looking, of course, but eventually we were forced to accept she'd disappeared as she'd said she would."

He looked at Anne. "I'd always hoped that someday, especially if she had children, she'd make contact again."

Anne smiled gently, leaned forward, and laid a comforting hand on his sleeve. "I've read the reports—the notes we make when we take in a new child. She died very suddenly of a virulent fever—she had no time to make any arrangements."

Portsmouth nodded. After a moment, Anne added, "If it's any help, I've seen the street she—

they—lived in. It's a poorer area but respectable, not the slums. She made her living by sewing and fine emboridery. I gather her husband died before Benjy was born."

Portsmouth raised a brow, but when Anne held his gaze steadily, he refrained from asking how she knew that.

She drew back, sitting straighter. "It seems abundantly clear that Benjy's your grandson. If you will give me a letter stating as much, and your intention of taking him in and seeing to his welfare henceforth, I believe I can have our solicitor deal with the legalities in short order."

Drawing breath, she fixed her gaze on Portsmouth's face. "I realize you might not have thought far ahead, but it would help to know what your plans for Benjy are."

"Plans?" Portsmouth blinked at her, his incomprehension quite plain. "No need to *think*! He'll go to Eton, then Oxford, just like all the Caverlocks. Neville's tutor can polish him up—" He broke off, frowned, then looked at Anne. "Incidentally, who taught him Latin? Never would have thought to hear such fluency coming from . . . well, no point making any bones of it, a child from the streets."

Anne beamed. "The Latin you may lay at my sister Penelope's door." She rose; she felt so happy, so relieved—and her and Reggie's continued presence would only delay a family reunion far happier than anyone had supposed. "I really don't think I need anything more aside from that letter." She held out her hand as Portsmouth rose.

"Perhaps you could post it to the Foundling House?"

"Aye. I'll do that." Portsmouth shook her hand, then Reggie's. "My very deep thanks to you both."

They took their leave of the other family members; Thomas walked them out to where Reggie's curricle stood waiting, shrouded in shadows in the drive.

"It'll be late before you reach town—are you sure you won't stay?"

Imogen had pressed the invitation, but both Anne and Reggie had firmly declined.

"The light's good enough," Reggie said as he handed Anne up. He turned to Thomas. "And I imagine tonight will be a moment best shared within the family."

Thomas smiled and didn't deny it. He raised a hand in salute and stepped back as Reggie shook the reins.

He steered the curricle down the drive, and out onto the road.

Anne was silent for the first few miles; he assumed she was reliving the unexpected resolution. A soft smile played about her lips; satisfied, he gave his attention to the narrow lane leading back to the Brighton Road.

They'd reached it and were bowling along in good style when he felt Anne's gaze, glanced at her swiftly, and realized from the steady seriousness of her gaze that she'd moved on and was thinking of other things.

More personal things.

He was forced to look to his horses. She shifted beside him and looked forward, too. He sensed more than saw her steel herself.

"What we spoke of before . . . I realize . . ." She stopped and hauled in a breath. "It seems likely you'll soon be Northcote, and then everyone will remember you're in line for the earldom—you could have your pick of the marriageable young ladies, even those from the highest families, or the incomparables, or the heiresses . . ."

He glanced at her; her face was set, determined.

She stared ahead; she didn't look at him. "Are you sure you wouldn't rather—shouldn't rather—marry one of them?"

He didn't need to think. "Don't be daft!" Irritation—masculine aggravation—rang in his tone; he made no attempt to mute it. "If you must know, the very thought has kept me firmly facing the other way for years. Sweet young things, huh! They *giggle*! Anyway—can you imagine it? A female like that would make my life a misery. I wouldn't know what to do with her. I don't want to marry anyone like that."

For one instant, the only sound about them was the sharp clop of the horses' hooves.

"I want to marry you." He stated it clearly.

He glanced at her just as she glanced at him, her eyes wide.

"You do?"

"Yes!" He would have glared, but his leader chose that moment to jib; he looked back to the horses—

With a horrendous *crack*!, a bolt of lightning cleaved the now darkening sky.

"Oh!" Anne grabbed the side of the curricle as the horses bolted.

Reggie held them, steadied them. Luckily they were on the main road; the macadam was smooth, and at that hour there were few other vehicles about.

The instant he had the pair trotting again, he glanced around—and swore. "We're never going to make it home."

Anne glanced at him; he nodded to the right, to where rain was sweeping across the fields beneath heavy, iron-gray clouds.

Thunder, low and menacing, rumbled up and over them. It wasn't that late, yet a blackness deeper than night was closing in.

Reggie swore again. Purley with its old inn was behind them, too far to go back; Croydon with its posting houses was too far ahead. He racked his brains . . .

Here he was, alone with the lady who would be his wife, and a storm was threatening. The initiative lay waiting to be seized . . .

"Croham Hurst!" Jaw firming, he looked ahead, to the right, searching for the line of hedges marking the lane. "There's a nice inn, small but comfortable—we can put up there."

Anne nodded. The wind had picked up; the scent of rain lay heavy on the air.

Large drops were falling when they pulled into the inn yard. An ostler came running, head ducked against the weather. Reggie jumped down, grabbed Anne, and lifted her down as the ostler hurried the curricle away. Hands locked, they raced for the tiny porch, reaching it just as the heavens opened and the rain came bucketing down.

They both turned and looked back at the sheer sheet of driving rain, then looked at each other—and laughed.

Still smiling, they entered the inn; the innkeeper, a small rotund man with a cheery country face, came bustling up to greet them.

"Well, now! You're lucky you're out of that. Turned proper nasty, it has."

"Indeed." Reggie couldn't stop smiling as they shrugged out of their coats. "My wife and I were visiting friends at Caterham—seems we left it too late to start back. Do you have a large chamber we might use for the night?"

"Oh, indeed, sir! Ma'am."

The man bobbed a bow at Anne; he didn't register the odd look on her face as she struggled to decide how to react.

"Our main chamber's at your disposal. All ready it is—I'll just get Bessie to light the fire, so all will be comfy when you go up." With an expansive gesture, the man threw open a door revealing a snug parlor. "We don't get much custom on nights like this and we're off the main way, so we'll have your dinner ready in a trice. You won't be disturbed in here."

Anne smiled a trifle weakly and entered. The instant she heard the door shut, she swung around and faced Reggie. "Wife?"

His expression as inconsequential as ever, he shrugged. "Jumping the gun a trifle, but it seemed wiser all around."

She didn't know what to answer to that. Before she could form any sensible argument, he asked her about the hurdles the Caverlocks might face in reasserting guardianship over Benjy.

Somehow that discussion, and other topics that flowed from it, lasted through the interval until their dinner was served, and through the dinner itself—a nice assortment of hearty country fare—until the moment when, the dishes having been cleared and tea served, a gust of wind howled about the inn and ferociously rattled the shutters.

"Oooh!" Anne shivered. "That sounds positively gothic." She paused, then added, "I can still hear the rain pounding and lashing."

In the armchair opposite, Reggie grimaced. He rose. "I just hope it stops before morning, or we might be mired here for a day or more." Taking her hand, he drew her to her feet. "Actually, I was thinking, once we get back to London we should take a trip north to Calverton Chase."

She glanced at him as he ushered her out of the door. "Why?"

"Well," Reggie replied, guiding her to the stairs, "aside from having a little chat with your brother, there's the undeniable fact that announcing our engagement just as the ton returns to town en masse is bound to set us in the eye of the storm. Far better, to my mind, to escape before we're stuck." Gaining the upper corridor, he took her hand, interlaced his fingers with hers. "Don't you think?"

She glanced up at him, at the faint lift to his

brows, looked past the superficial lightness of his face, into the seriousness of his eyes. He was asking far more than the obvious; they both knew it. "Is that a proposal?"

He frowned. "Actually, I saw it as a trifle further advanced than a proposal—we covered proposing before." He met her gaze; his brows rose a fraction. "A plan of action, perhaps?"

She had to smile. "Very well." She squeezed his fingers lightly. "We'll head to the Chase just as soon as we get Benjy's affairs in order."

"Good." Reggie turned her toward the door to the large chamber over the front of the inn. "We can time the notice to the *Gazette* accordingly."

He set the door wide, and she entered. Without a second thought. Without any of the missish hesitation or nervousness she'd expected would assail her. It was as if they were already married in fact, as if the ceremony were merely incidental, a superficial recognition of a union that had already in truth begun.

The room was as cozy as the innkeeper had promised. Dimity curtains covered the windows; matching hangings were gathered at the corners of a large four-poster bed. The covers were turned down; the pillows plumped high. The fire leaping in the grate threw warmth into the room; the flames sent flickering fingers of light dancing over the scene.

Anne stopped in the center of the room. She heard the door shut. An instant later, she sensed Reggie behind her, then his hands slid around her waist and he drew her back against him.

In the hearth before them, flames licked the

dark logs and sent sparks rising up the chimney.

The fire warmed the front of her; he warmed her back. He bent his head, she tilted hers as he touched his lips to her throat.

Raising her hand, she stroked his hair, soft, warm.

"Before, in Lady Hendrick's parlor, why did you stop?"

The caress of his lips halted, but he didn't lift his head; she felt his breath on her skin when he answered, "Because I didn't know if you'd made a decision—or if you'd been swept away by the moment." His voice was low, deep. "It's not as if we'd had any courtship—you hadn't had time to consider, either the act or its consequences."

His lips returned to her skin, their touch sweet, drugging; he didn't say more, spell out what he meant, but she knew, understood. Marriage wasn't a state he had any interest in trapping her in, no matter how much he wanted her. It had to be her decision, taken in full command of her wits.

A decision they were both aware was in the past.

She turned in his arms, lifted her own, and draped them about his neck. His lids rose, heavy over rather sultry eyes. How much he wanted her was there in the blue, there for her to see.

She felt a slow smile lift her lips, light her face. "We've known each other for such a long time."

"We've been would-be lovers for only three days."

"Time doesn't matter, not once one understands—sees." She held his gaze. "Once one recognizes the truth."

His arms slid around her, closed; he drew her to him. "I love you."

His gaze didn't waver; she smiled, assured. "And I love you. That's all that matters, isn't it?"

He searched her eyes, then bent his head and touched his lips to hers.

She kissed him back, offered her mouth, shuddered with anticipation when he took. His hands spread over her back, pressing her breasts to his chest, then slid lower, molding her to him, searching, learning, possessing.

The tangle of their tongues trapped her attention—the slow, hypnotic quality of the kiss; the steady build of heat between them captured her awareness, ultimately to the exclusion of all else. She didn't realize his fingers had been busy until he raised his hands and eased her gown from her shoulders. In a giddy daze, she drew her hands from the sleeves, let him peel the bodice down and away, let him loosen her skirts and let them fall.

Only when her petticoats followed and she stepped free of the frothing folds did she feel the touch of air cool on her legs, and realize—and shiver. He paused, hesitated, but she'd made her decision. Drawing in a breath, she boldly stepped back into his arms and lifted her lips to his.

He took them willingly; she felt the breath he'd held ease from him. Then he wrapped his arms about her, lifted her off her feet, and carried her to the bed. He tumbled her down and she giggled, the sound not as nervous as she'd expected. He shot her a look from under heavy lids and reached for her stockings, drawing first one, then the other, off.

Lying across the coverlet clad only in her fine chemise, she studied his face, conscious of a sense of freedom, of rightness, welling within her. Despite her nervousness in company, she'd never lacked for courage—never turned aside from a challenge.

This challenge was one she could wholeheartedly devote her life to.

When Reggie turned and sat to pull off his boots, she squirmed around and crawled toward the pillows, intending to burrow beneath the covers.

His hand closed around her ankle and anchored her. "No."

She turned back to him, brows rising, letting her head fall against the lowest pillow. The expression on his face was not one she'd previously seen—hard, uncompromising—intent.

"Stay there."

With a fell look, he released her and started to unbutton his shirt.

She tilted her head. "Are you going to be a dictatorial husband?"

He snorted. "In this sphere, yes." He didn't look back at her, but stood, stripped off his shirt, then his hands fell to his waistband. A second later, his breeches hit the floor, and he turned to the bed.

Before her eyes had finished growing wide, he was on the bed beside her. Then his lips were on hers—stopping her host of sudden questions at the source. Her hands touched his chest, then gripped, spread, slid, caressed. Passion flared, cindering any reservations she might have had, any last-minute hesitations. Within seconds she was convinced that nothing on earth was more important than being closer, getting closer, skin to skin.

His hands slid beneath the fine fabric of her chemise, touched, caressed, stroked.

Until she was on fire, until she pressed him back, seized the material, and drew the chemise off over her head.

He immediately pulled her to him, immediately lowered his head and drank the gasp of delight that the first touch of body to body wrenched from her.

Her hands, her whole body seemed to have a mind of its own, clutching, caressing, wanting. When he parted her thighs and stroked between them she gasped, clung, her nails sinking into his upper arms as his fingers parted her and probed, then slid in.

After that, she was conscious of nothing but rising heat, and a welling, driving urgency. Her skin was hot, flushed, alive, her breathing tortured.

He was the same, the same desire lit his eyes, the same passion drove him.

Then they came together and she cried out, arching as their bodies fused, melded, as the sharp pain ebbed and was swamped in heightened delight, swept away on the steady, unrelenting tide of need, of a glorious and dizzying passion.

It held them both, swirled about them as they danced, as they found the rhythm came naturally, the pace, each touch, each lingering of lips, each gasp something both new and familiar, sensually startling, emotionally revealing, yet comfortable and assured.

With open and unwavering confidence, they clung and journeyed on, senses awhirl, bodies attuned, until they reached the pinnacle where desire and physical sensation ended.

In ecstasy.

Gasping for breath, Reggie held himself over her and drank in the sight of her face, the blissful joy that suffused her expression, the delight that curved her lips.

Then her lashes fluttered, lifted; she looked up and met his eyes.

A long moment passed, the reality of what governed them, what had brought them here, to this, hung, as ephemeral as a shimmering veil, as real as a rock, between them, then he bent his head as she lifted her lips.

Love found and shared; that was, indeed, all that mattered.

The Matchmaker's Bargain
A Novella
Elizabeth Boyle

To Lydia,

for sitting at my feet for so many years
and happily snoring while I tapped away.
You were the best cat
a writer could ever wish for.

$\mathcal{P}rologue$

England
1818

$\mathcal{L}$eaning across the table, Esme Maguire squinted at her guest. Her eyesight wasn't what it used to be, but her instincts were rarely wrong. And right now they were telling her that the gel who'd stumbled up to her cottage during this wretched storm wasn't being entirely truthful.

"Lost, you say?" Esme mused. "And here we thought . . . well, never mind that. It's not like Nelson to be wrong, but still I'm glad you ended up on my doorstep, for it isn't a fit night to be out." From the lady's side, an indignant yowl rose, and she scratched the cat with an indulgent caress.

Yes, Nelson, you have the right of it, Esme thought.

The drenched young lady on the other side of the table stared down at the cup of tea in her hands. "Yes, after the mail coach became mired in the mud, the driver assured me there was an inn not far up the road, but I fear I wandered down the wrong lane. Thank you so much for taking me in." She shivered and took another sip of her tea.

Over near the fireplace hung her steaming gown—an expensively wrought piece of blue silk, and of far better quality than any of Esme's usual clients wore.

So, the old lady reasoned, she was no milkmaid or country girl, but most likely a lady. And from the state of her perfect hands, white and uncallused, one who had never toiled.

The mystery of her guest tugged at Esme's innate curiosity. "Lucky you are to have found your way here, Miss—"

The girl glanced up, her eyes wide. "Oh, uh, I'm . . . I'm . . . Miss Smythe."

"Miss Smythe it is then," Esme agreed. *For now.* "And I'm Mrs. Maguire. But you must call me Esme, for everyone does." She sighed. "Oh, but isn't it nice to have a bit of company on such a miserable night." As if to emphasize her words, a clap of thunder boomed overhead, shaking the timbers around them. "I don't get as many visitors as I like, and I do so love to have someone to talk to."

"Yes, company is lovely," the lady mused, as she glanced about the shadowy room.

"More tea?" Esme asked, even as she filled the lady's cup once again with the spicy brew. After she refilled her own, she settled back into her seat. "Now where is it that you're bound?"

Miss Smythe took a nervous sip from her cup. "Brighton."

Esme smiled. The tea was starting to work, because that was the first honest thing the girl had told her. "Oh, a bit of sea air, a bit of romance, I suppose," she mused. "Are you meeting someone there? Perhaps a young man?"

"Oh, nothing like that," the girl said hastily. "I fear I'm rather too old for such a thing."

Esme waved her hand at the very notion. Certainly this Miss Smythe was no schoolgirl, for she hadn't that dewy innocence about her, but she was hardly past her bloom, what with her rosy cheeks and bright eyes. "Too old for love, she says," she muttered in an aside to Nelson.

Nelson shot a glance at their guest before he switched his long tail and then returned his gaze to his mistress and let out an adamant meow.

"Nelson is quite right," Esme declared. "No one is too old for love. Even you, Miss Smythe."

"I hardly have time for all that," she said, politely covering a yawn with her hand.

"Time?" Esme asked. "Time is what you make of it. And I would imagine you have enough to find your heart's desire." She scratched Nelson again. "I could help you with it, if you like. For a small fee, that is." She held out her hand, her eyes fixed on the delicate little blue reticule before her guest.

"A small fee for my heart's desire?" The girl laughed, making just a tiny hollow sound, as she reached for her purse. "Well, I suppose it is the least I can do for your hospitality." As she passed the coins across the table, Esme's glance strayed in the direction of Nelson.

The foolish cat was grinning at the sight of gold—probably fancied a fine chicken and kidney pies with their newfound riches. Oh, yes, there would be a bit of that for him, but first and foremost they had to discover the truth about their new client.

"What would that be?" Esme prodded. "What would be your heart's desire?"

Miss Smythe yawned again. "I do beg your pardon. I traveled quite a distance today, and what with the storm and all, I fear I am quite tired."

"I suppose you are." Esme nodded toward a small cot in the corner. "Lie down over there, Miss Smythe. Sleep a bit. We can discuss everything in the morning."

The tea had done its work, for even as the girl's head touched the pillow, Esme could see the dreams that rose within her guest. Wishes that tipped and toppled as they danced through a Season in London.

Settling into her rocking chair and pulling out a pipe, Esme smoked and eavesdropped on the girl's dreams.

And of course into Miss Smythe's slumberous interlude strode a man.

"Isn't there always one?" Esme said, nudging Nelson, who'd climbed up into her lap.

The cat shook his head and then nodded at her to get on with her business. As far as Nelson was concerned, there was a fine dinner to be had out of all this.

So caught up in her own jest, Esme almost

missed a glance at the sort of man Miss Smythe desired. But when she did turn her attention to him, the elegant figure cutting a dashing path across Almack's stopped her cold.

A man with a carefree smile and a rakish gleam to his eyes. A man Esme knew only too well.

"How could this be?" she whispered to the large tabby. Even the unflappable Nelson appeared stunned. Yet there he was, Miss Smythe's heart's desire, as clearly as if he'd just walked through Esme's door.

And now it was up to them to see that the girl found her way into his heart.

Esme set the cat down, then rose and tottered over to the line of pegs on the wall, reaching for her cloak hanging there. Turning to Nelson, she motioned at him to follow her. "Storm or not; come along. We've got our work cut out for us."

The cat grumbled something under his breath, but followed his mistress out into the dark and wretched night.

A bargain was, after all, a bargain.

One

The next morning . . .

"$\mathcal{E}$sme, are you in there?" The door rattled on its hinges as something hard rapped against the solid oak. "Time to wake up, old gel. I come bearing gifts."

Miss Amanda Preston sat bolt upright in a narrow cot. For a moment she couldn't reconcile the deep voice outside with the odd dreams she'd been having, least of all determine where she was or why she was wearing a night rail that wasn't her own.

As the man outside knocked again, this time a little more insistently, the sharp sound jolted her memory like the claps of thunder that had rattled the cottage through the long dark hours.

The storm. She'd sought shelter here after she'd . . .

She blinked at the bright and merry sunshine pouring in through the windows. The morning radiance had chased away the shadows and eeriness that had lent the lonely cottage such a mysterious air the night before. Especially since it seemed her well-meaning, albeit odd, hostess, Mrs. Maguire was gone. Not even that peculiar feline, Nelson, lurked about.

Why, in daylight the entire place looked rather ordinary. Amanda would have sighed in disappointment had not the pounding started again, as well as the voice.

"Esme? Are you well? Come now, open the door. Her Dragonship sent me over with a basket of provisions, including a nice roast chicken for Lord Nelson, and by the smell of it, a batch of Mrs. Stocken's scones, which are making me nigh on faint. That, and this demmed leg." The last comment was muttered more like a curse. "Oh, playing hard to get, are you? I'm going to count to three, and if you can't get decent in that time, I'm still coming in."

Of all the impertinence, Amanda thought, until a jolt of panic raced through her. This man intended to come in, and she wasn't dressed. Not even moderately decent.

"One!" came the cry from the door.

Goodness, where were her clothes? She glanced first toward the hearth where they had hung the last time she'd seen them. There was nothing there now but a bundle of herbs. She dashed out of bed and ran right into a low table, sending it toppling over.

The rather boisterous laughter from outside did nothing to improve her mood.

"Who have you got in there, Esme? A lover? I'll

be jealous if you've been cheating on me." More laughter ensued. "Stow the bastard quickly for I won't stop counting just to protect your question- able reputation. Now where was I? Ah, yes—two!"

A lover? Last night her hostess had seemed so kindly, but now Amanda was starting to wonder about the lady's character if she had such forward callers so early in the morning.

Taking one more frantic glance around, she spied her gown neatly folded on the chair beside the bed.

In her haste, she'd bolted right past it.

If she felt relief in finding her gown, her panic returned tenfold. She stared down at her clothes and wondered what one did next. She'd never dressed herself a day in her life. Her mother had forbidden her and her sisters from ever doing anything for themselves. It just wasn't done, the lady had exhorted her daughters time and time again.

But it had to be done now. And quickly.

The pounding on the door started anew. "Esme? Are you well?" Now there was an anxious tone lac- ing the voice outside, something that spoke of friendship and respect and, well, concern.

She wondered if anyone was so worried about her now that she'd gone missing. Amanda snorted and decided worry was the least of the emotions that were probably echoing through the manor. Most likely the walls were reverberating with her father's complaints as to the "expense" of bringing her home, while her mother fussed peevishly about the possible scandal of it all.

Meanwhile, outside Esme's cottage, this man

didn't seem the least deterred by expense or propriety as he hammered on the door. "Three! I'm coming in whether you like it or not."

"Oh, no, please don't," Amanda called out as she frantically yanked her dress over her head. Suddenly instead of being her sister's best day gown, the elegant creation turned into a straitjacket, trapping her arms askew, not even allowing her a peek at Mrs. Maguire's anxious protector.

The door to the cottage creaked open. "Esme? Is that you?" The bemused questions were followed by footsteps and the tap of a walking stick. "I think not. I haven't seen a pair of legs that fine since the last time I saw the Revue in London."

A hot blush rose up on Amanda's cheeks. He was looking at her legs? She knew right there and then this trespasser was no gentleman.

All her mother's stern warnings about the evils of men rose in her ears like a cacophony of banshees. To answer their strident cries, she struggled to pull the dress down.

At least far enough to cover her knees.

Her ankles could wait, some little wicked part of her ventured.

"So who have we here?" The footsteps and tap of a walking stick drew closer.

"Sir, I beseech you to leave. At once," she pleaded through the tangled folds of her gown. "I am not decent."

"I beg to differ. From my vantage point, you appear quite fetching," came the whimsical reply. "But here, let me assist you. It wouldn't do for me to be caught with a half-dressed client of Esme's."

Client? Whatever did that mean?

Then like the storm from the night before, the old lady's words clamored in her head. *I could help you with it, if you like. For a small fee, that is.*

Oh, what kind of muddle have I found myself in now? Amanda struggled and wiggled and tried pushing her arms this way and that, searching for a sleeve or the opening at the neck. How could getting dressed be so difficult? "Oh, the devil take this," she muttered as yet another frantic attempt failed.

"Truly, I can help you," her mysterious benefactor offered. "If you would just—"

A pair of warm, strong hands caught hold of her waist. After the shock of being held with such . . . such . . . enticing familiarity started to wear off, Amanda panicked. Oh, she could see now why her mother's warnings had always been so strident; there was something altogether too tempting about being held thusly by a man. Something that made her want to lean into his chest, to reach out and touch him to see if the man surrounding the deeply sensual voice was just as promising.

What was she thinking?

"Unhand me!" Amanda cried, trying to get away. The back of her legs smacked into the cot, and she nearly toppled onto it.

Nearly, that is, only because of the unwanted help he continued to offer. His arms wound quickly around her waist and hauled her upright until she was pressed scandalously against his chest.

Really held, not at some proper distance, but

gathered in close without any regard for decency or manners or society's rules.

Amanda gasped as her body melded to his. In an instant, the warmth of his limbs sent a dangerous tremor of recognition through her. She was no longer just Miss Amanda Preston, but "fetching" and she felt it all the way down to her bare toes.

However, her mother's stern warnings and her years at Miss Emery's Establishment for the Education of Genteel Young Ladies overruled any further sense of adventure, and so she told him in the sternest voice she could muster, "Please, sir, unhand me."

"If you would only hold still, I could get you dressed," he said with such supreme confidence, she had no doubt that he was well-versed in the intricacies of ladies' clothing.

Yet why did she have to be the lady men wanted to help get dressed?

"Hold still," he told her again. "You've really got this in a dreadful tangle." His fingers, which had been diligently searching for a sleeve, instead brushed over her breast, sending a quake of delight and shock through her.

"Oh, my!" she gasped. Being held was one thing, but this . . . this sent her to a realm into which not even her mother's ominous warnings had strayed.

"Release me now!" she told him, this time in earnest, her hands finding the wall that was his chest and giving him a good shove.

It was enough to send him toppling over. She heard the clatter of his cane, but to her dismay, he had no intention of letting her go, and she fell with him into a heap on the cot.

"O-o-o-f," he said as she landed atop him.

If merely being with a man in her undress was ruinous, then this, without a doubt, would be her final undoing. She sat straddling him, her bare thighs against the thin leather of his breeches, her breasts pressed against his chest. And what she felt pressed to her thighs—so hard and all too masculine, sent her heart pounding at a dangerous rate.

When she'd fled her parent's house yestermorn, there had been a small, fervent hope that she would encounter her own bit of excitement. But never would she have believed that she'd discover it so quickly, or rather, that it would find her, and quite insistently, for that matter.

His hands found her hips and settled her exactly atop him. "I daresay if you wanted me beneath you," he said, the tempting promise behind his voice bringing a hot blush to her cheeks, "all you had to do was ask."

"I wanted no such thing," she shot back, even as the delicious heat of his body enticed her to move closer to him. "Truly, I did not want *this*."

Oh, now she could count lying as another of her newfound sins. That, and the unnamable desires this man stirred within her—irresistible notions of intimacy—the feel of his bare skin against hers, his confident touch, the whisper of his deep voice in her ears. If she didn't find a way to resist his spell, she'd be a fallen woman in no time.

Not that such a thing mattered to her anymore. But still, she couldn't erase Miss Emery's exacting and uncompromising lessons on propriety so easily.

So resist him she should. Er, would. "Sir, if you do not unhand me I'll—"

"If I must," he said, a hint of playful regret in his voice. Next thing she knew, his hands no longer cradled her hips, but were once again pulling and tugging at her dress. Before she knew it, her arms found her sleeves, and the gown popped down over her head without any further mishaps.

That is, until she glanced at her savior, or as her mother would say, despoiler, and realized she must be dreaming.

"Oh, dear. Oh, my," she sputtered as her heart sang with recognition and then lurched in despair.

The man beneath her was none other than Mr. James Reyburn.

But her anguish was for naught, because it was obvious he didn't recognize her. The quizzical look in his clear blue eyes told her only too clearly that he had no idea who she was. Like most men who'd ever met her, he'd put her out of his mind as quickly as the introduction had been made, and the sting of his failure to identify her now hurt no less than it had all those years ago when he'd danced with her out of desperation to be near another lady.

Oh, yes, for what man ever remembered Miss Amanda Preston, the all-too-forgettable daughter of Lord and Lady Farleigh?

The disappointment flooding the lady's lively green eyes was nothing compared to the stabbing grief that wrenched through Jemmy's gut as he watched her struggle to get away from him.

He didn't know why he expected anything different. Mayhap it was because he hadn't flirted with, let alone *held*, a woman in so long. How easy it had been to delude himself in those few seconds, in the thrill of the chase, in the intoxicating desire of having a woman in his arms, as to why he'd turned his back on such conquests.

For any young woman who looked at him, no matter how well-bred or disciplined she might be, could not hide her dismay at the beastly reminders the war had etched upon him.

The pain in his leg he could live with. The scar on his face he didn't mind, but a woman's regard, the kind that spoke of approval and desire, something that had once seemed like his birthright, he sorely missed.

"I must be away," the young woman said, as she scrambled up from the cot, unwilling to look at him. "This is hardly proper. I wouldn't want anyone to think that we . . ."

Then it occurred to him what the *real* reason for her alarm might be. Not so much his appearance, but . . .

He didn't even want to say it, it was so laughable. Not even Esme would dare such a bargain. "You don't think that I'm—"

"I don't know what you are, sir, but I am not . . . not . . ."

"Going to marry me?" he suggested.

This brought the chit's gaze spinning back to his. *"Marry you?"*

Well, she needn't sound so incredulous.

"I don't believe," she said, "that this situation calls for such drastic measures. I may not have much experience in these matters, but I doubt my clumsiness would be regarded as compromising enough to demand marriage. Indeed, if you think I've lured you here on some pretense—"

Jemmy had heard enough. He glanced around and spied his cane, which he caught up and used to rise from the bed. His leg wobbled beneath him, but he held his position as if he were facing the French. "Lured me here? I'm not the one lolling about Esme's cottage in her altogether awaiting her true love." His words came out bitter and harsh, more than they needed to be. He suspected it was the lingering sting of her rejection that spurred such venom, but if he was honest, he'd admit that it was fed mostly by his own disillusionment.

He'd believed in true love once. In happily-ever-afters.

"You're mad," she shot back, "if you think I'm here looking for a husband. What is it about this cottage that has everyone convinced I need to find romance?" She turned her back to him and finished smoothing her gown into place.

Unfortunately, the pretty silk fell all the way to the floor, and Jemmy cursed himself for helping her.

She truly did have a fine pair of legs, and it was a shame to hide them.

But that wasn't the point, he reminded himself. Besides, it wasn't as if he'd have an opportunity to view them again. "Romance is the only thing most people have on their minds when they come here," he told her.

She glanced over her shoulder at him, her

brown hair tumbling in a long curl down her back. "Whatever for?"

"Because of Esme," he said. He stepped a little closer to her. "You don't mean to tell me you didn't know that she is the matchmaker."

"A matchmaker? Ridiculous. Whatever would I be doing with a matchmaker? I simply got lost in the storm last night and stumbled upon this place. Mrs. Maguire offered me shelter, and when I was awakened this morning, rather rudely I might add, she was gone." She opened a plain leather valise and started searching through it as if tallying up her belongings. "Now if you are done with your speculations as to my character, I'll be gone."

Something about her indignation, her denial caught Jemmy's curiosity. "What would you expect me to think?" he asked her. "After all, this is Bramley Hollow, so it is natural to assume—"

Her hand froze over the latch on her traveling bag. "Bramley Hollow?" Her eyes widened in recognition.

So she really hadn't known. "Aye, Bramley Hollow."

"And this is—" She looked about the room, her gaze darting over the bundles of herbs hanging from the rafters to the heavy pot slung in the fireplace.

"Yes, the cottage of the matchmaker," he told her. "The matchmaker of Bramley Hollow."

From the look on her face, she was no longer lost. She knew exactly where she was.

"Oh, this is a disaster." Her hand now floundered about for something steady to grab hold of.

"Hardly all that." Jemmy slid a chair beneath her shaky legs. She sat down, her head resting in her hands. "As long as you didn't engage Esme's services, make a bargain with her, then you needn't worry that you are about to be dragged before the parson."

Her gaze flew up to meet his. "A bargain?"

"Yes, you know, over tea, I would imagine. She pours you a cup and offers to help you find your heart's desire."

"Tea?"

If the gel had been pale before, she hadn't a bit of color left now. "Don't tell me, you drank the tea?"

She didn't speak, only nodded.

Jemmy had been warned by his father from an early age never to partake in a cup of Esme's potent brew. It was how his own parents had ended up wedded. "I wouldn't be so overwrought," he offered. "As long as you didn't give her any money, then there is no harm done."

She closed her eyes and shuddered, as if trying to forget the evening in its entirety.

"You gave her money?"

"Just a few coins. It seemed the decent thing to do. She'd taken me in, after all. I thought she was naught but a lonely old lady with a fastidious cat to feed—"

"Nelson," Jemmy said, groaning. If Esme could be called a bit of an oddity, a century or so back the eerie Nelson would have qualified her for a nice toasty blaze in the village square.

"Yes, Lord Nelson. I thought a few coins would put her right for the time being. Just enough for a stewing hen is all. But I certainly didn't ask her to make a match for me."

"Are you positive?" he asked. "Absolutely positive?" Esme wasn't renowned for being all that open and honest about her transactions.

The young woman bit her lower lip and closed her eyes. "I fear last night is a bit hazy. But I do recall giving her a few coins after she offered to help me. But with what, I can't remember."

Now it was Jemmy's turn to seek out a chair. He slumped down and looked across the table at her. "You know what you've done, don't you? You've contracted a match!"

Her cheeks pinked. "I did no such thing. I was merely lost and sought shelter here, nothing more."

Jemmy stared at her. "Well, it turned into something more, now didn't it?"

The lady's chin notched up. "It's not like this sort of thing is done anymore. It was all just an innocent bit of conversation."

"Not in Bramley Hollow," he said. "A bargain is a bargain. And when a match is contracted, it must be completed." He paused for a second, feeling no small twinge of guilt to be the one to break the bad news to her. " 'Tis the law. You must be wed."

Her eyes widened again. *"The law?* Why, that is barbarous. You can't force a person to wed."

"No one is forcing you. You were the one who contracted Esme's services. But the law is quite specific on the subject. Once a match is engaged, an expedient marriage must take place."

"How can that be? Banns must be read."

"Not in Bramley Hollow," he told her. "The king granted the village an exemption from the Marriage Act, though only in weddings contracted through the matchmaker."

She shook her head at this unpleasant news. "I don't see how I can be forced to wed someone in such short order."

"Surely you know the legend of Bramley Hollow?" Having grown up under its auspices, Jemmy couldn't imagine anyone not knowing the story.

"Yes, yes, I know the tale, but I don't see why a thousand-year-old pledge need be honored. Especially since I was induced into this bargain by trickery."

"Trickery is how matchmaking got its start in Bramley Hollow—if that princess hadn't induced the baron to marry her, she would have ended up wed to that wretched despot. Her clever bit of matchmaking and the baron's loyalty have kept the village out of harm's way all these years." He smiled at her. "But just in case you are of royal blood, your father isn't going to sack the village if we don't hand you over, is he?"

She managed a wan smile. "I don't think Bramley Hollow need fear anything so dire."

"Relieved to hear it—I had visions of having to haul the family armory out of the attics."

"But don't you see—I don't want to be married," she said, bounding up from her chair. "I can't get married."

Something about her spirit tugged at his heart, almost more so than the memory of her soft thighs and long legs.

"Whyever not? You aren't already engaged, are

you?" He didn't know why, but for some reason he didn't like the idea of her being another man's betrothed. Besides, what the devil was the fellow thinking, letting such a pretty little chit wander lost about the countryside?

But his concerns about another man in her life were for naught, for she told him very tartly, "I am not engaged, sir, and I assure you, I'm not destined for marriage."

"I don't see that there is anything wrong with you," he said without thinking. Demmit, this was what came of living the life of a recluse—he'd forgotten every bit of his Town bronze. "I mean to say, it's not like you couldn't be here seeking a husband."

The disbelief on her face struck him to the core.

Was she really so unaware of the pretty picture she presented? That her green eyes, bright and full of sparkles, and soft, brown hair, still tumbled from her slumbers and hanging in long tangled curls, was an enticing picture—one that might persuade many a man to get fitted for a pair of leg shackles.

Even Jemmy found himself susceptible to her charms—she had an air of familiarity about her that whispered of strength and warmth and sensibility, capable of drawing a man toward her like a beggar to a warm hearth.

Not to mention the parts that, as a gentleman, he shouldn't know she possessed, but in their short, albeit rather noteworthy, acquaintance, had discovered with the familiarity that one usually had only with a mistress . . . or a hastily gained betrothed.

He shook that idea right out of his head. Whatever was he thinking? She wasn't interested in marriage, and neither was he. Not that any lady *would* have him . . . lamed and scarred as he was.

"I hardly see that any of this is your concern," she was saying, once again bustling about the room, gathering up her belongings. She plucked her stockings, gauzy, French sort of things, from the line by the fire.

He could well imagine what they would look like on her, and more importantly what it would feel like sliding them off her long, elegant legs.

When she saw him staring at her unmentionables, she blushed and shoved them into her valise. "I really must be away."

"Away?" He shook his head. "You can't leave."

"I'm certainly not staying."

He rose from the table. "You don't understand. You can't leave. If you do, you'll be breaking the law. The magistrate won't allow it, and I assure you the constable will have you in irons before you can cross the shire."

"And you, sir?" she asked. "Will you allow me to be wed against my will?"

"Well, I . . . I mean to say," he stammered. He'd never considered the idea. "That is, order must be maintained." Some answer, he thought. He sounded like a third-rate barrister who'd barely managed to make the bar, let alone find the Inns of Court.

"Yes, that is a fine opinion. Some gentleman you are." She tossed a glance in his direction, as if she were sizing him up to see if he were capable of stopping her. When she continued her packing, he felt more than just slighted.

"I care not what your antiquated laws require," she told him. "I will be well away from here before anyone misses me. As it is, I've tarried too long. Thank you, sir, for your warning, and now I bid you good day." She finished stowing her meager possessions and then plopped a straw bonnet atop her head and hustled out the door before he could even try to stop her.

So much for his arguments about maintaining law and order.

But more than that, he found himself unsettled by the quiet solitude of Esme's cottage that now surrounded him. Instead of wrapping him with a sense of calm, it only served as a unpleasant reminder of the empty, lonely void that was his life.

How was it that in such short order, this tart-tongued, spirited lady had left her mark upon him? Not that he was likely to discover what that mark might be, for he'd let her get away.

Demmit, he didn't even know her name.

But a few moments later she came rocketing back into the cottage, a frown creasing her fair brow, and she managed quite handily to toss his life upside down once again.

"Forget something?" he asked, trying his best to ignore the cheer of elation rising in his chest at the sight of her crooked bonnet and the tangled curls peeking out beneath it.

"Yes," she said, her booted foot gouging at the floor, her teeth nibbling for a moment at her lower lip. "Which way is it to Brighton?"

Two

"Brighton?" Jemmy replied. "Are you serious? That's a good fifty miles away. You can't go there unescorted."

Once again her chin rose stubbornly. "I don't see that it is any of your concern."

She was right, it wasn't. But still . . .

"What is in Brighton that is so important?" he asked. It was mere curiosity, he told himself. Not that he cared. Truly he didn't. But then again, what was she thinking traveling about the countryside unchaperoned? She had every appearance of a lady—from her expensive gown to her innocent blushes, not to mention the pair of silk stockings that would be too dear for anyone but quality—and therefore had no business gadding about the countryside without someone looking out for her welfare.

"I wish to . . . I mean to say . . ." She crossed her

arms over her chest. "I have a matter of some importance to conclude there."

Pretty and stubborn to boot, he mused. Yet despite the dead-eyed challenge in her gaze, he didn't miss the waver to her overly confident words. No, for all her bravado, this was a lady in trouble.

Demmit, he thought, his fingers curling around the top of his walking stick, if she needed help, all she had to do was ask. Then again, he reminded himself, she *was* asking him, if only for directions, that is.

Worst of all, in her defiance he saw a glimmer of something he recognized only too well.

The siren's call to adventure.

Are you mad? he wanted to sputter. He knew only too well what happened to fools who followed their folly. He had a worthless leg and scars enough to prove the point.

Yet, there it was in her eyes, in her stance, in the stubborn tilt of her chin, that bewitching notion of the unknown, the spellbinding temptation capable of drawing a man into the depths of hell without a second thought.

It was one thing to be mesmerized by a pretty chit—which she was—but even worse, before he knew it, her determination ignited a spark inside him, so much so that he felt the chill he'd carried since he'd fallen in battle, since his life and body had been ripped apart by that French mine at Badajoz, melt ever so slightly.

Oh, that warmth was heady, but also terrifying. In an instant, he knew he should point her south and forget about her. Forget that outside Bramley Hollow, life continued without him.

At the doorway she stood, tapping her foot with staccato impatience. "Really, sir, if you cannot, nay, will not, help me, I bid you good day."

Then she turned to flee again, and Jemmy found himself blindsided by a rush of panic that this time if he let her walk out the door, he'd never see her again.

Demmit. He had no reason to feel responsible for the chit, none whatsoever. One day it would be his duty to enforce the laws of Bramley Hollow, and here he was considering breaking a pledge that had been kept for nigh over a thousand years.

"Wait," he said before he could stop himself.

She stopped and glanced over her shoulder at him, her chin wavering just a mite. He suspected she'd walk every mile if she must. And if her determination caught him, it was her eyes that held his gaze, wrenched anew at his reluctance.

Green eyes. Oh, the devil take him. There was nothing he could do now. Green eyes had always been his downfall.

Perhaps if he took her to the nearest posting inn, say, Southborough, there would hardly be any crime in that? She was the one breaking the bargain, not he. In truth, his conscience would be in worse repair if he turned a blind eye to her plight and allowed a young woman to wander alone about the countryside. Why, she could be accosted, or worse.

He glanced up and found those green eyes filled with wariness, and worse yet, doubt.

Doubt that he could rise to the challenge. He pounded his walking stick to the floor. "Do stop looking at me that way. I'll help you. At least to get you to the nearest posting house."

Her sudden smile slanted into his heart like a well-aimed arrow. "Oh, thank you. You are too kind."

He tried to ignore the delighted sparkle in her eyes. He wasn't too kind. If he was, he'd take her the entire way to Brighton.

The entire way? Now what was he thinking? He shook his head and mustered every bit of common sense he possessed. *Just to Southborough*, he told himself. Then she'd be out of the shire and on her way to Brighton.

And out of his life. That notion didn't set well either, but he wasn't about to consider anything else. He didn't dare. Hadn't she looked up at him with something akin to horror when she'd first spied his face?

"I can't tell you how much your help means to me," she was saying. "Last night I rather despaired that I would ever see Brighton." Her smile widened, and he tried desperately not to bask under its glow.

"Yes, well, I wouldn't be so enthusiastic in your appreciation," he told her. "We haven't escaped your fate yet. And until we do, you remain bound by your bargain and under the jurisdiction of the magistrate, who I assure you will not look kindly upon your desire to leave Bramley Hollow unwed."

That was an understatement. The magistrate

would most likely throw them both in jail and toss the key down the village well.

Glancing around the cottage one last time, he spied his top hat under the table and stooped to retrieve it. For his labor, he was rewarded with a shooting pain down his leg.

The curse that threatened to issue forth was halted instantly as he glanced up and realized the lady had already stepped out into the sunshine. And what a sight she was.

The sunlight glinted on the curls escaping from her bonnet, igniting the simple brown strands with hints of red and gold.

Fire, like the lady herself.

For an instant, she stood there in those rays of sunlight, like an angel in an illumination, and Jemmy started to wonder if she were real or just some strange dream like the ones Esme's teas were rumored to produce.

Without even thinking, he moved toward her, to touch her, if only to assure himself he wasn't caught in some strange dream. As his fingers settled on the crook of her arm, she turned around to face him.

This time she didn't favor him with that look of loathing and dread that had been all too obvious earlier, but offered him a knowing glance, as if she were waiting for him to confess something that she already knew.

As if she knew all his secrets.

Jemmy's breath caught in his throat. Who the devil was she?

Besides, there was also something oddly familiar about her. She looked to be about his age, making it possible that she'd been out when he'd been in London playing the rake.

Had he flirted with her? Ridden past her in the park? Danced with her?

No, he would have remembered a dance, for her very touch sent his heart racing.

"Who are you?" he whispered. Suddenly the answer became very important. "Have we met?"

Her eyes widened, then her dark lashes shuttered away the tempest behind her green gaze. "If we had, wouldn't you remember me?" The flirtatious words tossed over her shoulder chided him. Gently she pulled her arm free from his grasp and blithely proceeded down the steps.

"Yes, yes, of course I would remember you. Still, if I am to risk my neck in this venture, at the very least I should know your name." Besides, he had to start thinking about her in some way other than "this pretty little chit."

"My name?"

"Of course your name," he told her. "When I am swinging from the Bramley Hollow gallows for saving you, what would my last words be if not your name?"

She laughed. "I hardly think your fate is so dire," she offered. "But if you must utter something, you can curse Miss Smythe."

"Miss Smythe," he said, testing it out. Then, remembering his manners, he bowed. "My name is Reyburn. Mr. James Reyburn. At your service, Miss Smythe."

It seemed rather trivial to make such a formal introduction after she'd been atop him, but sometimes social conventions filled in quite conveniently when all else failed. Especially when his thoughts were more inclined to linger over the memory of holding her in his arms, the soft curves of her . . .

"Um, well, we had best leave at once," he said quickly. Edging past her, he walked as rapidly as he could out to his cart. It was hardly the high-flyer phaeton he'd had in Town, but the cart required only one horse and was relatively easy to get in and out of, so he could handle it without assistance.

If Miss Smythe noticed his less than fashionable transportation, she said nothing, rather tossed her valise into the back and climbed up with a smile on her face, as if she were being escorted to court in a royal coach and matched set of eight.

Gritting his teeth, Jemmy climbed up, doing his best to look as capable as any knight errant, but his tonnish intentions only got him into trouble. As he tried to swing himself up, a bolt of pain shot down his leg and he fell back, landing in an ignoble heap on the ground, his cane clattering beside him.

"Blast," he managed to bluster, saving her ears from the truly blistering curse he wanted to use.

"Oh, dear me!" she exclaimed, clambering down from the cart in a whirl of blue silk. "Mr. Reyburn, are you hurt?"

"Nothing more than my pride."

"Here, let me assist you," she said. Before he could protest, she threw his arm over her shoulder and wrapped her own around his waist, hoisting him to his feet.

He turned his head and found himself face to face with her. This close, with the sunlight streaming down on her, he could discern every minute detail of her features, right down to the way her lips parted as his gaze went there, as if his glance were kiss enough to her.

It certainly wasn't for him. There had been a time when he'd have planted his lips on her sweet, perk pair and stolen a kiss without a second thought, then offered a grin and a wink as a less than sincere apology.

And while he hadn't done so in some time, he certainly was no Methuselah, and wasn't opposed to stealing a favor from a lady.

Especially one as pretty as Miss Smythe.

He tipped his head and made his move. Her eyes widened as he drew closer, but before he could complete his rakish endeavor, she did something that truly upended his intentions. He'd forgotten that she was holding him, and just as easily as she'd helped him to his feet, she let him go—dumping him right back on the ground in the same wretched heap in which she'd found him.

"What did you do that for?" he asked once he'd recovered from the shock.

"I daresay you know why," she said, brushing off her skirts in his direction. "How dare you!"

Jemmy swiped his fingers through his hair. Lord, he was out of practice.

"I'll not be one of your . . . your . . . your conquests, Mr. Reyburn. Don't think I don't know *who* you are, and *what* you are."

Well, demmit, it was just a kiss. Hardly a conquest.

Too bad his memory kept reliving the rare glimpse he'd gained of her long, tempting legs, and the way her round bottom and perfect breasts had felt pressed against him. If he didn't shake off these lascivious thoughts, a conquest would be only the beginning.

"I only wanted to—" he started to protest against his better judgment.

She held up her hand. "Don't even try to explain, sir. Your reputation precedes you."

He dusted off his jacket and reached for his tumbled hat. "What would you know of my reputation?"

"I can read. And the *Morning Post* detailed any number of your, shall we say, more notable exploits about Town." She at least had the courtesy to lean over and retrieve his cane. He thought for a moment she might use it like a governess and rap a lesson in manners into his thick skull.

But instead, like the lady he suspected she was, she offered it to him as if he had merely dropped it.

"The *Post*, you say. Lies, all of them." He laughed as he struggled to his feet—this time without an offer of help from Miss Smythe.

She made no reply, only those delightful brows rising again in scathing disbelief.

"Oh, maybe one or two of those accounts had a bit of truth to them," he offered, "though most were gross exaggerations." He started to brush off his jacket, but realized he was covered in dust, something his father's valet would have horrors over. But if there was any consolation, it would give the bored man something to do.

"I hardly doubt the report of you and Lady Alice . . ." she was saying.

Lady Alice? This Miss Smythe had a fine memory, for Jemmy had all but forgotten about that *on dit*. Not that he should have, his mother had rung a peal over his head for weeks over that momentary lapse.

"Fine. Perhaps I have had one or two well-reported dalliances, but I have always been a gentleman in my intentions," he said. "And as a gentleman, I'll apologize to you. I admit my manners are a bit rusty, and it was not the best form to try to take advantage of a lady who has sought my aid." She started to open her mouth to say something, but he stopped her. "However, I will not apologize for wanting to kiss you. That is entirely your fault."

"M-my fault?" she stammered.

"Yes. You are far too fetching, Miss Smythe, not to be kissed. And kissed often, I might add." From the way her eyes opened wide and a soft blush stole over her cheeks, he decided that perhaps he wasn't as rusty as he'd suspected. For good measure he winked at her.

She shook her head. "As incorrigible, as ever, sir. Now I see that exaggeration isn't solely the domain of the *Morning Post*. My fault, indeed!"

He felt something oddly like a sense of accomplishment. "Now that you've witnessed the true nature of my depraved character," he said, "do you still want a ride?"

Miss Smythe looked up at him, and after what seemed an interminable amount of time, she nodded. "Do you need help?"

His hand went to his chest. "Oh, you wound me, fair maiden. Here I am the one supposedly rescuing you and I've landed in the dust twice." He glanced around the yard. "I daresay I'm not that much of an invalid. I'll just move the cart over to the woodpile and use the block."

Her hands went to her hips. "Why didn't you do that the first time?"

Jemmy snapped his fingers. "Ah, feminine logic. I fear it was my own pride that prevented me from taking such steps. A man doesn't like to look infirm in front of a lady."

"You were worried about my good opinion?" Now it was Miss Smythe's turn to laugh. "How useful for you that you possess a fair amount of pride, Mr. Reyburn, for it seemed to soften your landing. Both times." She smiled again, then walked over to the horse, caught up its bridle, and led the docile animal over to the block. Without another word, she climbed into the seat and waited for him.

Capable, sensible, and possessing a sharp tongue. If he didn't know better, he'd think Esme had found her just for him.

Now that was utter nonsense.

He was about to step up onto the block when a flash of blue caught his eye. There blooming around the foot of it was a cluster of flowers.

Without even thinking, he reached down and plucked a handful of them, then stepped up on the block, caught hold of the cart, and pulled himself into the seat beside her.

It didn't occur to him that this time his leg never gave him even a twinge of pain.

"For you," he said as he handed her the impromptu bouquet. "With my sincerest apologies."

She took his offering, staring down at the flowers for a few seconds before glancing back at him. Then to his amazement, she burst out laughing.

"What is so funny?" he asked as he took up the reins. "Is something wrong with them?" He glanced over at the blossoms now clutched in her hand. They looked perfectly fine to him. Certainly not one of the faultless orchids his father grew, but they'd been offered sincerely.

"Nothing," she finally said. "They're perfect."

How perfect, he just didn't realize.

Amanda stared down at the flowers and wondered at the irony of his offering. *Forget-me-nots.* He'd given her a bouquet of forget-me-nots, while he'd forgotten her.

Utterly and completely.

But she hadn't forgotten him. Not once in all these years had a day passed that she hadn't thought of the only man who deigned to dance with her during her first and only miserable Season.

And now *he* was the one stealing her away from her dire fate. Oh, the absurdity of it plucked at her heart.

Why, he'd even tried to kiss her. She cursed her years at Miss Emery's school, lessons drilled into her that had prompted her (quite against her wishes) to dodge his attempt. Now she might never have another opportunity.

He tapped the reins, and the horse started off, ambling down the pleasant country drive. When they came to the main road, instead of turning onto it, he crossed it and set off across a barely used track.

"Where are we going?" she asked.

He nodded at the grassy lane before them. "This way is less traveled. Though it will take longer, we're not as likely to run into the magistrate or the constable. Can you imagine the scandal if we were to be tossed into jail together?"

Amanda glanced over at him. His mouth was set in a serious line, but there was a teasing light in his eyes that shocked her. He was flirting with her.

In her entire life, no man had ever flirted with her. Especially not one as rakish as Jemmy Reyburn. She wasn't too sure what she should do.

Flirt back, a mischievous voice clamored over her straitlaced thoughts.

No, I shouldn't, she told herself, resorting to the same fears and admonitions that had ruled her life for five and twenty years.

No, she couldn't think like that anymore. This was her adventure, her chance to live the life she'd always fancied . . .

She laughed aloud at the irony of all of it.

"What is so funny now?" he asked.

"All of this." She waved her hand at the cart

and the countryside. "I'm fleeing a matchmaker."

"You won't be laughing if we get caught," he reminded her.

She glanced up at him. "I assume, Mr. Reyburn, given your rather scandalous reputation, you will endeavor not to be caught. Besides, I suspect you could charm your way past a hangman's noose, as well as this magistrate who inspires such terror."

"You hold me in high esteem for someone who purports not to know me." His brows arched and he paused, as if waiting for her to enlighten him.

Amanda wasn't about to have him discover the truth, so she said, "You look rather capable."

"Hardly that. I can't even climb into a pony cart without a lady's assistance. A pony cart, mind you."

"Oh, bother that," she told him quite emphatically. "There is more to a man's measure than the carriage he chooses or how he gets into it—or out of it, as the case may be. What makes you admirable is that you're helping me, despite the obvious risk." For good measure, she winked at him, as he had done to her earlier.

"I have to admit this is entirely more enjoyable than listening to my mother prattle on all day about heirs and duty." He tipped his hat back and grinned. "In truth, I haven't had this much fun in ages."

"And why is that?" she asked. She couldn't imagine the Jemmy Reyburn she remembered not living a day of his life that wasn't filled with some great series of amusements or lively jests.

"I don't go to Town anymore, and I don't have too many visitors out here."

"And you never married?" she asked before she

could stop herself. It was none of her business, truly, but she had to know.

He looked away. "No."

Never married? She eyed him again. "Whyever not?"

"Because . . . well, you can see why," he said, nodding down at his leg. "I was injured in the war."

"I don't see why that should have any bearing on the matter," she told him. Certainly his injuries had been grievous, given the scar on his face and his dependence on his walking stick, but he'd survived, lived through it all. "It isn't like your life ended. You're a well respected gentleman. You could do anything you want with your life."

"Yes, except for the important things."

"And those would be?"

He shrugged his shoulders. "First of all, I'd have to find someone who doesn't mind this," he said, pointing at the jagged scar that ran down the side of his face.

She glanced over at it. "I believe it makes you look piratical."

"Piratical? Is that a word?" he teased.

"If it isn't, it is now," she told him. "What else?"

"What else, what?" he asked, glancing up the lane and not at her, evading her questions with as much caution as if she were the magistrate, his defenses rising up around him like a dark mantle of fear.

Amanda was stunned. He was afraid. Jemmy Reyburn was afraid to live. Outlandish!

"What else keeps you from finding a wife?" she pressed.

Jemmy sucked a deep breath. "For one thing, I can't dance. Can hardly get up the steps to most ballrooms, for that matter. Can't ride all that well, either." He paused for a moment, then shrugged his shoulders. "Actually, not at all. Rather hopeless, don't you think?"

If she wasn't mistaken, he was appealing to her to agree with him. To add her stamp of approval to his sorry case.

Amanda wound the strings on her reticule into a tight knot. Up until yesterday she probably would have shared his frustration with life—resolved to live to the end of her days trapped by her own deficiencies, or those that her mother liked to point out whenever the opportunity presented itself—which unfortunately was often. But that was until . . . until she'd learned the truth of her life, and made the fateful decision to take this enormous gamble at happiness.

A chance of a lifetime to discover the joy she'd longed for so very much. The very enchantment Jemmy seemed determined to toss away, because of what . . . a bad leg and a rather dashing scar?

Besides, the young man she remembered, the one she'd watched at countless routs and balls, would never have let such a minor infirmity stop him. The Jemmy Reyburn of her heart would have slain such a dragon with a teasing quip and a wink of his devilish blue eyes.

But this man beside her, she barely recognized. She'd read the gossip about him leaving London in the company of his mother's hired companion—it had been quite a scandal. Later she'd found an account about him being in Spain with Wellington's army, but how he'd gotten there, she knew not. His injuries she had known about as well, for they had been reported in a copy of her father's *Gentleman's Magazine*:

Mr. James Reyburn, Bramley Hollow, Kent, arrived at Portsmouth on the *Goliath* last month, having suffered grievous harm at Badajoz.

She'd committed the lines to memory, then spent the next year frantically searching the papers for some mention of him. Then after that, she'd waited impatiently through each Season hoping to see some word of his return to Town or even mention of a betrothal. But there hadn't been a single reference to the elusive Mr. Reyburn in all these years—and now she knew why.

He'd chosen exile from the exacting and critical eyes of society. He was right that he would be viewed with a less discerning eye by some, but surely he knew his character, his charm would leave him in good stead with the people who loved him.

But clearly he didn't believe that—couldn't believe it. And instead of pitying him, all that boiled up in her heart, in the tightness of her chest, was anger. White-hot anger. Like nothing she'd ever felt before.

She pressed her lips together, trying to stop the words that sprang forth, but they came rushing out anyway. "Perhaps it is time to stop feeling sorry for yourself and start living again."

He drew the cart to a quick stop, the horse letting out a neigh of protest. *"Sorry for myself?* You have no idea what I have endured or the pain I suffer." His face grew red with anger and indignation. "Start living again, indeed! The life I loved is gone. Lost."

She straightened and mustered every bit of resolve she could manage in the face of his bitterness. *Lost?* He thought his life was lost? He hadn't the vaguest idea what it meant to lose one's life.

And while she'd never been so outspoken in her life, with every passing moment she felt an odd courage filling her with strength and resolve.

She sat up straighter and looked him right in the eye. "Then if it is lost, I daresay that is your fault. Because you will hardly find it when you've convinced yourself you are better off hiding away in the country than taking advantage of the gifts you still possess."

Three

*J*emmy couldn't believe the chit's audacity. If his suspicions were right, she was running away from some sort of trouble, and here she was telling him to toss aside everything he held dear and start his life anew.

Why of all the—

Then a quiet voice whispered up from his heart, *Perhaps you've already begun.*

He shook his head. It wasn't the same thing. He was doing what any gentleman would do— assisting a lady in need. It wasn't the same as what she was suggesting.

Not in the least.

Then he looked into her eyes, at the passion behind her challenge. For the first time in as long as he could remember, he felt his heart beat, hammering in his chest. Not from struggling up the front steps of Finch Manor but from the thrill of living. Of being in the company of a woman.

Even a vexing one like Miss Smythe.

Gads, he'd spent the past hour flirting with the chit. He hadn't wooed a woman in so long, he was surprised he still remembered how.

He glanced over at the stubborn tilt of her chin. Lord, if he didn't know better he thought he should look for a gauntlet tossed between them.

"So what would you have me do?" he asked, almost afraid to hear what this hoyden would suggest.

Her eyes widened, as if she too were surprised by his inquiry. Though if she felt any hesitation, it didn't last long. "To start with, return to Town," she said, settling quite comfortably into her role as his guide. "I would advise you to partake in all the pursuits that young men do in London. *All of them.*"

He wondered if she truly understood what that meant. As if holding her in his arms, toppling onto the bed like a pair of lovers hadn't been enough reminder of what he was missing. But London? Therein lay a life of mistresses and willing widows. Of flirtatious pursuits and passionate nights.

He was loath to admit it, but what she suggested terrified him, right down to his unpolished and scuffed boots.

Go back to Town? To have the eye of Society upon him? What if he fell? Or just stumbled? He'd look the buffoon. And worse than being laughed at, he didn't want the pitying glances he knew would be directed at him, discreetly of course.

Hadn't Miss Smythe, once she'd gained a look at his scarred face, scooted out of his grasp with all due haste? Lesson learned there.

No, he'd been foolish to dream of military grandeur in the first place, and now he preferred to exhibit his mislaid and tattered ideals in private.

"I have no desire to go to London," he told her, picking up the reins and urging the horse forward again.

She laughed. "Liar. Tell me you wouldn't love to spend an afternoon at Tatt's? Or off in one of those clubs you men find so satisfying?" She paused for a second. "What does go on at White's? I would so love to see that infamous betting book."

"Inside White's?" He nearly dropped the ribbons. "That is certainly no place for a lady." Now he was convinced the chit was mad. A young woman inside those hallowed halls? Never!

"But it is for a gentleman?" she argued. "How is that? I've never understood the distinction." She crossed her arms over her chest and waited for his explanation.

"Well . . . well . . ." he began. "Oh, demmit, suffice it to say it is not a fit place for you. Or any lady."

"If I wasn't going to Brighton, I think I might want to discover the truth for myself."

That did it for Jemmy. He would see her on the mail coach for Brighton if he had to pay the fare himself and bribe the driver to keep her locked inside the coach until she was at the very edge of the sea, well and good away from White's.

They continued along the lane in silence and he tried his best to ignore the wicked smile tilting her lips. Gads, what the devil was she imagining with such a look on her face?

"Don't you want to hear what else I would do?" she offered just then.

"No!" he shot back. "It's bad enough I'm bound for the Bramley Hollow gallows, but I won't lose my membership at Brook's as well."

"At this pace you'll have us both dancing to the hangman's tune." She laughed and took the reins from him, giving them a confident toss. The horse responded by picking up its pace. "Besides, 'tis a long way to Brighton, and I haven't the time to tarry."

He retrieved the ribbons from her grasp, his pride once again piqued. He might not make an elegant leg, but he could still drive a cart. "What has you in such a hurry?"

That stopped her smug stance. "As I said before, the matter is personal."

So she wasn't going to confide in him. "If you won't tell me what is in Brighton," he said, "I fear I will have to come to my own conclusions."

"And those would be?"

"A lover."

She made an inelegant snort. "You and Mrs. Maguire. She thought I was going there to meet a gentleman as well." She sighed, her fingers twining around her reticule strings again. "That isn't why I am going to Brighton."

"A job, perhaps?"

She shook her head.

Jemmy sat back and took another long look at her. "Perhaps you are going to escape a wretched betrothal. I would venture your ne'er-do-well guardian has engaged you to a terrible and hideous old roué and you are running away to escape a disastrous future."

At this, she laughed again. "That only happens in French romances."

He shrugged. "I suppose so. But I still think you mean to escape a betrothal."

She shook her head and then looked away. "Nothing like that, I assure you," she said softly. "I've never been engaged."

Something about her wistful tone made him pause. "That seems impossible," he told her. "What is wrong with the men in . . . in . . . Where is it that you are from? I've forgotten."

"That's because I didn't say," she replied, once again smiling.

"Ah, yes. Another of your mysterious qualities."

She peeked up from beneath her bonnet, a blush stealing over her cheeks. "You think I'm mysterious?"

"Immensely," he told her, and was rewarded with another burst of laughter, sweet and entirely filled with joy. "In fact, I find you quite—"

They rounded a corner and as they did, his words fell to a halt at the sight before them.

A single man stood in the roadway, his hand in the air signaling them to stop. Behind him sat a large carriage filling the way, an obstruction capable of stopping even the most determined criminal.

"Who is that?" she whispered.

"Mr. Holmes. The village constable."

"And am I to suppose that inside the carriage is this magistrate you hold in such terror?"

Jemmy shook his head. "No. Worse."

"Worse than the magistrate?"

"Yes," he said.

"Who could be worse than this unholy magistrate you've told me so much about?"

"My mother."

"Lady Finch?" she gasped.

And from the way the color drained from her once rosy cheeks, he had no doubts she understood exactly what fate had in store for them.

The hangman would have been a far more welcome sight.

As Jemmy had explained hastily to Amanda, it would do them no good to make a run for it, so they had continued toward the barricade as if they were doing nothing more than taking a companionable morning drive through the countryside.

"Jemmy, you've found her!" Lady Finch exclaimed as he pulled to a stop before the frowning constable. "Excellent! Esme came by this morning just after you left, and when we arrived at her cottage there was no sign of you or the young lady." Her brows rose at the significance of such a situation. "But here you are safe and sound—both of you."

Used as Amanda was to her mother's critical eye, nothing could have prepared her for Lady Finch's sharp gaze. Heavens, she'd rather have to go through another tea with Mrs. Drummond-

Burrell in hopes of receiving vouchers to Almack's than face this all too discerning inspection.

From Lady Finch's furrowed brow and none-too-keen expression, Amanda suspected her false front was about to be uncloaked.

"Miss Smythe, I believe it is?" the baroness asked.

Amanda nodded, afraid to breathe even a word before the lady all the *ton* held in an unearthly terror. 'Twas said that even though Lady Finch had come to town only once in the last thirty years, she knew what the king had for breakfast before the man was served his plate.

If anyone could ferret out her true identity, it was Lady Finch.

"Where are your people, gel? Where do you come from?"

At this question, Jemmy turned to her, one of his brows quirked in a quizzical air. She'd denied him these answers, but in the face of the indomitable Lady Finch, they both knew there was no eluding the questions now.

"I'm . . . I'm . . . I'm from London," she offered.

Lady Finch huffed, then leaned over and tapped her cane on the side of her barouche. "Mrs. Radleigh, your assistance please."

A moment later a woman climbed down from the carriage, notebook in hand and pen at the ready. She was dressed in widow's weeds, with her face buried within the expanse of her black bonnet, so it was hard to determine how old Mrs. Radleigh was or what she looked like.

Jemmy leaned over and whispered, "My mother's secretary, poor chit. East India widow.

No family to speak of, so Mother took her in." He shook his head woefully, as if that were the worst fate to befall the lady. "Why, just the other day, the old dragon had her writing a—"

"What is that, James?" his sharp-eared mother called out.

"Nothing, ma'am," he said in a polite and deferential tone, though Amanda didn't miss the lingering sparks of mischief in his eyes.

"So, Miss Smythe of London," Lady Finch began as she elbowed Mr. Holmes out of her path and stalked toward the pony cart. "I will have your parents' directions in London. Now."

It was an order that brooked no refusal. "Number Eight, Hanway Street," she told the lady. She might have to answer the baroness's questions, but that didn't mean she had to tell the truth. Besides, it wasn't a complete lie. It was the house they had let six years ago during her Season, or as her father liked to call it, "that demmed waste of my money."

Besides, it was the only London address she knew by heart. And it would take even the indomitable Lady Finch some time to determine her falsehood. By then Amanda would be well on her way to Brighton.

"Harrumph! London, you say?" The lady thumped her cane to the hard-packed road. "You haven't the sound nor the look of a girl brought up in the city, but then again, I daresay you went to school in Bath, where they were able to rid you of those wretched Town affectations."

Amanda's mouth opened, despite her very

proper Bath education. How had Lady Finch
known where she'd gone to school? Why, she
might as well 'fess up right this very moment and
return home. Return to the dreadful future awaiting her there.

But before she could do anything so drastic,
something incredible happened, something so
miraculous that it gave her the faith to believe
that all was not lost. Not quite yet.

For as Lady Finch turned her attention to Mrs.
Radleigh, instructing her hapless secretary to
make a notation of the address and check it
against her previous correspondence, Jemmy
pressed his leg against Amanda's.

It was such a slight movement, at first she
thought he'd just accidentally bumped her, but
then as the pressure increased, Amanda slanted a
glance up from beneath her bonnet to find him
shooting her a quick wink.

"Hang in there, minx," he whispered. "Her
Dragonship is feisty, but my money is on you."
Then he leaned closer, so his lips were but a hair's
breadth from her ear. "And I haven't forgotten my
promise. I'll see you get to Brighton if I have to
take you there myself."

See her all the way to Brighton? Why, the very
idea was scandalous. Amanda didn't know what
to say. Not that she could have responded with
Lady Finch so close at hand.

Nor did it appear that the baroness was paying
them any heed, for she was engrossed in dictating
a long list to Mrs. Radleigh. ". . . and you'll need
to send a note to Tunbridge for those fellows who

played at Lady Kirkwood's *soirée* last winter. They were tolerable musicians and should suffice for a betrothal ball."

"A wha-a-at?" Amanda blurted out.

"Why, your betrothal ball, Miss Smythe," Lady Finch replied matter-of-factly. "Mrs. Maguire and I decided it is the most expedient means of finding your match. She is of the opinion that time is of the essence, and I"—she glanced from Amanda to her son and then back to Amanda—"share that notion."

"But I don't want to be—" Amanda's protest was cut short by a none-too-gentle jab in the ribs by Jemmy.

He made a great show of floundering with the reins as if he'd dropped them. "Oh, excuse me, Miss Smythe," he said. "How terribly clumsy of me. What was it you were saying? That you didn't want my dear mother to go to such bother? I agree. Really, Mother, is a ball entirely necessary?"

"I don't see that this is any of your concern, Jemmy," Lady Finch said, her sharp gaze still fixed on Amanda.

Amanda protested despite her aching ribs. "My lady, a ball is not necessary."

"It most certainly is," Lady Finch declared. "All the best young men will be invited. Just think, in two nights, you'll be happily wed."

"*Two nights?*" both she and Jemmy repeated.

Lady Finch cocked an iron brow. "And not a moment too soon, I assume."

"Uh-hum," the constable coughed.

"Yes, Mr. Holmes. What is it?" she asked.

"My lady, I'll have to take her into custody." He coughed again and shuffled his feet. "She was breaking the law. And the young master as well."

"Nonsense," Lady Finch declared. "My son was merely bringing Miss Smythe over to Finch Manor so she would have proper accommodations until the match is made."

The constable narrowed his gaze on Jemmy. "Is that so?"

"Certainly, Holmes," he told him. "What else would I be doing?"

Amanda had to admire his mettle. He said it as if he meant it.

"Seems a roundabout way, iffin you ask me." Holmes rubbed his chin and shot a glance around the cart at the lonely track behind them.

Jemmy grinned at the man. "Sir, if you had such a lovely lady at your side, would you take the most direct route?"

Mr. Holmes colored, as did Amanda. She glanced down at her boots to hide her astonishment. James Reyburn thought her lovely? Though it was probably just more evidence of his legendary skills of exaggeration, a part of her clung to a hope that he was telling the truth.

"That will be quite enough from you, Jemmy," Lady Finch scolded. "Miss Smythe, attend me in my carriage." She nodded at Amanda to get down. "Now."

From the set of the lady's jaw, Amanda knew she had no choice but to do as the imperious baroness bid.

But to her surprise, Jemmy caught her arm and held her in place.

"Mother, I see no reason why I can't continue escorting Miss Smythe home while you and Mrs. Radleigh see to your errands in the village. I am sure you have any number of things to—"

"Preposterous!" Lady Finch told him, coming forward in a brisk, no-nonsense manner and taking the situation in hand. She caught up Amanda's elbow and pulled her down from the cart. "Miss Smythe and I have much to discuss." Lady Finch led her away, tugging Amanda along when she dragged her heels. "My dear girl, I would like to hear your opinions on the flowers and the dinner menu for your ball. I believe a bride should have some say in the matters, though I've already instructed Cook on several points. However, I do think there is some leeway on the salads."

With the barouche looming before her, Amanda thought a French tumbrel might have been more appropriate.

"Mother!" Jemmy called out, lodging one more protest. "Miss Smythe may not want to be dragged about town. She would probably like a respite from her travels and I could—"

"Jemmy," Lady Finch said, "I think you've seen quite enough of Miss Smythe this morning. You can have the pleasure of her company tonight at dinner." With that, his mother prodded Amanda into the carriage. And to her shock, she could have sworn she heard the baroness muttering under her breath, "A little time apart ought to have him in a fine fettle."

She glanced over her shoulder at the baroness, amazed at her astute observation.

Leave it to Lady Finch to know that a little time is all I have left.

Four

Jemmy entered the dining room at precisely quarter after six, expecting quite a fuss over their now infamous guest. But the room was silent and still—with no one about, save his mother. Not even their loyal butler, Addison, who presided over every meal with a fierce attention to detail, was in sight. Only a small collection of trays on the sideboard containing sliced meats and cheeses, breads, and a few dishes of Cook's best sauces and stewed vegetables awaited him.

"Where is everyone?" he asked, filling a plate and taking his place at the table. What he really wanted to ask was "Where is Miss Smythe?" but decided against such a blatant question.

So much for his discretion. His mother's first glance, then second more inspecting one, said more than if he'd asked directly as to Miss

Smythe's whereabouts. "If you didn't insist on living down at the gatehouse, you wouldn't be late for dinner."

"I'm fashionable," he replied. "And it doesn't appear that I've missed all that much." He glanced around the empty seats. "So where is everyone?"

"Your father is repotting the specimens he got from Lord Bellweather, and Mrs. Radleigh is finishing up a few tasks. She should be down presently." She gave his appearance another once-over before returning her attention to the papers before her.

Demmit, he knew he shouldn't have come up to the house in a clean waistcoat and jacket. She'd most definitely gotten the wrong idea. And of course, she failed to mention Miss Smythe's whereabouts. Deliberately, if he knew his mother.

He ran his hand over his chin and winced when he came to the nick he'd given himself shaving. Still, in his favor, if his mother had an opinion as to his nattily tied cravat and pressed jacket, she said nothing—for once. He could only imagine the earful he'd be getting if he'd succeeded in convincing his father's valet, Rogers, to give his hair a trim.

Rather than offer her any further cause for speculation, he dug into his meal and kept his gaze pinned on the food before him.

But it wasn't long before he broke the silence between them, allowing his curiosity to get the better of him. "Mother?" he asked as nonchalantly as he could muster. "Where is Miss

Smythe? Aren't prospective brides allowed a last supper?" He managed a light smile as if he were just trying to make some pleasant conversation.

After all, it would be odd if he didn't ask about their houseguest, wouldn't it?

"She was a bit fatigued from our shopping trip and so I told her not to worry about making herself presentable for supper. Addison is taking her a tray."

A bit fatigued? He didn't like the sound of that. "I told you that she shouldn't be dragged about," he said, letting his temper get the better of him. "You've probably worn her out completely."

His mother's brow arched, and once again that knowing gaze fell on him. "I doubt that," she said with a bemused tone. "She appeared quite fit when I checked on her not a half an hour ago."

Well, she needn't smile about it, he thought. His concern had been naught but . . . Oh, demmit, he could hardly tell his mother that he'd made a promise to take the lady to Brighton. Yet how was he going to do that if his mother insisted on dragging the poor chit about and wearing her to a frazzle?

They ate for a time in silence, Jemmy considering all the ways he could smuggle Miss Smythe out of the shire. If only he had one of the Danvers brothers about. They always seemed to know how to take care of these clandestine matters.

Though if he were truly going to use them as examples, he should well consider that each time one of them had set out to help a lady he'd found himself married to the wily minx.

Jemmy wanted to groan.

Just then, Addison came in. "My lady, Mrs. Radleigh tells me that she found the extra china in the attic, and that along with the plate and silver Lady Kirkwood is sending over, we should have enough to seat all the guests for the midnight supper." The ever efficient butler noticed Jemmy's empty glass and immediately filled it.

The man must have known that he was going to need the fortification.

Jemmy shot a wary glance at his mother. "Just how many people do you plan to invite?" He took a sip of the rich burgundy, trying to appear as uninterested as possible.

His mother shuffled through her papers until she found the correct list. "The last count was one hundred and twelve."

"Wha-a-a-t?" he sputtered.

"Those are only the ones I'm positive will arrive in time. Though I do hope Lord and Lady Worledge can come," she said, barely sparing him a glance. "It is short notice, but one can always depend on Camilla to bring a crowd along—especially since all five of her sons are currently in Town." She paused for a moment, a calculating look on her face as she surveyed her list. She glanced up and smiled. "And not a one married."

Lord Worledge's rabble? Oh, this had gone too far. Jemmy tried his best to remain calm as he broached the subject with his mother. He failed utterly.

"That horde of idiots?" he burst out. "Are you

mad? The eldest is in his cups every waking moment, while the next one gambles without a care, or the means, I might add." He threw down his napkin and frowned. "How can you even consider any of that lot for Miss Smythe?"

"And whyever not?" his mother demanded. "The viscount shan't live too much longer. Lord knows, I have a hard time believing he's lasted these past few years, what with his gout and heart ailment. That only makes his eldest son all that much more appealing, despite his unfortunate tendencies toward drink. Imagine, your Miss Smythe a viscountess, and quite possibly a widow in short order."

"She is not 'my Miss Smythe'!" Jemmy said, a mite too adamantly, uncomfortable with the notion of Miss Smythe being married, let alone a widow free of society's restraints. "Truly, Mother, this is getting out of hand."

"How so?" Lady Finch asked, setting her pen down. "If Esme is to find Miss Smythe the perfect groom, she will need a good selection of eligible men from which to choose."

"But don't you think this is a bit much?" he asked. "Next thing you know, you'll tell me you've invited Prinny and the unmarried dukes."

"Oh, go on. Miss Smythe is quality, but she's certainly not royalty. Besides, Esme was quite specific about the sort of man she is looking to match with the gel. And I happen to agree with her."

"And you think you can get enough of this 'sort' here on such short notice?"

"Of course, or else I wouldn't be borrowing Lady Kirkwood's spare china service."

"But Mother, how do you expect the staff to handle all this? After all, we don't entertain." In fact, in his entire life he couldn't think of his parents ever putting on a ball.

His mother had gone back to surveying her list. "Then it is about time we did."

"Just like that, you think you can actually fill the house with prospective grooms?"

"Of course."

He didn't like the way she said that with such supreme confidence. Especially since his mother was rarely wrong when it came to predicting the whims of the *ton*.

Still, perhaps she was mistaken. There was one very important fact she wasn't considering. "And who will come? The Season has barely begun. I can't imagine now that everyone has settled back in Town, they will feel inclined to come back out to the country."

"Never fear," Lady Finch said. "When word gets out that your father and I are hosting a matchmaker's ball, London will empty. Besides, it isn't all that great of a distance to come here."

He knew only too well his mother was right—everyone and anyone who could afford a fast carriage would come down to Kent for such an evening. Not just prospective grooms, but marriage-minded mothers and their flocks of daughters as well, for where there were eligible men, mamas and debutantes were never far behind.

He decided to try another tack. "Have you thought that Miss Smythe may be viewed as merely a curiosity in this sideshow? Really, what mother would want to see her daughter bartered off in this fashion. 'Tis unseemly."

Even as he said the words, he knew he was defeated, for the knowing look on his mother's face said what Jemmy should have known.

A married daughter is a fine sight better than a spinster, no matter how she finds her way to the altar.

But he wasn't about to give up. Not yet. He still had a few more arguments to present. After all, it had been a long afternoon pacing about the gatehouse, waiting for his mother and Miss Smythe to return.

"Have you considered that Miss Smythe doesn't want to be wed?"

His mother's gaze rolled toward the ceiling, as if she were considering whether he was truly her son. "Jemmy, despite your aversion to matrimony, it is not the same for young ladies. Every girl wants to be married."

He shook his head. "But I think Miss Smythe may have misunderstood Esme's intentions, and if that is the case, marrying her off in this fashion would be a terrible miscarriage of justice."

"Harrumph!" Her snort of disbelief went well beyond her usual derision.

Jemmy persisted, even against his own better sense. "Besides, how will the village's reputation be served if it gets out that an innocent young lady was carted before the parson against her will? Not only that, her father may have a thing or two to say if his slip of a daughter is married off without his consent."

There, he had finally found a way out of this for

Miss Smythe. Perhaps her innocent age would serve her well.

His mother didn't look all that defeated. "She is five and twenty and therefore quite able to make a marriage without her father's consent."

His mouth fell open. "She's that old?" It left him a little unnerved that his mother seemed to know his Miss Smythe better than he did.

But she's not your Miss Smythe, remember?

"Really, Jemmy," she began, "it matters not how the bargain was wrought, only that it was made. You know that as well as anyone else."

The finality of her words might have cast a pall over any remaining arguments. But he wasn't his mother's progeny for nothing.

"I don't believe Smythe is her real name," he said, hoping his conspiratorial tone added to Miss Smythe's already mysterious background.

"Uh-hum" was all his mother murmured as she continued fussing over her various lists.

"We can't have Esme pawning her off on some unsuspecting fellow and discover she's mad as a hatter and poisoned two previous husbands before her arrival here."

At this, his mother set down her pen and stared at him as if he were the one gone round the bend. She let out a patient breath. "Jemmy, really, I don't know where you get these notions. Miss Smythe has the Bath manners of a gently bred young lady from a good family. And why she's left the shelter and protection of her relations is her reason and hers alone, but it is up to us to see her wed quickly and her good reputation secured." His mother straightened her papers and then looked him squarely in the eye. "If you believe a fraud has taken place, prove it. However, until then—"

"A bargain is a bargain," he said, repeating the village's fateful promise.

Jemmy knew it was entirely inappropriate, but after spending an hour dodging the staff and his mother, he made his way up to Miss Smythe's room and knocked on the door.

There was no answer.

"Miss Smythe?" he said softly. "'Tis me, Mr. Reyburn." He had to keep his voice down for her room was dangerously close to his mother's chambers. "Miss Smythe? Are you in there? I must speak to you."

There came no reply. No female admonition to be away from the sanctity of her bedroom, not even an invitation to come in.

Not that he'd been looking for one. He was only worried about keeping his promise to her. And in a timely fashion. It would be a far cry better for everyone if she was well away from Bramley Hollow. His quiet, well-ordered life was being turned upside down by her arrival, and he wanted his solitude back. Egads, the ball his mother intended to throw would have half the *ton* at Finch Manor. Old friends and flirtatious conquests. All here to view the wreckage of his misspent youth.

He clutched his cane more tightly. His leg throbbed from a day spent gadding about. Pacing about the gatehouse, climbing up to the attic to find the trunk with his old dress clothes—for he could hardly come up to dinner in his usual country togs—and then the last hour spent lurking about the backstairs. No wonder his leg hurt like the very devil, for he hadn't been on it that much since the day he'd fallen in battle.

Tapping on the door again, he whispered a little louder, "Miss Smythe, I need just a moment of your time."

Nothing but silence greeted him. He stared for a moment at the solid panel. Perhaps she'd fallen asleep or was suffering from one of those megrims that befell ladies. After all, she'd spent the good part of the day with his mother, and that was enough to do in most anyone.

It really would be in bad form to wake her. Yet . . .

He knocked on the door a little harder. "Miss Smythe, are you well?"

When yet again there was no response, another thought struck him. A premonition of disaster sinking into the pit of his stomach.

She'd left. Fled Finch Manor. *And without him.*

But even as he ran through the hundreds of routes she could have taken to the main road, how he would scour the countryside to find her, he heard a clunk of something falling to the floor inside her room, followed by a mild curse. Not much of an ear bender, but enough to make him smile.

Smile that she was still here.

"Miss Smythe, if you do not open this door at once, I am going to come in."

"Go away." There was another thump and clunk, and yet another curse.

This time he didn't wait for an invitation. He opened the door and made his laborious way into the room.

Miss Smythe stood in front of the window, holding it up with one hand. Not only was she dressed in her traveling clothes, but there by her feet sat her valise at the ready.

So she *was* trying to leave. And without his help. Jemmy squared his shoulders and wished his cane to perdition. Did she think him so useless that he was unable to keep his word?

"Oh, do stop gawking," she sputtered. "And find something to prop this window open."

"What are you thinking?" he said, stomping into the room, his leg now the least of his worries. To his horror, there was an oddly fashioned rope—made out of, if his guess was correct, the sheets from her bed. One end was tied to the leg of the grand four-poster that took up a good portion of her room, while the rest lay coiled nearby.

"Mr. Reyburn," she said, struggling beneath the weight of the half-open window. "Please, I need your help."

He crossed the room and took hold of it. She sighed, then bent over to retrieve her rope. But by the time she'd turned around, he'd closed the window and flipped the latch shut.

"What are you doing?" she said, nudging him out of the way and starting to struggle with the heavy casement again. "It took me a good half hour to chisel that open, let alone the time to make the rope. And what with every servant and bothersome fellow coming in here pestering me with your mother's questions, I haven't much time to spare."

"You can't go out the window with that," he said, pointing at her tattered sheets.

"And whyever not?"

He didn't answer, just picked it up and held a width between his hands. Then to make his point, he gave it a good tug and watched her eyes widen with horror as her well-intentioned knots pulled apart. "If the fall didn't kill you, Father would put you in irons for damaging his roses."

She wasn't thwarted for long. A wild light filled the lady's green gaze, and she caught up her valise and started past him. "I must be away from here, away from this madness."

He reached out and caught her, and without even thinking tugged her into his arms. "You aren't going anywhere, not without—"

She began sputtering something, and as he stared down at her all he could see was the fire in her eyes, all he could hear was the passion of her protests.

Her passion—that was what did him in. He wanted nothing more than to throw himself into the tempest that was so much a part of her character—to steal a kiss that he suspected would make a man forget that he didn't want to live.

And in that wild, delirious moment, suddenly all he wanted was to live—a life full of passion and adventure, everything he saw blazing there in her eyes. So this time he put aside any hesitation and caught her lips with his, kissing her hungrily.

Oh, it had been a long time, but he found that once he'd taken that devilish first step, his rakish desires had no trouble leading him back down the path of temptation.

And tempt him she did. While she continued to protest for a few moments, to his surprise, she didn't send him flying into a heap. Just as quickly as he had taken her into his arms, she was clinging to him. She opened her mouth to him and welcomed his kiss.

A sense of awe filled his heart. Jemmy forgot his leg, forgot that she was a guest in his parents' home, and kissed her thoroughly, tempting and teasing her until her arms wound around his neck, and she rose up on her tiptoes to get even closer to him.

Then came the unavoidable part of temptation, for once he'd tasted her lips, a kiss wasn't enough. His fingers tugged off her bonnet so they could splay in the silken strands hidden beneath. Emboldened by his success, he pushed aside her pelisse, his thumb tracing the neckline of her gown, down to the rounded curves of her full, firm breasts. Beneath his palm he could feel the hard peaks of her nipples, the hammering of her heart—thrumming with the same desire that had his blood pounding.

Reverently he cupped her breast and started to stoke a new fire within her.

At this, she broke away from him, one hand at the neckline of her gown, the other covering her lips, her eyes alight with a newfound awareness.

Then the realization hit him. Egads, she'd never been kissed. And while his next thought was to kiss her again, Miss Smythe had other ideas.

She backed away from him until she hit the dressing table chair. "Why not?"

"Why not, what?" he asked distractedly, his gaze fixed on her lips. He took a step closer to her, to those damnable, kissable lips.

She crossed her arms over her chest. "Why can't I leave? I thought you were going to help me."

Oh, that again.

"I will," he told her, dipping his head down to steal another kiss, but the lady wasn't as willing this time. She dodged him and shoved a chair between them. He counted himself lucky that she hadn't chosen to send him sprawling as she had earlier in the day.

"No more of . . . of . . . that," she sputtered, pointing at him with an accusing finger. "I doubt such foolery will see me to Brighton."

Jemmy grinned. "Ah, but it would make the journey more pleasant."

She blushed quite prettily.

He took a step closer to her. "I promised to see you out of this bargain, and I will."

"The sooner the better," she told him. "Before this betrothal ball of your mother's gets out of hand."

Jemmy flinched. Nothing better to warm a lady's heart toward one than being the bearer of bad news. "Too late for that," he warned her. "Mother's determined to empty London for your sake."

Whatever color had been in her cheeks drained away. "What has she done?"

"Invited most everyone. The house is going to

be overflowing. She's determined to make a spectacular match for you."

The bride-to-be shot a hasty glance back over at the window. He didn't blame her. If he were about to be offered up before society like a sacrificial lamb, not even Finch Manor's three stories and the thorniest collection of shrubbery in the land would keep him from escaping.

And neither would it prevent Miss Smythe, he guessed.

He shoved the chair aside and took her in his arms again. "I will help you," he insisted, mostly because the last thing he wanted was her leaving without him. Not for the reasons some might suspect. He tried telling himself again that it wouldn't do for her to go gallivanting across the countryside unescorted.

Why, it was scandalous and dangerous to boot.

Unlike being alone in her bedchamber and kissing her? his conscience prodded. He shook off that notion. His intentions were honorable. Well, almost noble.

Though if he was entirely honest, with her lithesome and delectable body pressed against his, he knew his intentions were anything but virtuous. More like agonizing. He wanted nothing more than to kiss her and not stop there.

"I must be gone," she said, struggling a bit in his arms, though even he knew that if she'd wanted to be away from him, she could have mustered the wherewithal.

"You can't sneak out now," he told her. "Not with everyone up and in a frenzy over this ball.

Why, they'll be at it until after midnight, I would guess."

Even as he said the words, he saw her catch hold of that one piece of essential information. *Midnight.*

Damn the chit. But before he could tell her not to consider leaving without him, there came a knock at the door.

"Miss Smythe! Miss Smythe! I have some more questions for you."

They broke apart, staring at each other, mirrored expressions of horror on their faces.

"Your mother," she whispered.

Jemmy groaned. Of all the perfect timing.

"Miss Smythe? Are you in there?" Lady Finch called out.

"A moment, my lady," she said sweetly. Then she turned to Jemmy and whispered, "Hide!" She glanced around the room until her gaze fell on the bed. Catching up the counterpane with her free hand, she dashed her valise under the bed. In a flash, the rope followed. Then she pointed to the dusty, cramped space. "You as well, sir."

Jemmy heaved a deep sigh but knew whatever discomfort he'd undergo to get down under her bed, it would be nothing to the deafening and painful peal his mother would ring over his head if she discovered him here.

Down he went, and once he was beneath the bed, she put the coverlet back in place and opened the door.

"Good evening, my lady."

"Yes, yes, Miss Smythe, good evening." His mother's skirts swished impatiently past the bed as she bustled in. "It is imperative we discuss the order of the dances."

Then to Jemmy's dismay, his mother went through an agonizingly long list of waltzes, quadrilles, and rounds, discussing whom Miss Smythe should partner with for each dance.

Demmit, why did his mother have to be so thorough? Meanwhile, dust clogged his nose, and he pinched it shut to keep from sneezing. Really, the upstairs maids were shamelessly neglecting their cleaning duties, but how could he complain since the inevitable question would follow.

And what exactly were you doing under Miss Smythe's bed?

To his relief, his mother finally dispensed with her list and was about to take her leave when she paused before the bed. It seemed she had one last bit of advice to offer, though it wasn't for Miss Smythe.

"Jemmy," she said, her slippered foot lifting the counterpane.

He flinched. There was no way to deny his presence, so he answered her. "Yes, Mother?"

"I'll give you five seconds to get out of this room, or I'll tell Lady Kirkwood that I suspect you of harboring a *tendre* for her daughter."

That was enough to send Jemmy scrambling up from beneath the bed and out of the room with only a breathless "Good night, Miss Smythe. Mother."

It wasn't until he was halfway down the driveway to the gatehouse that he recalled that he hadn't warned Miss Smythe not to attempt to escape on her own. Now he'd have no choice but to wait up for her.

And hope he could stop her before it was too late.

Five

*A*manda endured three more visits from Lady Finch, two from her harried secretary, and one last one from the housekeeper, who issued an admonishment that she "should 'ave been abed hours ago."

As if she could sleep. She was trapped in this reckless bargain, as well as by Lady Finch's determination to see her well matched. Dear Lord, why hadn't Wellington just sent the determined baroness to scold the French into an armistice instead of wasting so many years fighting? Amanda suspected the lady could have nagged Napoleon's army into a full retreat with nary a shot being fired.

And despite Jemmy's assurances that he would help her, she wasn't about to wait for his assistance—not after that kiss they'd shared.

Dire consequences might await her in Brighton,

but nothing in her innocent and maidenly dreams had ever prepared her for the searing heat of Jemmy's kiss, or the way her knees quaked beneath her.

No, she had to leave before he had a chance to bewitch her completely and leave her confessing her wretched circumstances to him. For despite his rakish reputation, Amanda had no doubts there was an all too honorable man beneath that devilish kiss—one who would put nobility and honor before everything.

And she didn't want his pity, his wretched integrity. But oh, how she longed for his kiss, his touch once again.

She dug beneath the bed and retrieved her valise. With the house finally as quiet as a rectory, she opened the door and made her way down the hall, resolute in her desire to flee.

Silently she bid a farewell to Lady Finch. Despite the baroness's machinations, the lady had shown her nothing but generosity and kindness. Amanda did her best to ignore the guilt creeping down her spine for running out on the lady's grand plans.

She tiptoed down the stairs and considered how she was going to get outside. Her father always had their house locked up at night tighter than Newgate, as if their quiet corner of Hertfordshire was filled with brigands just waiting for the opportunity to pillage their possessions.

But for some reason, she doubted the Finches held the same view of the world, and in confirmation of her suspicions, she found the front door unbarred and unlocked.

Silently she stole from their trusting home feeling like a veritable thief.

The moon shone a brilliant path down the drive. She smiled at this rare bit of luck and made her way toward the road at a fast clip, the gravel crunching beneath her booted feet, her valise bouncing against her leg.

As she got closer to the gatehouse, she slowed her pace, moving as silently as she could.

When they had returned from their shopping trip, Lady Finch had pointed it out, explaining that it was Jemmy's refuge from the world, from his family. In fact, the lady had told her quite a bit about her son without Amanda even asking. Laments about his injuries, his lonely years of self-imposed exile.

"If only he had something to live for," Lady Finch had said sadly as they'd driven past his bachelor residence. The lady's comments had explained much about the changes in James Reyburn, and left Amanda at sixes and sevens over the enigmatic man who scorned life, but kissed with a boundless passion.

To her disappointment, the house was dark and quiet. He hadn't even bothered to wait up for her, for surely he knew she wasn't going to sit around and wait for calamity to strike.

Drat the man, she thought. *Some hero he turned out to be*. Obviously her kiss hadn't meant as much to him as it had to her, for if it had he would have—

"Good evening, Miss Smythe," his deep voice called out, just as her foot was about to cross the sanctuary of Finch Manor. "Or should I say, good morning?"

She whirled around to find Jemmy perched on one of the great stone lions that sat on either side of the gate. He struck a match and lit a small lamp resting on the feline's head. The steady flame illuminated the night, imprisoning her in a circle of light.

But before she could reply, another voice rose from the copse across the road.

"And I would say the same to you, sir," came the voice of Bramley Hollow's persistent constable.

Holmes! Amanda's head swung in that direction.

"Now, now, now, what have we here?" he said, walking out from his hiding spot, casting a large, looming shadow. "You wouldn't be trying to escape, now would you, miss?"

Amanda glanced over at Jemmy, silently beseeching him to come to her rescue. He just couldn't let her be hauled off to jail. He wouldn't!

The wretch grinned at her. "Yes, Miss Smythe," he said, "do tell the good constable what you are doing out at this ungodly time of night."

"I was . . . well, I thought to get . . . what I mean to say is, that I needed . . ."

Jemmy carefully eased himself down from his perch and caught up his walking stick. "There you have it, Holmes. A logical explanation if ever there was one." He took Amanda's arm in his and swung her toward the house. "I suppose you've had enough air for tonight, haven't you, Miss Smythe?"

"Why yes, Mr. Reyburn," Amanda offered, her

heart skipping a traitorous beat at the heat of his touch.

"Just a moment there, sir," Holmes called out, catching up Jemmy's lamp and holding it high enough to cast the light in their direction. "The lady was escaping, and that's against the law."

Jemmy stopped and turned around. "Do you think, Mr. Holmes, that if she were escaping she'd be so foolish as to go out the front door and down the drive?"

Holmes scratched his chin. "Suppose not."

"Exactly," Jemmy told him, tapping his cane to the ground. "Miss Smythe was doing nothing more than soothing her bridal nerves with a little fresh air. Isn't that so?" He squeezed her arm, sending a reckless thread of warmth through her limbs. Why, he made her feel as if she could outwit the devil himself.

"Uh, yes. A walk," she told the constable. "I was taking a turn in the garden and . . . and I . . ."

"Became lost?" Jemmy suggested.

"That's it exactly," she said. "I became terribly turned around. I fear I have the most wretched sense of direction."

Holmes's lips drew into a skeptical line. "Then I would ask, miss, do you always take your traveling bag with you when you go for a walk?"

Leaning forward, she cupped her hand to her mouth and said in a loud aside, "I didn't want to leave my belongings unattended. I don't like to speak ill of Lady Finch's staff, but I would hate to lose my poor and meager possessions to thievery."

Jemmy coughed and sputtered, and she couldn't tell if it was from indignation or ill-concealed humor at her poor lie.

Holmes didn't look all that convinced either. "And you, Mr. Reyburn, sir. What are you doing out here?"

"Stargazing," Jemmy told him. To prove his point, he reached inside his jacket and pulled out a small telescope. He held it up for Holmes to see. "A passion of mine."

"Humph!" the constable said. "That may be well and good, but I'll still have to take the lady in. I'm not about to risk her making another wrong turn and ending up on the mail coach to London."

"I wouldn't do that," Amanda rushed to assure him. It wasn't entirely a lie. She had no intention of going in the direction of London.

"Sorry, miss, but the law is the law." He reached out to take her valise, when to her utter amazement, Jemmy stepped in front of her.

"Miss Smythe isn't going anywhere, Holmes."

Amanda's breath stopped at his commanding words. First his kiss, now this possessive stance. All for her?

The constable's jaw worked back and forth. "But sir, you know the law as well as I do. She was escaping, and that's that."

Jemmy remained rooted in place, feet firmly planted. "She has done no such thing. As long as she remains on Finch land, she hasn't broken any laws." He drew an imaginary line between the two lions with his walking stick. "Inside this threshold, she is under my family's protection."

Holmes's eyes narrowed, and Amanda knew the man was caught in a wretched tangle. What could he do? Go against the word of the future baron?

"So be it, Mr. Reyburn," he replied. "But if I catch her outside the gates, it's to jail she goes until she can be properly wed. A bargain is a bargain, and my family's been protecting Bramley Hollow for eight generations on that understanding. No one has broken a vow in all those years, and I mean to see her wed like she was promised." He glanced over at Amanda. "And, miss, don't fear for your possessions. I'll be about. Nothing or *no one* will go astray before your match is made."

"You are a credit to the village, Mr. Holmes," Jemmy assured him, as he started to drag Amanda back up to the house.

"Mr. Reyburn, I—"

"Not another word, Miss Smythe, not until we are well out of earshot of our determined constable."

She nodded and continued walking.

If it had been under any other circumstances, she would have thought she was dreaming, for the evening was made for romance, if not a poorly executed escape.

The moon shone bright and full of face, while the stars offered only a pale twinkling of secrets overhead. On either side of the drive, flowers lent their own fragrant air—the spice of early roses, the sweet scent of lilacs, the elusive air of peonies.

And beside her, through the magic of the moonlight and the romance of the stars, Jemmy walked along determinedly. *Jemmy Reyburn.* She couldn't believe it. After so many years of wondering about him, now here was the man himself. All at once she wanted to ask him a bevy of questions. Did he like poetry? Had he ever dreamed of seeing the ruins at Pompeii? What had Spain been like?

And most importantly, had he ever loved someone?

As she had him . . . albeit from afar.

She continued along silently, her mind full of questions, her lips pressed together for fear of confessing too much to this man who unknowingly had been the hero of her lonely days and empty nights.

"You shouldn't have tried to leave," he said, breaking the silence.

Hardly the words of love she so longed to hear at least once in her dull and unremarkable life, but what did she expect from this man? He who kissed her senseless and called her "fetching" one moment, then barked at her the next with such dark passion.

"You needn't concern yourself with my problems, Mr. Reyburn," she said airily. "I won't have you go to jail for my sake."

"I don't plan on going to jail for you, for I wouldn't have been so foolhardy as to go out the front gates."

So much for her knight errant. No braving the dragon or storming the walls in a blaze of fire on the promise of attaining her slender hand. "And what other route was I to take?" she asked. "I don't know the countryside, as evidenced by my arrival at Mrs. Maguire's cottage last night. But I do know the way to the nearest mail coach, and it is out those gates." She jerked her thumb over her shoulder, where Holmes probably still remained encamped in his lonely and determined vigil.

Jemmy groaned and shook his head. "How did you intend to get to the coach? Walk?"

He needn't sound so incredulous. Perhaps she hadn't thought out all the details, just as she hadn't when she'd fled her parents' house. Certainly there were difficulties to face when one took hasty action—as evidenced by this matchmaker muddle—but this slight delay aside, she knew one thing for certain, she needed to be gone from Finch Manor—for without a doubt if this man kissed her again and, by some miracle of fate, asked her to stay, she would. And that would spell disaster.

For her, and more importantly, she sensed, for him. "Well, yes, I did intend to walk."

Instead of going in the front door, he led her around the side of the house and stopped in a small garden. "Miss Smythe, you have amazing faith."

She notched her chin up a bit higher. "I fear I possess little else."

There in the moonlight she spied a dangerous light in his eyes. "Oh, I wouldn't be so sure of that," he said.

His confession sent shivers through her.

"Do you know what could have happened to you—out on the road, at night, alone? There are men out there who, well, suffice it to say they aren't gentlemen when it comes to unescorted, unprotected ladies. You could have come to grievous harm." His brow furrowed. "I would never forgive myself if anything happened to you." His hand brushed over a curl that had escaped her bonnet, and gently, protectively, he tucked it back inside. Then his hands went to her shoulders. His fingers, warm and steady, held her with determined resolve. "Promise me not to try anything so foolhardy ever again. At least not without me."

Without him? She couldn't think of anything else she would want more. To spend the rest of her days with him. Oh, it sounded like heaven. Then she looked into his eyes and saw a dangerous passion there.

Something to live for.

Oh, no, not that. She couldn't be that for him. There wasn't time. Not before . . . The hope in his eyes tugged at her. Why couldn't he see that it wasn't possible?

"I can't stay," she whispered, panic and anguish rising in her chest.

He misunderstood completely. "I know. I'll help you. I gave you my word I would, and yet—" His words came to a hesitant halt.

"And yet what?" she asked, despite her resolve to leave.

"I don't want you to go."

There it was, the words she longed to hear. How was it that now, of all times, the enchantment of the stars had drifted down and worked their magic on him?

She didn't know how or why, but his grasp shifted, from holding her at arm's length to pulling her into his embrace.

"God help me, you drive me to distraction," he murmured, before he leaned over and claimed her lips in another kiss.

She tried to tell herself to stop him, that this was desperate folly, but from the moment his mouth captured hers, Amanda felt as if she were being swept heavenward once again. She couldn't do anything but sigh with elation and give herself to him.

His tongue boldly teased her lips, and she thought she would go wild with hunger for him—tasting him, letting him devour her.

Amanda had never imagined a kiss could be so intimate, so wildly delicious. She celebrated by winding her arms around his neck. Her body folded wantonly against his. Oh, bother her fears, her worries. She'd never have another chance to do this . . .

His hand pressed at the small of her back, pulling her closer. She felt the length and breadth of his chest, his body up against hers. This was what living meant.

Amanda's heart pounded, dangerously so, and she wondered if she should stop. Stop before . . .

But how could she? Jemmy might have changed, but his kisses tasted of the impetuous rake she remembered from her Season.

A rake capable of making all her dreams come true, right now, this very night.

Yet the pounding in her chest grew more furious, more frightening, and Amanda wrenched herself out of his grasp.

What was she thinking? She shouldn't be doing this—not if it meant . . .

"No," she whispered. *Not now.*

He stared at her. "What is it?"

"I must be gone." She backed away from him. "I must be away from here." *From you.*

He caught hold of her once again. "What is it? What has you so frightened?"

"I'm not afraid," she lied. Terrified was more like it.

"Yes, you are." He pulled her close, into the warm and safe confines of his steady embrace. "I feel foolish, I don't even know your name."

"Amanda," she told him impetuously. "My name is Amanda." She took a deep breath, and then another. Oh, goodness, if only her heart would stop beating so violently, if only she could catch her breath. Then perhaps she could think straight. What was she doing, telling him her name?

"Amanda," he repeated, as if tasting it on his lips as he had her kiss. "It fits. Fair and pretty."

"Hardly that," she managed to say, trying very hard not to be delighted at the sound of it on his lips, at his praise.

"That and more, my sweet Amanda."

Oh, this was worse than she'd imagined. Having Jemmy kiss her was one thing, but to have him holding her so and whispering endearments into her ear and asking her to stay—

Not when—

"I can't," she said, pushing at his chest.

"Can't what? Stay?" He nestled her securely in place and then kissed her forehead. "I don't know how or why, but you've brought the light back into my life. Never fear, I'll take care of Her Dragonship and all this betrothal ball nonsense in the morning. And then we'll find some way to—"

"No!" she told him, wrenching herself free. Her eyes brimmed with tears. "I can't stay here."

"Why not?" he demanded.

"I just can't." How foolish she sounded. But what else could she tell him? The truth?

"Is it me?" he asked. "I know I've been a little forward and all, but, demmit, I haven't felt this way . . . well, ever."

"No, it isn't you." She glanced heavenward. *Never you.*

"Then what is it?" he demanded. "Is there someone else?"

"No!" Amanda told him.

"Then why won't you stay?" he asked, catching her before she realized what he was doing. He didn't even hesitate, but caught her mouth in a passionate kiss. A hot, demanding kiss that sent her heart fluttering anew. By the time he tore his lips from hers, she was gasping for air. "Stay with me, Amanda. Brighton will always be there."

"Yes, but I won't be," she whispered as she tore herself out of his arms and ran for the door.

"Stay with me, Amanda," he beseeched. "Be my life, my heart."

She paused at the doorway, clutching the latch and gulping back the sobs that tore at her heart, then confessed the secret she'd tried so hard to keep locked away.

"I can't stay with you because I haven't a life to give you. I can't stay with you because I'm dying."

Six

The next morning Jemmy was still berating himself for not immediately following Amanda into the house and demanding an explanation.

Amanda dying? The woman who had breathed life back into his existence about to lose her own? It was unfathomable.

And what had he done? Stood in the garden gaping after her like a floundering trout. And by the time he'd gained his senses he'd found the side door locked, as well as the front door.

Short of the impossible—climbing the trellis to her window—he'd had no choice but to wait until morning to discover what could be done for her.

"I won't allow it," he muttered as he stalked into Finch Manor the next morning, past the usually unflappable Addison.

"Allow what, sir?" the butler asked.

Jemmy ran a hand through his hair. "Nothing, Addison. Is everyone at breakfast?"

"Up and gone, I daresay," the butler told him. "Your mother arose very early, and is now in the ballroom with Miss Smythe and the dancing master."

Jemmy started for the stairwell.

The butler shot a puzzling look at him. "Have you forgotten something, sir?"

"Not that I'm aware of," he replied, and stalked up the stairs to the ballroom, any thoughts of breakfast left behind.

Even as he made his way to the first landing, he could hear someone playing a waltz on the pianoforte. Mrs. Radleigh, most likely, for she was about the only one in the house who had such talent. The passionate and tempting music sent a ripple of anticipation all the way down to his toes.

It made him want to dance. Dance with Amanda.

Ridiculous notion, he thought, gripping the handrail. As ridiculous as the idea that she was dying. With resolute determination to get to the bottom of this nonsense, he finished climbing the stairs.

He entered the room expecting to see Amanda gracefully dancing across the floor, but what met his searching gaze was organized chaos. Footmen scurried about carrying massive arrangements of greenery, roses, and orange blossoms—Jemmy wondered what his father would say about his precious orange trees being raided for their sweetly scented blooms. A maid, her arms laden with linens, dashed around him. It seemed the entire household occupied the ballroom, what with their cleaning and decorating the long un-used room. The Holland covers were gone, the long curtains on the windows were flung back. Even the doorways to the balconies were open, and he wondered wryly if, like Amanda's win-dows, they'd had to be chiseled open.

As he made his way through the busy throng, he found his mother in the middle of the ball-room directing the mayhem like a field marshal sending her troops into a do-or-die battle.

And there was no sign of Amanda until he heard a despairing cry from the other side of the room.

"Non! Non! Non, mademoiselle!"

The lovely music ended abruptly, Mrs. Radleigh's fingers hovering over the keys. Jemmy's head swiveled in that direction, and to his delight, there by the pianoforte stood Amanda.

His breath caught at the sight of her. Her glori-ous hair was coming down in a shambles of curls, while her cheeks were pink from dancing. There she was, so lovely and vibrant, so very much alive, that he couldn't believe she had the right of it—she couldn't be dying.

"I am so sorry, monsieur," she was saying. She held her skirt up so her slippers peeked out from beneath the hemline. "I fear when I lose sight of my feet, I never know where they may land."

"My toes, mademoiselle! Your foot landed on my toes," the fussy little man said. His hands went to his hips as he complained further, "How many times must I say it, my toes are not for dancing upon."

The flurry of activity in the ballroom paused at this petulant display.

Lady Finch bustled forward. "Bother your toes, Monsieur Suchet. She only needs to dance well enough to leave her chosen groom able to walk down the aisle unassisted." Then she shot a glance around the room at her eavesdropping staff, and in an instant they were once again in motion, loyal servants hard at work to see their mistress's demands met.

Amanda hadn't noticed him as yet, and Jemmy watched her intently. How could she be dying? The flush of pink to her cheeks, the sparkle in her eyes belied her doomful prediction.

"I've never been very good at dancing," she said to Lady Finch. "My apologies, monsieur."

"You must listen to the music," Monsieur Suchet was saying, tapping his finger to his ear. "Listen, mademoiselle."

"I do," Amanda said, "but while my ears hear one song, it always seems that my feet are dancing to another."

Jemmy wanted to laugh at the incongruity of her logic. He suspected that being contrary was very much a part of her.

"Start the music again, Mrs. Radleigh," Lady Finch said, waving her handkerchief at the pianoforte.

The lady picked up where she'd left off. The dancing master heaved a loud sigh, then began counting aloud to the beat. After a few false starts, he and Amanda began twirling around the room.

The waltz didn't last long, for very quickly there was another stumble on the floor. The pair broke up, and the fastidious dancing master erupted into a flurry of angry French.

This time when Amanda glanced up from examining the damage to the dancing master's boots, her gaze met Jemmy's. In an instant, the passion from the night before glowed with recognition.

He wanted nothing more than to march across the room and kiss her until the fires he'd ignited last night rekindled . . . convinced him that he'd misheard her.

That she couldn't be dying.

"One last time, mademoiselle," the dancing master said between clenched teeth.

"Yes, I would love to," she said, but her words were for Jemmy and for him alone.

Mrs. Radleigh began to play, and the dancing master took Amanda in his arms. Slowly, he moved her through the steps of a waltz.

Instead of watching her feet, Amanda watched Jemmy. And he, her. Airy and light, she swung about the room, her gaze never leaving his. He'd held her less than a handful of times, but he knew every curve of her body, could almost predict the way she moved.

Please, let her live, he prayed silently. *But most of all, let me love her.*

Just then the last notes twinkled from the pianoforte, and Amanda and the dancing master came to an elegant stop.

"Monsieur, you've done it!" Lady Finch declared, clapping her hands and grinning, as did all the servants—probably from relief that this critical step in finding Amanda's match was finally concluded.

The dancing master made his bow to Lady Finch, then departed, limping and muttering a litany of complaints as to his poor beleaguered fate, lost and adrift in the graceless ballrooms of England.

In the meantime, Jemmy's mother had been taken aside by the seamstress and was consulting on laces, while Amanda stood frozen in place glancing shyly at him. After a few moments she started for one of the chairs.

Dear Lord, his mother had probably pushed Amanda's frail health to the very brink.

"Addison, please get some tea for Miss Smythe," he ordered as he passed the butler on his way to her side.

The man nodded and went to fetch a tray, while Jemmy crossed the room, taking in every detail of the lady. How stray tendrils of her hair curled around her ears, how her brow furrowed as she rubbed her feet. He would have kissed that crease away if his mother and the entire staff hadn't been in the room.

Oh, damn them all, he'd kiss her anyway.

"What are you doing—" she began to say as he knelt before her.

"Shh," he told her, taking her foot in his hands and rubbing it. "Don't tax yourself." He looked into her eyes and nearly drowned in those beautiful green depths. "Tell me it isn't true."

She said nothing, just looked away.

"How long?" he managed to ask. Gads, he who had longed and prayed for death in his narrow cot in Spain now found himself angry and willing to fight any battle to snatch Amanda away from its cold clutches.

"Days, maybe weeks," she whispered, still unwilling to look at him.

"And you are going to Brighton to see a doctor?"

She shook her head. "No. For the sea."

He wasn't quite sure he'd heard her correctly. "Sea bathing will save your life?"

At this she smiled. "No, nothing will do that, but I would like to hear the waves and surf once before I die. And perhaps," she said, pulling her foot free from his grasp, "put my toes in the water."

His heart constricted. Of all the possibilities he'd considered for why she wanted so desperately to go to Brighton—employment, a lover—never once had he considered some fanciful dream to stand on the shore.

And as much as he intended to be the one who made sure her every wish was granted, he also wanted something else. Something more.

He took her hands in his. "I'm going to take you to London. I'll find you a doctor. Someone who knows of these things, someone who knows of a cure."

She shook her head. "I've already seen the doctor. And he was quite positive that there is nothing to be done. Well, except to wait."

Wait? Wait for her to die? Jemmy wasn't going to stand for that. "Are you sure?"

Nodding, she bit her lip and looked away. "I was ill all winter. A decline, my mother called it. Recently I just couldn't get out of bed, and she feared I was about to die, so she summoned the doctor. All the way from London and at great expense."

Now it was Jemmy's turn to nod. "She must

have been overcome with worry. No wonder she sought out someone so qualified."

To his shock, Amanda laughed. "Not for the reasons you would think." She looked away again, and this time when she glanced back at him, her eyes brimmed with tears.

"What is it?" he asked. "What other reasons would there be to call a doctor other than to see you live?"

Amanda swiped at her cheeks and forced a small smile to her lips. "My mother's reason had nothing to do with me and everything to do with my sister."

"Your sister? Is she ill as well?"

She laughed again. "No, not at all. Actually, she is due to come out this Season. My mother feared that if I died before then, it would put the family in mourning and my sister would have to put off her debut until next year. My parents hope to see her well-matched and heard rumors the Earl of Symmons was coming to London to look for a bride this spring. My passing would have put a terrible crimp in their plans."

Jemmy dropped her hands and stared at her. He'd never heard anything so outrageous in his life. No wonder she didn't believe in him—with such a family to look after her.

Across the room, an overburdened maid collided with a footman, and the vase she carried smashed to the floor. Lady Finch hurried into the fray, directing the mess to be cleared and soothing the flustered servants.

Jemmy rose and ran a hand through his hair.

"First of all, I am going to put a stop to all this nonsense. Then you and I are going to—"

Her hand caught his arm. "No."

"What do you mean, no?"

"No. You cannot call this off. It is giving your mother a great deal of pleasure to put on this ball. Let her have her moment of glory."

"But you cannot be wed. Not to anyone else but—" He stopped over the last fateful word. *Me.* His near confession caught his heart. Marry Amanda?

If someone had told him just two days earlier he was going to meet the woman of his dreams, let alone marry her, he would have scoffed at the notion as pure tomfoolery.

But now he understood how love happens. As his father would say, one moment there is merely a tiny seed, and then you turn around and something spectacular and unexpected has blossomed, seemingly out of nothing.

Nothing more than a wrong turn on a country lane. A storm that drove her to seek shelter. A morning ride to visit a friend. A bargain with a matchmaker.

A bargain he intended to see broken. Just as he intended to find a way to see Amanda live a long and happy life.

"Miss Smythe! Miss Smythe, where have you gone to?" his mother was calling.

"I'm here, my lady," she replied. She leaned closer to Jemmy. "Do not disappoint her. For my sake."

What could he do but agree when she turned

her pleading gaze upon him? His heart melted, and if this was what Amanda wanted . . . but that didn't mean he was going to let her be married off.

He caught her hand in his once again. "We'll slip away just before midnight," he told her. "There will be so many people coming and going, we'll be able to elude our determined constable."

"You'd do all that, risk so much for me?" she asked.

He nodded. "Until then," he promised, pressing a quick kiss onto her fingertips.

"Jemmy, quit pestering Miss Smythe," his mother said, crossing the room. As she passed the butler who had just arrived with a tea tray, she said, "Addison, tea! How perfect. Please put it in the music room and then find Mrs. Maguire for me. I want her opinion on Miss Smythe's ball gown." With the tray set aside and the butler dispatched, the lady turned her attention to Amanda. "Come along, my dear. Mrs. Hanley is here for your fitting. She might not be some fancy imported mantua maker, but I'd put her handiwork and taste up against the best Bond Street seamstress. I think you'll find the gown she's designed exquisite."

"Mother, I—" Jemmy called after them.

Amanda swung around, her eyes wide with alarm and betrayal.

He had to put a stop to this nonsense—didn't she see that? But one more pleading glance from her green eyes stopped him.

"What is it, Jemmy?" his mother snapped, her patience wearing thin. He suspected the old dragon had the day planned out to the last second to see this wretched ball pulled off without a hitch.

Amanda shook her head, her lips forming two words. *No, please.*

"Jemmy, I haven't all day," his mother was saying.

"Yes, well, I wanted to say . . . that is, I wanted to ask . . ." He took a deep breath and spit out the first stray thought that came to mind. "I would like the honor of dancing with Miss Smythe in the opening set."

"Then ask the gel and be done with it," his mother said. "But one dance, and that is all you get."

Amanda's eyes sparkled and her mouth curved in a sly smile. "I would be honored, sir."

"Bah! What nonsense," Lady Finch said, waving her hand at her son. "Now go make yourself useful, Jemmy. Your father has wandered off again. Go see to it that he's found and is reminded to be in attendance tomorrow night. I won't have Lady Mitton spreading rumors again that I've nagged Lord Finch into exile." With that, she had Amanda hustled into the music room where an impromptu dressmaker's shop had been set up.

Amanda turned and smiled at him. *Thank you.* But only too quickly the double doors were closed on this all too female domain, shutting Jemmy off from her.

"Nelson, will you look at all the flowers? They add the right touch, now don't they?"

Jemmy spun around to find Esme standing in the doorway, a basket in hand and that odd cat of hers poking his head out from under the lid.

"Her Ladyship is in the music room, ma'am," one of the maids told her.

Esme nodded and started off in that direction, but Jemmy stepped in front of her.

"This match must be called off."

Esme glanced up at him, made an inelegant snort, and sidestepped around him.

Jemmy wasn't about to be ignored. "Amanda, er, I mean, Miss Smythe isn't capable of making a marriage."

The matchmaker stopped and glanced up at him. As did all the staff in the room.

Esme noticed their interested gazes and caught Jemmy by the arm, steering him out to one of the balconies.

"What is this nonsense?" she demanded as she closed the door behind them.

"As I said, Miss Smythe is incapable of making a match."

"Why's that?"

Jemmy glanced away. "Her health prevents it."

"Meow," Nelson called out.

"Exactly," Esme agreed. "She looked well enough yesterday."

He wasn't about to lower himself to arguing with a cat, so he stared Esme in the eye and ignored her feline companion. "Her looks are deceptive. I have it from the lady herself that she is dying." He had promised Amanda that he wouldn't tell his mother, but he hadn't said anything about not telling the matchmaker.

But if he thought that Esme would see Amanda's failing condition as a detriment to marital bliss, Jemmy was wrong. Very wrong.

"Dying, you say? We all are, my dear boy. One way or another." She turned around to leave, but he caught her arm and stopped her.

"You don't understand. She's ill. Truly dying." Gads, he was loath to say the words, let alone hear them. "Don't you see, she can't be matched."

Esme shrugged. "I see no such thing. Now if you will excuse me, I have—"

Jemmy held firm, unwilling to let her go. "I won't have Amanda spending her last days with someone she doesn't love."

At this, Esme smiled, her face awash in wrinkles, but her blue eyes rang sharp and clear. "She won't be."

"But Esme—"

"Shh," she told him, patting his sleeve and soothing him just as she had when he'd been a young boy and come to her with his troubles. "Don't fret so much. You'd be amazed at what love can heal." She pulled her arm free from him and picked up Nelson's basket. "Now, I'm sure you have things to do, don't you? I know I've a dress to examine." She shook her head. "Ah, matchmaking used to be so easy, but now it's all gowns and hair and proper number of waltzes. Bah, I should retire." She toddled off, her litany of laments meant obviously for Nelson and not Jemmy.

As he watched her go, he grit his teeth. He'd have no help from that quarter, but then he should have known better. But damn them all, he wouldn't let Amanda be matched without a fight. He stormed out of the room, plans whirling in his mind for a midnight escape.

Which of the horses in the stable were the fastest . . . where to change their mounts . . . how to hide his curricle from Mr. Holmes . . . and the most discreet posting houses along the route.

Demmit, he didn't even know if he could still drive his curricle. Then he laughed. If he couldn't, he'd bet his last farthing Amanda could— practical, wonderful minx that she was.

As he left the room, he realized everyone was staring at him as if he'd gone mad. He had, he wanted to tell them. As mad as the king. Instead he grinned for one and all, then continued storming out of the room, with the servants gaping after him.

For who among them had seen the young master without his cane since he'd returned from Spain?

Seven

*F*or all her secret yearnings to discover a bit of passion before she died, Amanda never imagined that she would find it in the arms of, of all people, Jemmy Reyburn.

Was it too selfish and too much to believe that he could care for her as passionately as she did him? Truly, it was too much to hope for.

He hadn't appeared at dinner that evening, and Lady Finch had kept her busy up until she'd dropped into her bed, dazed and exhausted.

But in the morning there had been a note and a spray of orange blossoms on her nightstand, their sweet, tangy scent enticing her out of her slumbers, while his missive had left a blush on her cheeks.

I would risk a kingdom for your freedom. The gallows for yet another kiss from your lips.—J

She'd pressed the flowers to her nose and inhaled deeply, then glanced around her room and wondered how and when he'd been able to place them there.

That he'd chanced so much, to secure her the flowers and leave a note for her eyes only, told her that he would indeed risk it all for her.

But why? Because he loved her or because he pitied her plight? She didn't know if she was brave enough to stay and discover the truth.

For most of the day Amanda reminded herself time and time again of all the reasons that she shouldn't remain at Finch Manor for a single moment longer. Yet each instance when she gathered up her courage to slip away, there was Lady Finch or Esme or Mr. Holmes nearby. Each was a problem, but the most insurmountable obstacle was Jemmy.

Gads, one look at his craggy features, his strong shoulders, the determined line of his lips as he went about making his furtive plans, and her resolve crumbled.

So in her indecision, the day passed, and now it was just a scant half hour before the ball was to begin. Not that she'd have much chance of escaping now, for she was trapped in her room as the dressmaker and Lady Finch fussed over her gown, while a multitude of other servants hovered about, each at the ready to help the next Bramley Hollow bride be matched.

Not that she could fault their efforts to see her wed. One of the maids, who had "a way with hair," spent the better part of the afternoon fussing over Amanda's usually wayward strands until

the talented girl had created a waterfall of perfectly curled tendrils. Then with a deft hand,
she'd tucked Jemmy's orange blossoms around
her head until they made a fairylike crown of
white.

Amanda stared into the mirror in awe at the
magic the girl had wrought. Dull brown hair that
had always made her look mousy now shone with
a lustrous glow from the tart lemon juice the maid
had used as a rinse.

Then there was her gown, and what a creation it
was! Lady Finch's dressmaker had chosen an
emerald-green silk that gave new fire to her eyes,
lent a dramatic background to her fair coloring
and the Titian tint of her hair.

"Oh, miss," the maid enthused, "you look like a
princess. Wait until your groom sees you." She
giggled. "Whoever he may be."

A groom? Her heart skipped a beat. She should
be on her way to Brighton right this very minute,
not standing about being trussed up for this impromptu Marriage Mart.

Yet Esme had been right. Dreams could come
true. After all, hadn't she been able to see Jemmy
again? But this ball was pure folly. Her identity
could be revealed by any number of the guests,
though if she were honest, she wondered if any
of the *ton* would remember her. There was an
irony in the fact that her health had started to fail
when she'd been told she wasn't going to be in-
cluded in their party when the family went to
London for her younger sister's Season. How
she'd longed to return to Town just once more,
her dreams still holding to the tiniest of hopes

that perhaps she might find someone who could love her. But those dreams had been shattered when her father had said that he'd spent the money on one Season for her, and he wasn't about to waste more "trying to make a silk purse out of a sow's ear."

But look what one silk dress had done—turned her into a princess—like the one in the Bramley Hollow legend. Truly, she barely recognized herself—so she had to believe that no one— possibly not even her family would recognize her.

Yet it was more than just the dress that was different about her. She'd certainly lost a lot of weight over the winter, what with her lack of appetite. Perhaps it was as she'd told Jemmy the other night, that in learning about her imminent death, she'd left all the boring vestiges of herself behind as well.

Having spent her entire life being usurped by her lithesome and blond sisters, she felt as if for the first time she'd been able to set her dreams free. Not that this new gown didn't help. Her mother had never seen any reason to dress her in anything but hand-me-downs, since it was unlikely that she'd attract an eligible *parti* worthy of such expense. Her sisters' ill-fitting gowns, let out to the very edge of their seams, had never felt as this gown did—the emerald silk flowed over her new figure and showed it off like nothing she'd ever worn. And it breathed with life—the color setting off her eyes and hair. Her sister Bethany's old gowns, all whites and pastels, had done nothing for her coloring, save leave her looking pasty, blending her into the sea of other debutantes. The only exception had been Regina's blue silk, which Amanda had taken the day she'd left because she'd always thought the gown might make her look pretty.

Lady Finch stood nearby, rummaging through a jewel case she'd brought in. "Ah, here they are."

One of the maids gasped as the lady plucked from the velvet confines a spectacular diamond necklace.

"Just as I remember them," Lady Finch declared. "Fit for a bride." She held them up to Amanda's throat.

Never before had Amanda seen such glorious, glittering jewels. "My lady," she said, her hands going to her mouth to cover it from gaping. "I can't wear *those*."

"Nonsense," Lady Finch told her, coming behind her and putting the necklace around her neck. The largest stone rested just above where her mother would say her gown became "indecent," while the other gems, surrounded by intricate gold settings, sparkled their way up and around her neck.

Lady Finch glanced up at Amanda's reflection and smiled. "This is not just any necklace, but the Finch Diamonds. I received them on my wedding day. They are said to have been a gift from Henry the Eighth to the wife of the eleventh baron, whom the king had an eye toward seducing." Lady Finch chortled as she did the clasp. "The wily lady managed to retain her virtue, prevent her husband's head from being separated from his neck, and most importantly, keep the diamonds—without having to visit the king's bed."

Even as her trembling fingers trailed over the treasure, Amanda protested again. "My lady, I can't wear this. What if—"

"Stuff and nonsense!" the lady exclaimed. "They were meant to be worn by someone young and beautiful. And you are both. Besides, they are said to bestow the bearer good fortune, and tonight I wish for you your heart's desire."

Her heart's desire. If only the baroness knew what that meant.

Guilt assailed Amanda. How could she accept such a kindness? She reached back to undo the clasp and return this undeserved gift. But Lady Finch stopped her, closing her fingers over Amanda's hands.

"Please humor an old lady and wear them," she said softly. "I haven't a daughter to see into society, nor a son who is inclined to go out and find a wife. Indulge me this one pleasure—to see the diamonds worn as they ought."

Amanda's eyes began to well up. Lady Finch had done more for her in the last forty-eight hours than her own mother had done in a lifetime. And how was she about to repay the baroness? By sneaking away and breaking the bargain that the Finches held so dear.

"Lady Finch, I-I-I don't know how to thank you for all your kindness."

"There is no need to thank me. You've done more than you already know." The lady patted her on the shoulders then dabbed at her own moist eyes with a lacy bit. "Now, now, no more tears. You'll have me going on like a watering pot, and that wretched Lady Mitton will spend the rest of the Season telling the entire *ton* that I've reached my dotage."

Amanda laughed, then wiped away her own tears and wondered if the lady would regret her generosity when the midnight announcement came and Amanda had long since fled Finch Manor and the only real home she'd ever known.

Addison's usually strong voice was growing hoarse as he continued to announce the guests, while Lord and Lady Finch greeted old friend and new alike.

Jemmy couldn't remember another time when Finch Manor had entertained so many people. He'd been kicked out of the gatehouse so Lord Worledge and his wretched entourage of family and friends and hangers-on would have lodging, while the main house was bursting to the seams. Their neighbor, Lady Kirkwood, had generously opened her doors to any number of guests for the night, for it seemed nearly every member of the *ton* had taken the long drive from London to Bramley Hollow for Lady Finch's unprecedented ball.

On Esme's advice, Amanda was not part of the receiving line. The wily matchmaker wanted her to remain unseen so that speculation and antici-pation would run rife.

Much to Jemmy's chagrin, the woman's plan was working. With all the mystery surrounding the bride, the house was also crawling with every fortune hunter and lordling with pockets to let, as well as a few *cits* hoping to improve their social standing through Lady Finch's good favor.

He'd have a hell of a time getting Amanda out of their greedy grasps once she was announced, but do it he would. He was only too glad she was stowed away in the music room, behind the door on which he lounged, guarding it with single-minded determination—especially given the company milling about.

"Say there, Reyburn," an old acquaintance called out.

Jemmy racked his brain to remember the man's name.

Bemley? No, Denley. Bother, that wasn't it either.

If he hadn't been particularly fond of the fellow before, the man's next questions didn't do much to make him anxious to renew the acquaintance.

"Where is this gel to be matched?" The fellow turned his head right and left as he scanned the crowd with an assessing eye. "Hear tell she's an heiress." He nudged Jemmy in the ribs. "Is she a worthy filly? A fine bit? Knowing my luck, my mother's badgered me down here for another one of these *cit's* nags—all teeth and no bite, if my name isn't Fently."

Fently! That was it. And heir to an earldom if Jemmy remembered correctly. Oh, his mother had been busy inviting the "right sort."

The pompous fellow had his thumbs stuck in his waistcoat. "I'll dance with her, mind you, but only because Mother expects it. Then I'm off to find some sport—that is, unless this bride is worth the effort."

Jemmy straightened. Had he been so shallow and crude?

No, better not to answer *that* question. If there was any relief to be had, it was that Amanda had never known him in his London days. Now he was ashamed of how he'd treated the poor debutantes standing in the wings of Almack's.

But there was one good thing about his dashing days, he knew how to answer the fellow in his own language and what words would send the reluctant bachelor packing.

He wagged his finger at Fently to lure him a little closer. Nothing like the appearance of a confidential conversation to garner every gossip's attention. As Fently struck a nonchalant pose—so as not to attract too much attention, but acting quite the opposite, like a magnet for the curious—Jemmy shook his head as mournfully as possible and then leaned closer. "I told Mother not to go to all this trouble, but when do they ever listen?"

"That bad, eh?" Fently's staged whisper drew three more potential grooms into their fold—best of all, the trio was as gossipy as his mother. "You'd best hear this," he told the newcomers.

Ah, yes, Jemmy thought. *This will do the trick.* He glanced around, making a great show of trying to preserve the confidential nature of their conversation. "On the other side of this door"—he jerked his thumb behind him—"is a gel as cowhanded as they come," he said loud enough to catch the attention of two other young gentlemen, who immediately stopped and joined the growing crowd. "Now don't say I didn't warn you," he told his curious audience, "but I 'spect this is the only way they could find to marry the gel off." He shot them a knowing look, and they all nodded in understanding. "In my opinion, by midnight there won't be a fellow left in the manor, 'less he's so far into his cups he'd be inclined to marry my father's three-legged foxhound." He shook his head. "I for one will be long gone by then. Can't stand listening to the wailing and tears—in which I understand this one is rather inclined to partake—mostly 'cause she hasn't a farthing to her name."

"Poor chit," one soft-hearted fellow said.

"Poor chit? Poor us," a Corinthian in the back complained. "Been lured down here on false pretenses. An heiress, indeed!"

"In truth, if there is anyone who should be pitied, pity me," Jemmy told them, adding another long mournful sigh to his act. "I've got to dance the first set with her. The dancing master left this morning nursing a broken foot, and I've only got one good one left." He tapped his boot with his walking stick.

At this, his companions laughed.

"Wouldn't be in this fix if it weren't for my mother," he complained further. "She's had me dancing attendance on the lady ever since she arrived." He cleared his throat. "James," he said, effecting a rather good imitation of Lady Finch, "please show Miss Smythe around the Orchid Room." Laughter followed. "James, Miss Smythe will require a dancing partner for the opening set; I expect you to do your duty." He waved his hand at them. "As if my time with Wellington wasn't enough service for one lifetime."

"Exactly, my good man," one of them declared.

Fently cleared his throat. "I think we've been had, my good friends. I'm for going back to the inn. The only way to save this wasted evening is a rousing game of loo and enough port to dull the memory. What say the rest of you?"

His compatriots were of a like mind. "Oh, aye!" one of them said.

"Count me in," came the enthusiastic chorus.

Fently turned to Jemmy. "Shall we save you a chair, Reyburn?"

"Most decidedly." Jemmy pointed at the double doors that led to the garden. "I'd suggest using the side door over there. You'll be able to make your escape that much quicker."

Fently grinned and slapped him again on the back. "Missed you in Town, Reyburn. Do come around, and I'll introduce you to this pair of dancers I've had my eye on. Twins, I tell you. Best part is, we won't have the dilemma of which of us gets the lesser one." He laughed and strode through the room, his bold, gallant manners parting the way for him and his boon companions.

Relieved he and his lot were gone, Jemmy tugged at his cravat and shifted in his coat. They were both too tight and hardly comfortable. There had been a time when he wouldn't have felt dressed unless he was turned out to the nines, but country life had shifted his priorities and his sensibilities.

As had Amanda.

He'd gone nearly half the day before he realized he hadn't reached for his cane once. In fact, he realized he'd dropped it in the garden when he'd kissed her and hadn't needed it since.

Her passion had filled him with life and a desire to live that spread through his limbs as swiftly as her tempestuous response.

Looking up, he watched half a dozen of the fellows slipping into the night. Jemmy smiled inwardly. Gotten rid of most of the likely fellows and a few fortune hunters to boot.

His little speech had done the trick.

Unfortunately, more so than he could ever have suspected.

Amanda had stood in the music room awash in panic, until she'd heard Jemmy's deep, soothing voice on the other side of the door. She'd pressed her ear shamelessly to the panel, feeling relief at having him so close at hand. She should have learned her lesson from the other day that eavesdropping would only cause her pain.

But this was Jemmy, her Jemmy, and she smiled as she heard him greet an old friend. But the balm of his voice didn't soothe her nerves as she had hoped.

His cruel boasts and jests had answered all her worst fears. What had he called her? *Cowhanded.* Well, granted she wasn't the best dancer, but he needn't be so cruel.

How had she been so foolish to believe him . . . and his kisses? He'd pursued her at his mother's behest, he'd made her feel beautiful so she would believe in the fairy tale happily-ever-afters that Bramley Hollow prided itself in.

Amanda swiped the tears off her cheeks as she hastily backed away from the door. Despair clutched her heart as she dashed up the servants' staircase, down the dark hall to her room, and yanked and pulled herself free of her ball gown. She tossed her own day gown back on and sniffled one more time.

How could she have believed that Jemmy was the hero she'd created in her careless dreams and not the selfish coxcomb she'd been unwilling to see? He'd merely toyed with her heart as a diversion from his lonely country existence.

Pity me. I've got to dance the first set with her.

"Ooh," she gasped, the sting of his words piercing her dismay. If the doctor's pronouncement of her impending death wasn't enough to do her in, Jemmy's betrayal should have. Instead she shook with anger. Anger that she'd wasted what precious little life she had left in Bramley Hollow. She yanked on her pelisse and retrieved her traveling valise from under the bed.

"Well, Mr. Reyburn," she said. "You needn't fear for your toes any longer."

"And now, I would like to introduce our guest of honor, Miss Smythe," Lady Finch called out, waving her hand toward Jemmy, who then turned and opened the door to the music room.

Except the room beyond was empty.

He glanced at his mother, and then at the still crowd. "Must have the wrong room," he joked. "Just a moment."

As he poked his head farther into the empty chamber, one thought echoed through his mind.

She'd left. Left him.

Glancing back at the ballroom, he forced a grin on his lips and blithely said, "Seem to have lost our bride. Demmed inconvenient, but I'll find her."

A volley of laughter followed, and Lady Finch hastily motioned for the musicians to start playing. From the look on her face, Jemmy knew it wouldn't be long before she called out the local regiment to retrieve their guest of honor.

Determined to beat his headstrong mother at her own game, he raced toward the back stairs, up the flight, and down the empty hall to the guest room. There he found the door open and her room deserted. A glance under the bed confirmed his worst fears, for her valise was missing.

"Demmit," he cursed. But why had she left? He'd promised her that he would see her safely to Brighton. On the floor near his feet lay her ball gown in a crumpled heap. He bent and ran his fingers over the silk. It was still warm to the touch.

If that was the case, she couldn't have gone far. He went to the window and found his suspicions rewarded by the sight of her stealing through the rose garden, heading toward the south meadow, valise in hand.

At least she hadn't decided to try the main drive again. Jemmy imagined Holmes had worn a groove into the road there from his constant and vigilant pacing.

Jemmy dashed from the room, amazed at how

well his leg was cooperating. He knew now that Amanda had been right—he had lost his life when he'd stopped living it, just as his leg had stopped working when he'd given up trying to make it work.

As her arrival in his life had brought joy to his heart, she'd also forced him out of his careful daily schedule. He'd done more walking and climbing and hurrying about in the last few days than he had in years, and his leg felt as if it were awakening from a long sleep.

Yes, Amanda had done much for him. And once he caught up to her he'd thank her, and then beg her to stay with him until the end of his days. For even if she had only a few months to live, she'd remain in his heart until the day he left this world.

Jemmy didn't have to travel to the ends of the earth to find his ladylove.

Mr. Holmes had accomplished that for him in short order. By the time Jemmy had reached the kitchen, the constable was coming through the door with the protesting bride-to-be in tow.

"Unhand me, sir. This is an outrage. I am a guest of Lady Finch's."

Jemmy had to hand it to Amanda, she had nerve.

He supposed that was one of the many reasons he loved her. And while he would thank Holmes later for saving him the trouble of having to chase her halfway across his father's lands, he could take over from here.

"Good job, Holmes," he told him. "But you can let the lady go now. I'll see her to my mother's care." He tried to catch Amanda's eye, to reassure her, but after her first tentative glance in his direction, she looked away.

What was that on her cheeks? Tears? She'd been crying? If Holmes had harmed her in any way . . .

"Oh, I won't be falling for that trick again, sir," the constable was saying. "The only person I'm releasing her to is the magistrate."

Jemmy groaned. Oh, this was going to turn into the *on dit* of the Season if Holmes went marching into the ballroom with the supposed Bramley Hollow bride nearly in shackles and charged her with running away from her own betrothal.

For one thing, they'd never get rid of their houseguests then. They'd probably all stay for the ensuing trial, considering the spectacle it would make.

But Holmes was a man determined, and he continued into the house, ignoring Jemmy's protests, as well as Amanda's.

"Ma'am," he called out as he came closer to the ballroom, having caught sight of Lady Finch greeting a bevy of late arrivals. "A word with you."

She turned and took one look at the tableau before her and hustled forward, drawing the threesome into a small parlor across the hall.

Inside, Esme rose from a chair, her gaze flitting first from Holmes to Amanda to Jemmy, and then back to Amanda's traveling clothes. But she said nothing, not that she would have had the chance.

"What is the meaning of this?" Lady Finch blustered, closing the door behind her.

"A misunderstanding, Mother," Jemmy told her.

"I don't recall asking you," his mother said in a

dangerously cold tone. He didn't think he'd ever seen his mother so angry. "Holmes?"

The constable puffed up, proud to have his tale finally heard. "Caught her, ma'am. Escaping. Trying to leave afore her match was made. She had her bags packed and was making for the road." The man paused, glancing at Amanda and then Jemmy. "And this isn't the first time I've caught her trying to escape her bargain."

One iron brow rose. Lady Finch turned to Jemmy. "Is this true?"

"Yes," he said. "But there is a reason, and if you would just hear me out—"

She raised her hand to stave off any further protests. "Not another word, James. I see quite clearly what is happening." She turned to the constable. "You say, Mr. Holmes, she was leaving—just as she is now."

The man nodded. "Night afore last. But this time, I caught her red-handed. So if you would be so kind as to get His Lordship to swear out a complaint, I'll be more than happy to lock her up until Mrs. Maguire can find her match."

"Lord Finch has been called to his conservatory, a broken pipe or some such nonsense. He'll be out with his orchids all night."

"But I need a writ from the magistrate if we are to see this done right."

"There's no need for the writ, Mr. Holmes," Lady Finch declared. "Leaving her betrothal is one thing, but we have a more serious crime at hand. I want this girl arrested for thievery."

"Thievery?" Jemmy and Amanda both burst out.

"Amanda is no thief," he continued, taking her by the arm and pulling her behind him.

His mother's eyes widened at his familiar use of her name, but she said nothing on the subject. Instead she continued to address Holmes. "Arrest her, I say, for she left my home with the Finch Diamonds. The girl is a thief."

Amanda's hands went to her throat, pushing back her blue pelisse and revealing the glittering evidence that convicted her more quickly than a hired jury.

But Jemmy could also see that from the surprise on her face she'd completely forgotten she was wearing them.

"Oh, my lady, I'm no thief. It's just that I was in a hurry and—"

"Bah!" Lady Finch said, now in complete high dudgeon over the matter. "I will not listen to your excuses. Not only are you breaking your bargain, you also decided to take advantage of my generosity and steal from me." Her hand fluttered over her forehead, and she wavered on her feet, until Holmes rushed forward and helped her into a nearby chair. "The ball is ruined. My good reputation lost. I'll be the laughingstock of the *ton*."

"Don't you think you are putting on the brown a bit, Mother?" Jemmy said. "Amanda panicked is all, bridal nerves and such. She's more than willing to go on with the ball and the match, but that's hardly possible with her in jail." He slanted a glance in his mother's direction and could see her military mind working over how best to salvage her fête.

"My lady," Holmes protested. "This is but another dodge. Your son is an accomplice, and under the law should be jailed as well."

"That would be demmed inconvenient, sir," Jemmy told him, "for I'm slated to dance the first set with the lady."

Amanda looked about to add her own protest to the plan, but outside in the hallway, a trio of voices rose that seemed to strike her dumb.

"I told you, Cedric, we would be late. Now we won't be announced properly," came the strident tone of a very vexed lady.

Unlike everyone else, who turned toward the door, Jemmy watched Amanda, and with each word argued outside, she grew paler and paler.

She knew these people.

"Demmed waste of money," an older man with a gravelly voice complained. "First that charlatan from London you insisted I summon, now running down here, and for what? Why, it's a wretched crush in there, Marianne."

The anxious and whiny voice of his wife rose in pitch. "All the better to find Regina a match. With all the young men here, think of what we'll save if we can arrange an understanding tonight and not have to go to London for the Season."

"Mother! You promised I would get a Season!" wailed the obviously unhappy Regina. "I will not be bartered off like some—"

"Bah!" Cedric complained. "You'll be wed, gel, and when I say. Now we're here, aren't we? I see no point in leaving, especially since I've gone to the expense of driving all this way—not until we've seen what prospects are about. Make for a tidy savings if we got rid of you tonight."

"Oh, no!" Amanda whispered, so softly that Jemmy doubted anyone else heard her. But she recovered from her shock quickly and spun around to face the constable. "Take me to jail," she demanded. "I confess everything. I was trying to escape being matched and I was trying to steal these diamonds. Now I demand to be taken to jail, right this moment!"

The only person not gaping at her was Esme, who smiled as if suddenly everything was going as she'd planned it all along.

Holmes, having gathered his wits back together only too quickly, appeared more than happy to comply, while Lady Finch looked positively murderous.

Jemmy took one glance at the set of Amanda's jaw and knew she'd rather go to jail than face whatever awaited her in the ballroom. Or rather, whoever.

But how could he allow it? Lock a dying woman away for the night? What if something were to happen to her? If she became ill, or worse . . . He wasn't about to leave her to meet her fate alone. "Mr. Holmes," he said, "if you are going to arrest Miss Smythe, then you must take me as well, for I have aided and assisted the lady in her plans to escape."

Holmes rubbed his hands together in delight at having yet another confession dropped into his lap, but that didn't stop him from looking to Lady Finch for confirmation.

After all, she was the magistrate for Bramley Hollow in everything but name.

She waved her hands at her son. "Oh, take him as well, Holmes. And good riddance. A night in jail might bring them both to their senses."

Eight

The jail in Bramley Hollow had been built centuries earlier, a sturdy building meant to contain even the most heinous of criminals, but over the course of its existence it had held very few inhabitants. An occasional drunkard, and as legend had it, an infamous murderess, however for the last hundred years or so it had only seen the passing of the broom from one Holmes descendant to the next.

The lack of inmates didn't mean the two side-by-side cells, separated as they were by great iron bars, weren't kept ready and waiting. Inside each sat a narrow cot covered with a wool blanket, and a bucket for, well, for necessary business.

Holmes, quite taken with the gravity of the crimes laid before his prisoners, saw to his duties with the utmost vigilance. That wasn't to say he was completely without compassion, for he'd hung an extra blanket between the cells to afford Miss Smythe a measure of privacy and given her a candle to keep her from being frightened.

Then he'd locked the cells and the doors tight and sought his own bed. After several days of watching his prey, he was glad to have this recalcitrant bride well at hand—if only to grant himself a much needed good night's rest.

Amanda glanced at the flickering flame of her candle and sighed. So this was where her grand adventure would end. A solitary jail cell, with the only man she'd ever loved locked away next to her. He might as well have been cast away in a Paris dungeon, what with these iron bars between them. Now she'd never get to . . .

She shook her head. Not that he would have been so inclined to take advantage of her—he'd only been flirting with her out of pity. Cowhanded, indeed! And to think that she had really been starting to believe that all her foolish dreams might come true.

Hugging her knees to her chest, she struggled not to cry. Especially not in front of him.

"The least you could have done was not confess everything before our first dance," Jemmy complained from his cell. "I was looking forward to it. 'Tis years since I've danced."

"Harrumph," she shot over her shoulder. "Save your flirtations for someone who doesn't know better."

She heard his cot creak as he sat up. "What the devil do you mean by that?"

"It means I heard everything. Everything you said about me to your friends. You called me 'cowhanded.' And how can I forget 'Pity me, I've got to dance the first set with her,'" she said. "So please save your breath, for I know only too well that you never really wanted to dance with me." Amanda swiped at an errant tear that spilled from her eyes despite her best efforts to hold it at bay.

"You heard all that and thought . . . You believed that I . . ." Much to her chagrin, he began to laugh. "Oh, you darling girl, no wonder you left."

"Of course I left. I wasn't going to stay and be humiliated."

He crossed the cell and plucked down the blanket that separated them. His fingers reached out to touch her shoulder, but she pulled out of his reach, scooting across her cot until she sat at the very edge. "Amanda, my dearest Amanda, I didn't mean a word of it. Not a one. Don't you see I had to tell those feckless fools a real banger or they would have stayed around and discovered the truth."

"Save your pretty speeches. I care not what you say," she told him, tugging the blanket up and around her shoulders. "I know what the truth is—you never cared for me. You only pitied me, and barely that."

"Demmit!" he sputtered. "Well, if you must know, I said those things because I was afraid. Afraid, I tell you."

"Harrumph!" But after she sputtered her disbelief, she spared him a glance and spied the look of utter despair on his features. Not that she cared, truly she didn't. Yet the passion in his voice called to her, gave her hope she knew she shouldn't dare give any countenance. And out of that hope, she ventured a quiet question. "Afraid of what?"

"If you must know," he told her, "I was afraid you'd arrive in that ballroom and realize you could have your choice of men. Any man you wanted. And if that was the case, why would you want me? For that matter, why would anyone want me—a useless, lame, scarred recluse."

His words resonated through her. *Why would anyone want me?* She knew what that felt like only too well, for she'd thought the same of herself until the day she'd landed by happenstance in Jemmy's arms.

Slowly she rose from the cot and turned to face him. What woman would want him? Any woman with eyes, she thought as she gazed upon him.

Still dressed to the nines, he had every appearance of an elegant gentleman, from his dark coat, snowy cravat, and richly embroidered waistcoat, down to the snug breeches that fit him perfectly. There was the strong line of his jaw, chiseled and rugged, the breadth of his shoulders, his piercing gaze, all of it spoke of masculine strength and promise, enough to send any feminine heart aflutter.

But more than that, she saw the honesty in his gaze, heard the anguish in his words, felt the nobility of his intent as if it were the sheltering blanket wrapped around her shoulders.

His scars? His leg? What did they matter?

And yet he couldn't believe that she, of all people, would see beyond his outer flaws. To her they were only more evidence that this was a man who lived his convictions, chased after his ideals rather than just boasted endlessly and uselessly of them over port and cigars.

"That's what you think of me? That my feelings for you are so . . . so . . . fickle?" She crossed her arms over her chest. "If that is so, why would you want *me*?"

They stared at each other, both set in their own stubborn resolve, both too afraid to be the first to confess the truth that could mean their happiness or their unending despair.

"Oh, bother," he said, waving his hand at her. "Forget I said anything. Think what you like of me." He stomped back over to his cot and flopped down on it, lying on his back and staring up at the ceiling. "I still would have liked to have that dance."

"It wouldn't have been our first," she shot back, nudging her slippered toe against the cold stone floor. "We danced together years ago at Almack's." What did she care if he discovered the truth now? With her family so close, it wouldn't be long before all her secrets were laid bare.

Besides, once he realized that she wasn't the mysterious Miss Smythe, but merely plain old Miss Amanda Preston, his interest in her wouldn't be as keen.

"We danced? How could that be?" he argued, rising up on his cot. "I would remember dancing with *you*."

The way he said it, she didn't know whether to be insulted that he didn't remember her, or delighted that he thought her so special.

"I assure you, we danced," she said. "Though I'm not surprised you don't recall me. I was quite forgettable back then."

He glanced up at her and smiled. "I would

never describe you as forgettable, and I can't believe that I danced with you and wasn't completely and utterly charmed."

She bit her lip and wished he had been. That he'd fallen in love with her that very night and they would have had all these long years together. And now . . . now it was too late.

"You wanted to dance with Lady Alice and she was already spoken for. There was room for an extra couple in her line, and so you set out to take advantage of her company, if only for the few seconds it would afford you. I was the closest female available, and so you asked me to dance."

He groaned and buried his face in his hands. "I didn't! Tell me I wasn't such an arrogant lout."

"You were," she teased.

"But *you*, I would have remembered you," he insisted, rising from his cot and crossing the cell. His fingers wound around the bars as if he wanted to tug them out of his way so he could pull her into his eager embrace. "You are not easily forgettable."

"I'm not the same woman." She shrugged. "Heavens, I'm not the same woman I was a week ago. Apparently learning of one's imminent mortality has a way of changing a person. Challenging them to make up for lost time." She glanced directly at him. "At least it had for me."

"Hmm," he mused. "I fear it had the opposite effect on me. I'm still a fool, I'm still unable to—"

She held up her hand to stave off his words. "It matters not what happened then or tonight. I don't think you a fool." That he truly thought her beautiful and memorable and kissable filled her soul with a joy she'd thought lost a few minutes ago.

"It matters very much," he shot back. "I was an idiot back then. How can you ever forgive me?"

"There was never anything to forgive," she said softly. And she meant it. She *had* been forgettable, allowing herself to get lost behind her sisters' beauty, cowed by her mother's criticisms, relegated to obscurity by her father's parsimony. "If there was anything to forgive, you must believe that you've repaid me these past few days in ways you will never imagine."

He shook his head. "I don't see how. I've blundered your plans to go to Brighton. Gotten you arrested, and now . . . well, how will I be able to see that you wiggle your toes in the waves?"

"Going to Brighton wasn't the only item on my list," she told him. "I've discovered quite another dream come true here in Bramley Hollow."

She moved closer to the bars. He stood facing her, clutching the ancient iron bars, and so she twined her fingers around his. His hands were warm and strong, and his strength once again lent her the courage to take the reins of her life.

To seize what was before her.

Meeting his gaze, Amanda saw only too clearly his hunger for her. *For her*, she marveled. He wanted her as passionately as she desired him. She didn't waste a second.

She leaned forward until her lips met his. It wasn't the same as when she could feel his body against hers, but his kiss welcomed hers hungrily, and it sent the same warm tendrils of desire trailing down her spine.

When his tongue drew a tempting line across her lips, she opened her mouth to him, inviting him in, like opening the door to an eager pirate hungry for plunder.

She rose up on her toes, as she sought to claim every bit of his kiss that she could with these wretched bars separating them. His arms reached through and pulled her closer, stroking her back, teasing her hair out of its elaborate display and into a tumble of curls down her back.

His touch left her weak and trembling, her heart thundering with passion. His lips teased hers, drew her into a heady, tempestuous tangle of wanton desire and passion. Oh, how she wanted him, wanted him to kiss her until this trembling, teasing need found release.

Then to her chagrin, he drew back for a moment. "If it wasn't for these demmed bars, I'd have you—" He stopped himself. "I mean to say, I'd—"

She caught hold of him, dragged him back to her lips, and kissed him anew. Then she asked him, "You'd what, Jemmy? What would you do to me?" She stared into his stormy gaze and willed him to tell her what he'd do.

"I-I-I'd—"

"Make love to me?" she asked, hopefully. "Ruin me beyond redemption?"

He nodded slowly. "Yes, you wicked girl. That is exactly what I would do."

She caught hold of the bars that were now her enemies and rattled them with all her might. "This isn't fair," she cried out. "I have waited all my life to be ruined, and I will not be thwarted now!"

He laughed and caught hold of them as well and joined her in her lament.

"Decidedly unfair," he called out to the heavens. "Release the lady that I love."

And all of a sudden a shower of dust fell down on them.

But Amanda hardly noticed. "The lady that you what?"

"Never mind that," he told her. "Grab hold of this bar again."

"I will do no such thing," she told him. "Not until you tell me again what you just said."

He paused, grinning at her, a mischievous, rakish light glittering in the blue of his eyes. "I love you, Amanda. I love you." Then he winked at her, and nodded toward the cell bars. "Now will you just grab hold of this one again and give it another good shake."

"You just told me that you love me, and all you want from me is to shake that bar?"

"Yes, very much so," he said, studying something up at the top of the cell.

"Don't you think that's a little unusual," she said, glancing up at the ceiling as well, but seeing nothing that appeared more interesting than what he'd just said. "Really, Jemmy, usually when a man makes such a declaration he does so on bended knee, or at least follows it with a kiss," she hinted.

"Greedy girl," he teased. "You can have that and more, if you will just help me."

"Help you do what?"

"Get this bar loose. I think this one may be enticed to break free."

"Truly?" She glanced up at the tiny shower of mortar falling down on them as Jemmy gave it another good shake. "Why didn't you just say so," she said, grabbing the bar enthusiastically and putting every bit of strength she possessed to break it free. And come free it did—the centuries-old plaster crumbling down atop them. And when the neighboring bar proved just as easily removed, Amanda had enough space to slip between the bars and find herself locked in the happy prison of Jemmy's embrace.

Nine

"*R*uin me," Amanda pleaded as she looked up into Jemmy's gaze. "Love me tonight."

"Tonight?" he whispered, as he gently fingered a stray tendril of her hair. "Not just tonight, but for always."

As he said the words, she knew without a doubt that these were not the beguiling and false promises of a rake, but the vow of a man who loved her. Truly and deeply loved her above all else.

"Me?" she asked, still unable to grasp the notion of it. Jemmy Reyburn in love with her? Her long-held misgivings and uncertainties knew such a notion was preposterous. But the woman she'd become in the last few days, possessing the confidence gained by a man's admiring eye, and better still, his kiss, did her best not to listen to those niggling voices of doubt.

"Of course, you," he said, dipping his head and catching her mouth in a searing kiss.

The moment his lips touched hers, her fears fled in the face of his fiery passion. Never before had she felt so alive, and now Amanda understood what it meant to live.

She met his kiss with her own demands, leaving her tentative innocence behind as well. If she was to live, she would do it with all her heart. And so much more . . .

As his tongue dipped to stroke hers, she moaned, welcoming his invitation. He tugged her closer, drawing her up against his chest. His body felt hard and so masculine against hers, and so very welcome.

As were his hands, as they moved over her, stroking her back, running over the curve of her hips and then up her sides, his thumbs casting a lingering line over her breasts. He cupped her breasts, teasing first one nipple, then the other, until they were both taut and hard. His touch sent a tangle of desire tumbling and unwinding through her, leaving in its wake a breathless, trembling need.

She moaned and arched up to meet his touch. But to her chagrin he stopped.

"You're trembling," he said. His hand paused over her heart, which beneath his touch pounded dangerously. "Do you think this is wise?"

"Please don't stop," she said, her fingers curling around his hand, and drawing it up to her lips.

"But didn't the doctor warn you of just this?"

he asked, pulling his hand free and putting it back over her heart.

"He said to beware my heart," she told him. "And I have no doubts that right now it is in good hands." She edged closer to him, so her hips met his, so her body pressed against the hard evidence of his desire. "Love me, Jemmy. Love me tonight," she beseeched him. To urge him further, she reached down and stroked him, amazed at her own wantonness and even more dazzled by the desire it brought forth—in him and her.

Jemmy closed his eyes and groaned as she touched him. But he didn't stop her.

Emboldened, she continued to tease him, drawing her fingers up and down the length of him, leaving him straining in his breeches.

How she longed to touch *him*, not just the wool of his breeches. To feel the steely length in her hands, to feel it within her, to let him ease the ache between her thighs by filling her, teasing her past the clamor of need that his kiss had awakened.

Unlike most young ladies, she wasn't ignorant of what happened between a man and a woman. Her older sister had taken great delight after her marriage in regaling her two younger sisters with all the mysteries of the marriage bed. But the sweaty, ridiculous mechanics her sister had described scarcely resembled the passion Jemmy evoked, the heated frenzy his touch promised. And Amanda's curiosity knew no bounds.

"Ruin me, Jemmy," she whispered.

He groaned as her hand swept over him again.

His mouth took hers, and he devoured her in a breathless kiss. Any tenderness he might have held was gone, as his hand slipped inside the décolletage of her gown and freed her breast.

She bit her lips together to keep from crying out as he took the hardened peak in his mouth and sucked and lapped on it until she thought her legs would buckle beneath her. With each sweep of his tongue, with each pull of his lips over the pebbled flesh, her thighs trembled, her breath caught in her throat in short, staggering gasps.

His deft fingers found the laces on her bodice and quickly undid them, freeing her from its confines and giving him ample leeway to explore her at his pleasure. His lips sought her again, trailing teasing kisses behind her ears, down her neck, and back to her breasts. It was like a waltz of passion, with each movement more provocative than the last.

How and when, she knew not, but she found herself undressed down only to her stockings.

For a moment he gazed upon her, and she held her breath.

"Demmit, Amanda, you are the most beautiful woman in the world."

"Truly?" she whispered.

"Oh, aye," he said, with almost a reverent air to his words. "I don't deserve you. I don't deserve what you are offering."

"I think I'll be the judge of that," she told him, her fingers tugging at his coat, tossing it aside, and then setting to work on his waistcoat. Her fingers faltered over the tiny buttons, and he pushed her hands aside and ripped it free from his body, sending a shower of tiny pearl buttons across the cell floor.

She laughed, then eagerly helped him. As he tugged his shirt free from his breeches, she pulled and unwound his cravat, their hands and arms tangling in happy purpose.

As he flung his shirt over his head, Amanda wondered that *she* should deserve *him*. She laid her palm upon his chest, and marveled at the heat and strength emanating therefrom. Slowly she touched him, reverently she explored him with her fingertips, tracing a path through the triangle of hair at his chest, over the flat plain of his stomach, to the top of his breeches.

"Amanda, I—"

Her gaze flew to his, and she placed a finger on his lips to still his words. They held an air of reluctance, and she wasn't about to lose her chance now.

This time when she pressed herself into his embrace, her body melded to his, her breasts brushing against his bare chest. She had never imagined such a feeling, such a mingling could occur.

It was as if they were becoming one. One to the other.

"Tonight, Jemmy," she reminded him, running her fingers over his chest. "You gave your word."

"Aye, I did," he said, his voice filled with smoky promise. And with that, he caught hold of her and gently lowered her to the cot.

As he knelt before her, his fingers toyed with the ribbons on her garters. "I've wanted to do this from the first day we met," he confessed.

Amanda thought back and remembered his lingering gaze on her stockings as she'd been packing them. Then she'd been embarrassed that he'd seen them. Now she wanted nothing more than to have him remove them.

And he did, untying one of her garters and setting the stocking free, rolling it down her leg, his fingers lingering over the curve of her calf, the arch of her foot. Amanda sighed with languid joy. She lay back on the bed and held out her other leg for him, but for this one he had other ideas.

His teeth caught hold of the ribbon and tugged it free, then with his teeth drew it from her leg.

And if she thought he was done, she was mistaken, for once the stocking was tossed aside, his mouth began tracing a hot trail up her leg, going from one to the other. Slowly he climbed up her limbs, leaving kisses on her calves, behind her knees, on the soft skin of her thighs.

Then to her shock, his mouth nuzzled over her most private place, his warm breath sending a message of passion. Her mouth fell open, but she couldn't speak, for he didn't stop there, his hands prompting her thighs to part while he continued to kiss and whisper over the petals of sensitive flesh between them. And as she opened herself to him, she tried to breathe, she tried to make sense of the passion spiraling out of control.

Then his tongue lapped over her, sending her hips bucking up to meet him as if of their own volition. He laughed and ran another long lap of his tongue over her.

This time she couldn't restrain herself. "Jemmy, oh, dear. Oh, my!"

If his kisses before had held a passionate promise, this intimate invasion invited a torrent of need, a thunderstorm of tremors.

He continued to tease her, leaving her panting and tense. She reached behind her and caught hold of the bars, grasping for something to hang on to as she felt herself rising upward on a tempestuous spiral of blinding arousal. When his kiss changed from teasing laps to suckling her, it became her undoing.

She felt tossed from a precipice as her body exploded in desire, the throes of it racking her with pleasure she could never have imagined.

"Jemmy, oh yes!" she cried out, reaching hold of him and pulling him up onto the cot, until he covered her.

She clung to him, wrapping her legs around him, riding out the waves in the confines of his arms.

"Oh, I never imagined," she whispered once they had begun to subside.

"And we've only just begun," he promised.

Amanda grinned. Mostly because he was a man who understood how to keep a bargain with a lady.

Jemmy watched the contented smile spread over her sweet features and smiled.

She stretched beneath him, her long, lithe legs wound around him. How he ached to bury himself inside her. To stroke a new fire between her thighs. But he knew this was her first time, and he wanted to ensure that the night was a long, plea-surable interlude.

He nuzzled her breasts again, and was re-warded with mews of pleasure. Her fingers wound through his hair, holding him there to en-joy the bounty of her perfect breasts.

And once he heard her panting with renewed need, he sought her lips again, and kissed her deeply.

Amanda, his tempting passionate Amanda. Jemmy had never thought that making love could be so fulfilling, but with her it became sacred, like keeping his promise to her. And keep it he would. In the morning he'd marry her with all due haste, then he'd hie her off to Brighton for a honeymoon by the sea.

And then . . . well, he wasn't going to consider the future beyond that; for now he'd feel blessed with the time he was allowed to share with her.

She shifted restlessly beneath him, her fingers moving over the top of his breeches, seeking out the buttons and undoing them, slowly, torturously.

He leaned up to help her, but she shook her head, her enticing gaze meeting his. There in her eyes, he saw her sensual delight as she explored his body. He didn't know which was more excit-ing, her bold touch as she pushed his breeches away, or the surprise that glowed in her eyes as her fingers spread across the front of his groin, sliding through the thick tangle of hair, then en-twining themselves around his manhood, hard and eager for her claiming.

She smiled, feline in her pride, and began to

stroke him with her hand, her other reaching up and pulling his head down to hers for another long, languid kiss.

Jemmy thought he would lose himself in the pleasure of it all. His hands roamed over her breasts, marveled at the silk of her skin, ran down to touch her where she was once again hot and wet—as ready for him as he was for her.

"Amanda," he said huskily, "let me love you."

"Yes, Jemmy," she said. "Oh, please."

He shifted above her, catching hold of her hips and pulling her close. Amanda made a mewing sound of pleasure, then wound her legs around his hips. He entered her slowly, stroking her gently, letting her discover the pleasure that came when a man and a woman joined together.

Her eyes closed, and her head rolled back. Her hips arched to meet his, to bring him closer, deeper into her tight, hot confines. "Oh, Jemmy, oh, Jemmy, that feels so good."

Aye, it did. Jemmy held his own desires in check, waiting until she was writhing and moaning beneath him, then he drove himself into her, breaking her maiden's shield.

Her eyes fluttered open in surprise, and he covered her mouth with his, lest she cry out—not that anyone was likely to hear them.

"Shh, my love," he whispered into her ear. "It only happens once."

"Then what happens after?" she asked him coyly.

And Jemmy showed her, pulling himself almost out of her and slowly filling her anew, his lips teasing the nape of her neck, catching hold of her mouth, and stroking her tongue with his.

She arched and moaned, meeting his rhythm with her own rising needs.

He could feel her mounting crisis, from the way her fingers clung to his shoulders, to the ragged thrusts of her hips. She reached back and caught the iron bars and clung to them anew.

"Love me, Jemmy," she begged. "Love me hard."

And he did, driving into her, her cries of ecstasy ringing through the quiet of the night and leading him to his own release. It pulled him from the darkness and led him into a glorious light, just as she'd done the day she'd walked into his life.

He drove into her, filling her until it was hard to tell where his body stopped and hers started. Their hearts, pounding and thundering, were like a chorus. Amanda continued to writhe and tremble in his arms, glorious evidence that she was still in the throes of her climax.

He kissed her again and continued to move with her, until finally the last shuddering vestiges of her release faded into memory.

She sighed and wound her arms around his neck. "That was so remarkable."

"You are remarkable," he told her, wrestling her closer to him—if that was possible. "Amanda, I love you so very much."

"And I, Jemmy, love you."

"But I am so different from—"

"Shh," she told him. "I love *you*. The man I discovered in Bramley Hollow. You have given me my life, let me find my heart, shared with me your soul. You made me feel beautiful."

He kissed her, softly, slowly, thankfully. "Make you feel beautiful? You are gorgeous."

She shook her head. "Not like one of those London ladies."

"Amanda, forget those shopworn cats—their beauty is purchased on Bond Street and fades like yesterday's flowers." He toyed with a strand of her hair. "Your beauty is that you don't realize how lovely you truly are—and it shines from within. It glows in your eyes, it radiates from your heart. It is like a gift that has awakened me. You let me find my heart, my life . . ." he glanced down at his scarred and once broken limb. "My leg. You've taught me to walk again. Not just up stairs and across the lawn, but to walk with the living."

She grinned and reached down to stroke his bare thigh. "Your leg does seem quite improved."

"Aye," he said, marveling at how limber and mobile it was becoming. "Perhaps my leg is like your beauty," he said, nuzzling her neck and then stealing a kiss from her willing lips. "When it isn't put to good use, it doesn't stand a chance of being seen."

"Then thank you for helping me shine," she whispered, and reached up and kissed him, and with a nudge of her hips, let him know she was ready to shine again.

Amanda didn't know when they'd fallen asleep, but it was the creak of the jail's front door that awoke her the next morning. Beside her, Jemmy stirred but didn't awaken. At least for the moment he still clung to the peace and serenity of his dreams.

She glanced around and realized not only was she still naked, but she was unclothed with Jemmy.

Whatever she'd said last night about her desire to be ruined was all well and good, but in the light of day it was hardly proper.

No matter the fact that her days were numbered, it was hard to shake four years of a Bath education at Miss Emery's.

"I left them right in here," the constable was saying. "Right and proper, of course."

And if being caught by Mr. Holmes wasn't enough to send her to her eternal reward, the voices that followed his should have done her in right there and then.

"Of course it is proper," Lady Finch said. "My son is *always* a gentleman!"

"Right and proper, she says!" a man huffed. "Lady Finch, this is an outrage. To even suggest that our Hortensia is—"

Amanda's mouth fell open. "*Father*," she stammered, diving under the wool coverlet in hopes it would cover her completely. Or better yet, the stone floor would open up and swallow her into the depths of perdition.

"Hmm," Jemmy murmured, finally stirring. "Come here, love," he whispered huskily, his arm winding around her and tugging her beneath him. He kissed her before she could protest, before she could tell him to stop.

To tell him they were no longer alone.

But in truth, she needn't have worried, for her mother did that for her.

"Dear God," the woman shrieked. "Your son has some doxy in there!"

Amanda peeked out from beneath the blanket. "No, Mother, 'tis me."

"Hortensia!" her father bellowed. "Get out from beneath that libertine!"

"That libertine," Lady Finch shot back, "is my son, and I will not have you implying that he's . . . he's done any—" She glanced in the direction of the cell and flinched. "Jemmy, come out from beneath that blanket and explain yourself."

"I would, Mother," he said, "but I fear I haven't any clothes on."

Lady Farleigh made a choking sound, her gloved hand covering her mouth. "Thank heavens we left Regina in the carriage so she wouldn't witness this . . . this . . . atrocity. Oh, we are ruined, utterly so!" She spun around to Lady Finch. "I blame you, Evaline Reyburn! My daughter was the epitome of good sense and moral fiber until she came into your son's lascivious clutches. Why, I wouldn't doubt he lured her from our home by some fiendish trickery."

Lady Finch buried her face in her gloves and shook her head.

"Reyburn, you come out from there immediately," Lord Farleigh said, rattling the iron bars. "I demand satisfaction."

Amanda was glad that Holmes hadn't managed to get past his shock and dismay at his prisoners *in the same cell*, to unlock the door yet. There was no telling what worse debacle would ensue given her father's current state.

Jemmy caught up the extra blanket, and with some dexterity, wound it around his waist, and stood to face the viscount. Amanda had to admire his mettle. There weren't many people who dared stand up to her father in one of his "states," as her mother liked to call them.

"Sir," he began. "I am not going to meet you on some grassy knoll. I hardly think that will accomplish—"

"Who said anything about a duel?" Lord Farleigh blurted out. "I want you out of there and before the archbishop this very morning. Your rakish days are over, you rapscallion. You will marry my daughter immediately! And you will take her without a farthing. I'll not be throwing good money after bad."

Amanda groaned. Leave it to her father to get to his most fundamental concern. His money.

And besides, she wasn't about to see Jemmy forced to marry her. It seemed a moot point considering how little time she had left. "Father, there will be no wedding!"

"No wedding? You've gone mad, gel. You'll be wed this very afternoon," Lord Farleigh declared.

"No, I will not," she said, struggling to sit up and keep herself covered. It was the first time in her life she could ever remember defying him, but she hadn't been about to be bartered off by the matchmaker, and she certainly wasn't about to be bullied into a wedding by her father.

"What did you say?" he asked, his features incredulous that anyone would contradict him.

"I will not marry Mr. Reyburn." Amanda remained firmly rooted in place. Though it did help to have a locked iron door between them.

"You damned well will—" he sputtered, shaking his fist at her.

Jemmy spun around and stared at her. He had much the same murderous look on his face that her father's held. "And why not? What the devil is wrong with marrying me?"

She smiled at him. "You know very well why I won't marry you."

"It matters not to me if you are dying," he told her. "I have every intention of marrying you and have since . . . well, I suppose since I met you." Then he grinned. "The second time, that is."

"But can't you see? It is because I am dying that I can't marry you." Amanda couldn't bind herself to him, only to leave him so quickly.

"Dying?" Lady Farleigh asked. "Who is dying?"

Amanda shot a glance over her shoulder. "Mother, I know what the doctor told you. I overheard, well, I was eavesdropping and heard him tell you that I hadn't long to live."

"You were *eavesdropping*?" her mother asked, as if that were the worst tragedy before her. "What has happened to you, Hortensia? You used to be such a docile, decent girl. Now you're eavesdropping and gadding about the countryside, and . . . and . . ." The lady looked down at the makeshift cot on the floor and the discarded clothing and shuddered. "And now this? Have you not thought, Hortensia, what this will mean to your sister's chances this Season?"

"Hortensia?" Jemmy asked, glancing at her.

Amanda cringed. " 'Tis my first name. Amanda is my middle name."

"Still, Hortensia?" He shook his head. "It doesn't fit you in the least."

"So I've said for years," she replied, glad to hear that someone finally agreed with her on that point of contention.

Lady Farleigh let out a long-suffering sigh. "There is nothing wrong with the name Hortensia. She was named after Lord Farleigh's aunt, who offered to dower one of our daughters if we used her name."

"And then changed her mind," Amanda shot back.

"Only because she said you'd never need it," Lord Farleigh said. "Come up to no good, she told us, and she was right."

"It is hardly my fault that I'm dying," Amanda replied.

"Dying?" her father said. "Why do you keep blithering on about this dying nonsense?"

"Because I heard Dr. Albin tell you that there was nothing he could for me, that my heart was nearly gone."

Lord Farleigh blinked. "You foolish girl, he said no such thing. Least not about you."

"But I heard him," she insisted, looking first to her father, then her mother. "I heard him say my case was hopeless. I was standing on the staircase and he was in the morning room with you both, explaining what he'd discovered."

"Oh, dear. Oh, my," her mother said. "Dr. Albin wasn't discussing you, Hortensia." She edged closer to the jail cell and lowered her voice. "He was discussing your father's hunting bitch, the spotted one. Oh, what is her name?"

"Spotty?" Amanda offered.

Her mother smiled and nodded. "Yes, Spotty. You know how your father is. Thought it a waste of money when the doctor came down and said your condition was only just a *malade imaginaire* and nothing that a good Season in London wouldn't cure. So since your father had gone to all the expense of having Dr. Albin up from London, he had the man examine Spotty." She turned to Lady Finch and explained. "She'd been so listless all winter. The dog, that is. Dr. Albin listened to her heart and said she wouldn't last through the summer."

"Damn sad thing, if you ask me," her father added. "Had to pay his outlandish fee, find out there was nothing wrong with Hortensia, *and* learn my best hunting bitch was a goner."

"So I'm not dying?" Amanda asked.

"No, heavens not," her mother said.

She turned around, her now perfectly good heart pounding in her chest. Would Jemmy still want her now that he knew she wasn't dying? And worse yet, if he did want her, would he be willing to marry her as Hortensia? If only to make it legal and binding.

Her father began another blistering harangue about the expense of finding her, her ruined state, and how he wasn't going to pay her fines to the magistrate.

"I'm not dying," Amanda whispered to Jemmy,

her parents forgotten, Lady Finch and Mr. Holmes just part of the background.

Much to her relief, he was grinning from ear to ear. "So I heard."

"This means I have some time," she told him.

"Enough to marry me?"

She nodded, tears filling her eyes. And with that, she went again into his arms and kissed the only man she'd ever loved.

Her father rattled the cell door and demanded their scandalous display be put to an end. But unfortunately for the viscount, Mr. Holmes had misplaced the keys.

With a huff, he washed his hands of his errant daughter, took his wife by the arm, and left Bramley Hollow, vowing to write Miss Emery the moment they returned to Farleigh Hall and demand Hortensia's four years of tuition be returned in full.

After their carriage was long gone from the village, Mr. Holmes produced the missing keys, conveniently stowed in his coat pocket, and released his infamous prisoners.

With a little privacy, the pair found their clothes and made themselves decent. As decent as two young people in love could be, for it was all they could do not to look into each other's eyes, or touch each other's cheek.

Once they were dressed and stepped outside, Amanda immediately went to the baroness. "I am so sorry to have ruined your ball, my lady."

"Nonsense, child," Lady Finch declared, winding an arm around her shoulder and giving her a hug. "It was a spectacular success. Not only will your abrupt departure and arrest be the most oft-repeated tale for years to come, I believe there were three matches made last night." She glanced over at her son and at her soon-to-be daughter-in-law and laughed. "Make that four."

Epilogue

*A*manda Reyburn tripped up the front stairs of the Brighton inn, having spent the early morning walking along the shore. As she passed through the common room, the innkeeper tipped his hat to her and pressed a packet of letters into her hands.

"Is my husband awake?" she asked.

"No, ma'am," he said.

She grinned and dashed up the stairs to their room.

As promised, Jemmy had married her the very afternoon Holmes had released them from the Bramley Hollow prison, and without a moment's delay had tossed her into his long unused curricle and carried her off to Brighton for their honeymoon.

A month later, they were still encamped at the

lovely little inn by the shore, spending their days walking beside the waves and exploring the shops in town, and their nights . . . well, those were spent before the fire in their room, getting more and more acquainted.

It was such an idyllic time, both of them were loath to leave.

Pausing before the door to their room, she listened to see if her husband was stirring, but only silence greeted her. That would mean he was still abed, a thought that made Amanda grin.

She knew the perfect way to help him greet the morning.

Before she went in, she quickly leafed through the letters clutched in her hand and spied one in particular that caught her attention. Tearing it open, she read it in disbelief.

She entered their room and closed the door behind her.

Jemmy stirred in the bed and rolled over. His tousled hair and shining blue eyes spoke of the night they'd just spent nestled in each other's arms, making love, sharing dreams of their future life together.

"Come, my sweet wife," he said, throwing back the counterpane and patting the empty space beside him. "Come back to bed with me."

"What?" Amanda asked, distracted by the letter in her hand.

"What do you mean, what?" Jemmy shook his head. "Must be time to return to Finch Manor if my bride is already forsaking my bed."

She laughed. "No, it's just that I've received a letter and I cannot believe what it says."

"Do tell," he said. "Then perhaps you'll reconsider my offer." He waggled his brows at her.

Tossing aside her bonnet and pelisse, she joined him in the bed and read aloud from her letter.

" 'Tis from my Aunt Hortensia," she explained.

"The one you were named after?"

"Yes. And she's written the most amazing letter." She paused for a second and bit her lip. "Though I am embarrassed to read it. I fear she's rather blunt in her observations."

"You've met my mother—I think I can shoulder a bit of blunt criticism."

She shrugged and then read the letter to him.

"My dearest Amanda—"

Jemmy stopped her right there. "She didn't call you Hortensia?"

Amanda held out the letter. "That's only the beginning. Listen to this:

"My dearest Amanda,

Your parents have written me of your disgraceful conduct and your hasty marriage to Mr. Reyburn. In light of all this, I must say I was quite overcome . . . with admiration for you. You have finally lived up to being called Amanda, and not by this horrible name with which I have been burdened all my life. I never thought your parents would dare name a daughter thusly, but then given your father's skinflint ways, I don't know what I was thinking. All that aside, I had always hoped that one day you would find a way to get past such a wretched moniker and discover a love that would fill your heart with joy, much as I had with my Oswald. Now it seems that you have.

My only concern is that mother-in-law of yours. Evaline Reyburn can be a bothersome, meddlesome woman, and I don't want to see her interfering with your happiness. As such, I am reinstating my promise to see you dowered. I have instructed my solicitor to place the sum of five thousand pounds in a bank account that is to be at your disposal. That rapscallion you've married cannot touch it, but you will have full discretion to do with it as you please. The remainder of my estate with be placed in trust for the endowment of your daughters. Raise them well and see them happily married, is all I ask.

And you as well be happy, my dear child, and enjoy this money with all my love.

Your ever loving,
Aunt Hortensia"

When Amanda finished reading, she stared at Jemmy, and he at her.

"Five thousand pounds," she said. "Can you imagine such a sum?"

"Well, yes I can," he said, plucking the letter from her hands and pulling her into his embrace. "What do you plan to do with it?"

She cast a glance out the window, to the sea beyond and to world that awaited them. "I want to go," she told him, "to all the places I've always dreamed of seeing."

"Are you taking me?" he teased, nuzzling her neck with kisses.

Swatting his shoulder, she laughed, then pressed her lips to his, seeking his kiss, his warmth. "Of course I want you with me. I want to explore Venice, and Athens, and Paris, wherever our whims carry us. And I want to see it all with you."

"Then I am at your command, Mrs. Reyburn," he said, bowing his head to her. "I shall carry your trunks wherever your heart desires. And in the evening I shall warm your bed and keep you safe."

"And my heart, Jemmy. Promise me always to be in my heart."

He nodded. Then pulled her gown from her, slipped her delicate stockings from her legs, and when she was gloriously naked, showed her exactly how he would keep such a bargain . . . in Venice, and Athens, and Paris.

And sometime later, when the sun was high in the sky, they stirred from their bed and Jemmy held her close as they gazed out at the sea.

"Five thousand is quite a bit of money," he said.

"What would you do with it?" she asked.

"Build a wall."

She glanced up over her shoulder at him. "A wall? Whatever for?"

"For the gatehouse. I think twelve feet high ought to do the trick. And I think your aunt would approve."

"And why do we need a wall around the gatehouse?" she asked, almost afraid to hear his answer.

Jemmy winked at her. "To keep my interfering mother out, of course."

Amanda laughed. "Yes, I think even Aunt Hortensia would approve of such a rapscallion expense."

The Third Suitor
Christina Dodd

One

Wildbriar Inn, on the coast of Dorset, England
September 1847

Leaning over the high porch railing, Harry Chamberlain looked down into the flowering shrubbery surrounding his oceanfront cottage and asked, "Young woman, what are you doing down there?"

The girl flinched, stopped crawling through the collection of moss, dirt, and faded pink blossoms, and turned a smudged face up to his. "Shh." She glanced behind her, as if someone were creeping after her. "I'm trying to avoid one of my suitors."

Harry glanced behind her, too. No one was there.

"Can you see him?" she asked.

"There's not a soul in sight." A smart man would have let her go on her way. Harry was on holiday, a holiday he desperately needed, and he had vowed to avoid trouble at all costs. Now a girl of perhaps eighteen years, dressed in a modish blue flowered gown, came crawling through the bushes, armed with nothing more than a ridiculous tale, and he was tempted to help. Tempted because of a thin, tanned face, wide brown eyes, a kissable mouth, a crooked blue bonnet, and, from this angle, the finest pair of breasts he'd ever had the good fortune to gaze upon.

Such unruliness in his own character surprised him. He was, in truth, Edmund Kennard Henry Chamberlain, Earl of Granville, the owner of a great estate in Somerset, and because of the weight of his responsibilities there, and the additional responsibilities he had taken on, he tended to do his duty without capriciousness. Indeed, it was that trait that had set him, eight years ago, to serve England in various countries and capacities. Now he gazed at a female intent on some silliness and discovered in himself the urge to find out more about her. Perhaps he had at last relaxed from the tension of his last job. Or perhaps *she* was the relaxation he sought.

In a trembling voice, she pleaded, "Please, sir, if he appears, don't tell him I'm here."

"I wouldn't dream of interfering."

"Oh, thank you!" A smile transformed that quivering mouth into one that was naturally merry, with soft, peach lips and a dimple. "Because I thought that's what you were doing."

Harry winced. "A good shot."

"I'll be on my way," she whispered, and started to crawl forward. "Warn me if he appears before I am away."

Harry nodded and looked around. His cottage afforded him a lovely view of the white sand beach, where waves rolled in eternally, soothingly, blessedly. Chalk cliffs rose on either side of the beach, and there the waves battered the rocks. He could hear the piercing cry of terns as they dove for smelt, and a breeze ruffled his dark hair, carrying the scent of brine and freshness. He wanted to sink back into the porch swing, to stare out at the ocean . . . to stretch his aching shoulder where the bullet had torn through muscles and bone, and wonder what next he would do with his life.

Instead he looked down. The girl was still there, struggling to unhook her bonnet from one of the stiff, clinging branches. "Take it off," he recommended.

"I can't. The ribbon is knotted." She jerked at the bonnet.

He heard a ripping sound. Another shower of petals fell off the rhododendrons, her bonnet dropped in the dirt, and a mass of curly blond hair tumbled around her shoulders.

"Good God," he whispered. In an instant, the fall of hair transformed her from a frightened English girl to a kneeling houri, waiting to service her master.

He shook his head to dispel the vision. Obviously he'd spent too much time among the sheiks and Bedouins of the East if he was imagining erotic tableaux here in the heart of sunny Dorset. And obviously he'd spent too much time alone if he lusted after such a hoyden.

But the tightening in his groin could not be denied. He did lust. When he got back to civilization, away from this backwater inn with its charming guest cottages and its windswept cliffs, he would have to do something about his condition. Take a mistress, perhaps. Or accede to his mother's wishes and take a wife. Or both.

Unaware of his wandering thoughts, the girl picked up the bonnet and stared at it, shaking her head. "Oh, dear. Miss Hendrika will be most unhappy about this."

He didn't want to ask, but the habits of a lifetime were too strong. "Who is Miss Hendrika?"

"She's my chaperone."

"Where is Miss Hendrika?"

"She's at the inn, finishing her breakfast."

"Ah." The inn stood behind the cottage at the very top of the hill overlooking the beach, a white-painted, two-story affair that looked like a larger version of his cottage, with a porch that ran the length of the building and chairs and rockers set out for the guests. That was whence the girl had undoubtedly come. "Aren't chaperones supposed to . . . chaperone?"

"She's rather old and a little dotty, and truth to tell, I think my stepmother told her not to bother chaperoning me too closely in hopes one of the suitors would compromise me."

That frank speech settled it. This girl lifted the malaise that had plagued him since he'd been shot. And although he was not dressed to receive guests—he had discarded his jacket and his cravat as soon as he returned from breakfast—she would have to sit with him for at least a little while. Harry descended the steps and reached into the shrubbery, offering his hand. "Come up on the porch and explain."

She eyed him doubtfully.

In a commanding tone, he said, "Really. I must insist."

"So I noticed." She crawled out and stood, brushing at the dirt caked on her knees and once again affording Harry a lovely view of her bosom. "But Lord Jenour-Redmond will certainly see me if I remain there."

"Jenour-Redmond?" Harry knew him, and he could scarcely credit that that witless, graceless marquess was a suitor for the hand of this vivacious girl. "Why him?"

In a voice overflowing with tragedy, she confessed, "I have a fortune."

"Dreadful." He watched with appreciation as she rose to her full height.

With the precision of a government agent— which he was—Harry summed her up. Five foot four, one hundred and twenty pounds distributed in quite an attractive manner, and blond hair that she was trying to return, not very successfully, to its original position coiled at the back of her head. Her eyes were brown. No, dash it all, they were sparkling amber, of such a vivid hue that he immediately returned to imagining erotic scenarios involving her, him, and a mouth that looked delectable to the extreme.

He would have to be careful with this girl.

She was perhaps a little older than he'd first suspected. Normally he would have never said anything, but he saw nothing normal about this situation. "You're twenty-two."

She paused in the act of peeling off her soiled gloves. "Yes! How did you know? Most people think I'm younger."

The gap between eighteen and thirty—his own age—was insurmountable. The gap between twenty-two and thirty was not so large, and made him feel less like an elderly letch leering at an innocent child's breasts. Thank heavens, for he couldn't stop leering—at the breasts and at the narrow waist below, and at the legs that, beneath the petticoats and skirt, must be long. "There is a touch of experience about you that no eighteen-year-old gently bred girl would have."

Her narrow chin set and lifted, and indignation sounded clearly in her voice. "Sometimes they try and kiss me, but I don't like it."

"They?"

"The suitors."

"Let's sit on the porch." Taking her hand, he assisted her up the steps and seated her on the wide swing. "Your suitors try to kiss you?" Smart men.

"Other men, too, but it's the suitors who seem to think they *must* try." She wiggled her nose as if that amply expressed her opinion, then expressed one anyway. "I'll tell you frankly, kissing is not as agreeable as the romantical novels make it out to be."

More fascinated than amused, he said, "Really?"

"For one thing, any reasonable looking man immediately becomes overly large at that distance, and one may view every fault."

"You're supposed to close your eyes," Harry informed her gently.

"There's a good idea." Sarcasm dripped from her tone. "He's already got me in a clinch, he's pressing his lips to mine, and I'm to close my eyes so I can't see what other tortures he has in store? Perish the thought."

"You've been kissed by bunglers. Someone needs to kiss you correctly." Ignoring her startled intake of breath, Harry went to the door and called his valet. "Dehaan, would you bring a glass of lemonade for my guest?"

"A guest? You have a guest?" Dehaan's Dutch accent thickened with excitement, and he stuck his head out the door. In a tone of awe, he said, "It's a woman."

Harry gave him a push before he could say anything untoward. "Yes, and she's thirsty."

"Ya, ya, I will do it right away. And cakes, too, in case she is hungry. We don't want her to run away and say we are not hospitable." Dehaan frowned meaningfully at Harry. "Do we, sir?"

"No, we don't. Now go and get the lemonade." Damn the man! He had been Harry's man of all trades for over five years, and he loved romance so well, he should have been a Frenchman. Now Dehaan's eyes gleamed with matchmaking fervor, and as always, that meant trouble. Returning to the girl, Harry apologized, "Dehaan thinks I spend too much time alone."

"Do you?"

The lady had a bluntness about her that took his breath away. "I have a lot on my mind." Like what to do with the rest of his life—which might also be the reason his mother had insisted he come here.

Actually, if he really wanted to know why his mother had insisted he come here, all he had to do was read the letter. He'd found it packed in his clothing, but he hadn't read it yet—these letters were his mother's usual method of breaking bad news to him. Just so she had told him, the first time he went off to school, that she had asked his godfather to watch over him—and watch over him Lord Atlay did, much to the youthful Harry's embarrassment. The first time he went abroad, she told him to bring her a damnable hat from Paris, and so he had, although he'd been forced to stuff a flower in the bullet hole near the crown. This time . . . there was no telling what she wanted this time, but it could wait while he relaxed with this girl.

And gave her advice. "Next time you have no wish to be kissed by a suitor, before he closes in, kick his knee—hard."

"Ouch." She rubbed her own knee in sympathy.

"Yes. That will discourage him. If he's close, use the flat of your hand and smack his nose."

"What does that do?"

"Breaks it, if you do it right. Allow me to introduce myself." He bowed and gave her the pseudonym he'd used to check into the inn. "I'm Harry Windberry of Windberry Court, in Derbyshire."

She rose and curtsied. "I'm Lady Jessie Macmillian, daughter of Viscount Macmillian of Suffolk."

Harry lowered his brows. Macmillian. Macmillian. The name was familiar . . . Viscount Macmillian must be one of his mother's many acquaintances, for somewhere back in the recesses of Harry's mind, memory stirred. But the memory was old, and Harry could drag nothing forth except the sense of unpleasantness. Nothing treacherous, just . . . unpalatable.

"Please, may we be seated?" she begged. "I've been on the run all morning, and I'm exhausted."

With a shrug, Harry gave up searching for remembrance, and returned his attention to Jessie. "On the run from Jenour-Redmond?"

"Yes, and he's just the first of three." She rubbed one slippered foot against the back of her leg, giving him a glimpse of her shapely ankle. "My father gave me an ultimatum. Choose one of them, or he'll choose for me."

Dehaan bustled out with two glasses of lemonade on a tray and a plate of the tea cakes they served at the inn, and with a bow and a gleaming smile, offered them to Lady Jessie.

"Thank you." She took the glass and put it on the small table at her elbow. "Mr. Windberry, I know that, as a lady, I'm supposed to pretend to have the appetite of a bird and leave you the most"—she piled fully half the cakes on the small plate—"but I'm starving."

This time Harry's grin took over his face. "Please, take all you like. I'm not so great a fool as to judge a miss by the number of cakes she eats."

"You're very handsome when you smile. I do think it ridiculous that ladies are held to such an arbitrary standard. My stepmother scarcely touches a crumb in front of my father, but you should see the trays she has sent to her bedchamber."

Harry thought he detected a compliment in the gush of words, but he wasn't quite sure, and he wasn't sure he wanted to know. This woman had already despoiled his morning without even trying. What she could do if they discovered a mutual admiration, he didn't dare imagine. So he seated himself in the chair against the wall, the one that gave him the broadest view of the grounds. He took the glass and two of the cakes. When Dehaan put the plate down at Jessie's elbow and disappeared back into the cottage, Harry said, "Tell me about these suitors, and why they're seeking your hand here rather than at a society party supervised by your parents."

Lady Jessie chewed, swallowed, and blotted her lips. "I have been out for four years, and after only one Season Papa announced he was tired of paying so much for a lost cause. You see, Papa is rather thrifty."

Harry suspected that was a euphemism of unusual tact.

"So I've not been in society these last three years. Then Papa married again, and my stepmother convinced him sending me here would be an economical way to establish my betrothal, and heaven knows she doesn't want to be seen at a party with me. She says it's because I'm tactless. I think it's because I may be twenty-two years old and a spinster on the shelf, but compared to her, I'm a babe in the cradle."

Throwing back his head, Harry burst into laughter. Tactless? This girl was as blunt and direct as a cudgel!

"I suppose I shouldn't have said that." But Lady Jessie didn't seem to suffer undue remorse, and she watched him with a tiny smile on her lips.

"I suppose not." Still he chuckled. He couldn't

remember the last time he'd laughed like that. His job was grim and dangerous, so he had become grim and dangerous. Now, as he watched her consume another cake, he experienced a loosening of tension, a desire to laugh and talk—as long as it was with her.

"These are good." She licked her fingers. "Especially the lemon curd."

"Your suitors," he prompted.

"But it's so pleasant here. Must we speak of them?"

"I think, if I'm to suffer a visit from Jenour-Redmond, that we must."

She sighed. "Even at the time of my debut, my father didn't think I could be trusted to pick out a husband. So he would pick them out, and they were invariably dull, stable, older men, friends of his who were willing to put up with me for my fortune."

Harry could easily imagine the kind of men the viscount called his friends. "Go on."

"Whenever I found someone I could love, my father got rid of him." She examined the toes of her black walking boots. "Usually with a bribe."

"True love, indeed."

"Not true love, but at least some excitement! Anyway, you see the problem. I can marry a young, ne'er-do-well fortune hunter of my own choosing, or an old, dependable fortune hunter of my father's choice. The ne'er-do-well would make me miserable. The dependable one would bore me to death." Putting down her plate, she leaned forward and took Harry's hand in hers. "As far as I can see, men are never interested in their wives for themselves, only in what their wives can bring to them. I don't like to hurt your feelings, Mr. Windberry"—she patted his fingers—"but your gender is entirely untrustworthy."

"Lady Jessie, you have dealt a grave blow to my masculine pride." He watched with fascination as, once again, that little smile flirted with her lips.

"I believe you're laughing at me, Mr. Windberry."

"I believe you show a great deal of wisdom, Lady Jessie." Turning his hand, he clasped her fingers in his. "But pray tell, if your suitors are here and in pursuit, what good does it do to try and avoid them?"

"If none of them ever find me, I won't have to reject them."

"That's not going to work. You can't stay at the resort forever, hiding in my shrubbery."

Her lips trembled. All the beautiful fire in her eyes was extinguished. "I suppose not."

A movement around the side of the cottage caught his eye. "And I believe, my dear Lady Jessie, your first suitor has caught up with you."

Two

*J*essie turned her head so quickly, her neck cracked. Mr. Windberry was correct. Jenour-Redmond was limping past the rhododendrons, his gaze fixed on her as he extinguished the beauty of their glorious pink blossoms with his presence.

In a panic, she turned back to Mr. Windberry. "Please, please don't leave me alone with him."

"It *is* my cottage."

Was he being uncooperative? For all his open laughter and kind words, she couldn't read this man. There was an edge to him, as if beneath the sympathy he hid a razor. He commanded rather than spoke, and always his eyes were watchful. Not that he didn't focus on her. She had no complaints about that. But at the same time, she would have sworn he observed the flight of every bird, the movement of every creature within view of the cottage. "You mean—you'll do as you like, not as I say?"

"No, I mean—no one's going to chase me off of my porch."

"Oh." Placing her hand on her bosom, she heaved a sigh of relief. So all she had to do was stay here and she'd be safe from Jenour-Redmond's disgusting, slobbery kisses. Although Mr. Windberry would have her believe some men's kisses were acceptable, or even enjoyable.

Mr. Windberry's?

He squeezed her fingers again. "Chin up. It won't be so bad."

She shot him a glare that should have withered him in his chair. Instead he smiled at her so mockingly she realized he was forcing her to seek courage.

What a man. If only her father would find her a fortune hunter as gorgeous as Mr. Windberry, she'd go to her wedding with more resignation. She snuck another glance at him. Indeed, she'd appear at her wedding with bells on her toes.

Black hair, swept back from his rugged face. A blunt nose, broken and healed. Broad lips, so soft and full she wanted nothing more than to kiss them over and over until he revealed all the secrets he knew about lovemaking. And those eyes . . . blue, magically, fabulously blue, an ocean of blue that concealed his thoughts, his feelings, until she would have done anything to coerce him into revealing himself.

For he carried himself with a strength and arrogance that drew her like a diamond displayed on black velvet. If he wished, he could rule the legions, he could control the tides . . . he could love a woman until she no longer remembered her name, until she abandoned pride, until her body was no longer her own and she would do anything he commanded for the pleasure of his mastery.

She gazed into his blue eyes, trying without words to lure him into a single kiss of incredible passion, when—

"Lady Jessie, I have been searching for you all over the estate."

Jessie deflated. It took an effort of will to look away from Mr. Windberry, but she managed, and the buzzing in her head told her she'd been holding her breath.

Of course, such lascivious thoughts about Mr. Windberry, an unknown gentleman and most definitely not one of her suitors, proved that her father's criticisms were true—she did have a light mind, unsuitable for making decisions of such importance as that of her future partner in life.

But it also proved she recognized a real man when she saw him—and Jenour-Redmond did not fulfill those requirements.

He was tall, thin almost to the point of emaciation, with a prominent Adam's apple that bobbled as he spoke and a voice so deep he sounded as if he were speaking into a well. He cut a comical figure, except for his title, which was marquess, and his ancient lands, which required her riches to prop them up. Of all her suitors, he was the one who most desperately wanted to marry her, and he might, perhaps, be the best husband— if she didn't mind being held in lower esteem than a stable of horses and an estuary full of fish.

"My lord, how good to see you." She extended her hand to Jenour-Redmond, who pressed far too arduous a kiss upon her knuckles.

His gaze flicked down toward the stains on her knees, and up to her lopsided coiffure, but he said, "You're beautiful, as usual."

"You're elegant, as usual," she returned.

Jenour-Redmond *was* elegant, clad in a eye-popping waistcoat of purple trimmed with gold fleur-de-lis, a royal-blue jacket, and matching striped trousers. His boots shone, and his black, high beaver hat proclaimed him a man of style.

"Elegant to a fault." Mr. Windberry's tone insinuated Jenour-Redmond had chosen his wardrobe badly for such casual circumstances.

The glance Jenour-Redmond flicked at Mr. Windberry made clear his contempt for Mr. Windberry's costume. "What are you doing here, Harry? Playing the merchant?"

In a noncommittal tone, Mr. Windberry answered, "Soaking up the scenery, Gerald."

Startled, Jessie asked, "You two gentlemen know each other?"

"Only too well," Jenour-Redmond said with crushing disdain.

Harry watched Jenour-Redmond steadily and in a manner that bespoke contempt—and Jenour-Redmond squirmed. Which surprised her, for Jenour-Redmond was far above her on the social scale, and thus even farther above a mere mister.

Turning his back to Mr. Windberry, Jenour-Redmond gave him the cut direct—not that Mr. Windberry seemed to care. "Lady Jessica, we should adjourn somewhere more private where we may pursue our courtship."

"I dare not, my lord." *Not if you were served on a silver platter with an apple between your ample lips.* "That wouldn't be proper without a chaperone, and since she is not present, I fear I must rely on this gentleman's kindness to protect my reputation."

With an almost audible clatter of bones, Jenour-Redmond rushed to sit beside her. "Your sentiments do you honor, Lady Jessica."

As Jenour-Redmond tried to grasp her hands, Jessie kept them moving, and the chase reminded her of a marionette's pursuit.

Apparently it reminded Mr. Windberry of something similar, for he leaned back and grinned.

She threw him an exasperated glance, and in her moment of inattention, Jenour-Redmond managed to grab her. His clammy hands painfully crunched her knuckles together, and he drew her unwillingly to her feet. As he led her toward the far railing, she wanted to dig her heels into the boards of the porch. But that would be foolish, an act of defiance when she had sworn to herself and her papa that she would, for once, be sensible. Yet when Jenour-Redmond tried to pull her closer and whisper in her ear, she skittered backward—and into the corner formed by the house and the railing. He followed close behind.

Trapped! Silently she told herself, *See? That's what happens when you get flustered.*

"My darling." His already bass voice lowered

258 *Christina Dodd*

dramatically. "You must know how I feel about you."

About my money. But she couldn't say that.

"Your father has given me grounds to hope I have engaged your affections. Hope, as I have never hoped in my life."

My father is a despicable liar. No, she couldn't say that, either.

Jenour-Redmond hunched his shoulders and lowered his head in the general vicinity of her face. A gust of sausage and kippers made her jerk back. She bumped her head against the wall.

He didn't notice, or if he did, he didn't care. Pinching her chin in his fingers, he brought her face back to his. Afraid to close her eyes for fear he would consider it encouragement, she stared at him. At the large pores on his nose. At the gray hairs poking out of his ears. At the damp, blubbery lips so close to hers. "Lady Jessica, I confess myself swept away by your beauty, coerced into improper behavior by your"—his gaze dropped to her neckline—"character."

She shook in a brief gust of laughter, then cut a glance toward Mr. Windberry, expecting him to share in her merriment.

He sat with his finger beside his nose, watching Jenour-Redmond with a killing gaze.

Jenour-Redmond continued, oblivious to her amusement and Mr. Windberry's displeasure. "Your father has already granted me permission, so I apply to you for your hand in marriage."

At last! Her cue. "My lord, while I regret—"

"But first, I can no longer resist snatching a single kiss from your succulent lips."

Taken by surprise by his uncharacteristic audacity, right here in front of Mr. Windberry, she forgot Mr. Windberry's instructions and tried to jam her elbow into Jenour-Redmond's chest. Alas! Too little, too late. His long arms wrapped around her back. He pulled her against him and pressed such a hearty kiss on her, he crushed her lips against her teeth. She would have made a gagging sound, but that would involve opening her mouth. She wished she could breathe, but she could hold her breath for a long time before she would allow him to touch her with his . . . Dear heavens, was that his tongue?

She shuddered, a long shiver of repulsion that shook her from head to toe.

And from the chair against the wall, Mr. Windberry drawled, "Darling Jessie, are you trying to make me jealous? Because it's working, and if Jenour-Redmond doesn't unhand you right now, I'm going to have to kill him."

Jenour-Redmond did unhand her, so quickly she was dizzy. He stumbled backward, all the way across the porch. The whites of his eyes showed as his gaze swiveled toward Mr. Windberry. He reached beneath his cravat with one finger and tried to loosen it. "Is she . . . are you a suitor, too?"

"No suitor would dare take the liberties with a lady that you have been taking." Mr. Windberry spoke with stinging disdain. "And in front of another gentleman!"

Jenour-Redmond didn't glance at Jessie, and for the first time Jessie realized that unexpected kiss was more in pursuit of some ancient competition with Mr. Windberry than interest in her.

She wiped her mouth on her sleeve to dislodge the taste of the odious lord.

"Are you calling my breeding into dispute?" Jenour-Redmond demanded of Mr. Windberry.

"Your breeding is impeccable, as we all know," Mr. Windberry answered. "It's your manners . . . and your bravery . . . that require bettering."

Jenour-Redmond doubled his fists.

Mr. Windberry observed him, and in a tone that mocked and insulted, he asked, "What are you going to do? Call your servants to thrash me?"

Straightening his skinny shoulders, Jenour-Redmond said, "I should say not! If I wished to thrash you, I'd do it myself. But this chit isn't worth fighting over." He flicked his gaze at Jessie's dishabille, then at Mr. Windberry's informal dress. "Not if she's already been in your bed."

Jessie gasped in dismay. Such rumors would bring her terrible disgrace!

Standing, Mr. Windberry paced toward Jenour-Redmond.

Jenour-Redmond scrunched himself into a corner, his head tilted, his lips open as he gasped like the bony fish he so resembled.

Jenour-Redmond's stiffly starched cravat made a crunching sound as Mr. Windberry gathered it in his fist. "Lady Jessie has done no more than offer me the kindness of her conversation, and if I hear of you spreading gossip to the contrary, Jenour-Redmond, please remember how long it took you to recover last time I was forced to teach you some manners."

Jenour-Redmond nodded.

Mr. Windberry shook him. "What did you say?"

Speech poured forth from Jenour-Redmond in a fearful torrent. "I do remember. I won't say a word about you and Lady Jessica. In fact, if you don't mind, I won't tell anyone I was even here."

"Yes." Mr. Windberry let him go and dusted his fingers and stepped back. "That will save you the embarrassment of rejection."

"Precisely." Jenour-Redmond bobbled his head at Mr. Windberry, bowed to Jessie, and sidled along the porch railing, all the way to the stairs. Once there, he turned and fled toward the inn.

Jessie was torn between expressing her amusement at Jenour-Redmond and her admiration for Mr. Windberry. She chose admiration for Mr. Windberry. Extending her hand, she walked toward him. "You must allow me to express my undying thanks. I fear if he had caught up with me when no one was about, he would have done everything in his power to force a marriage upon me."

Mr. Windberry took her hand and cherished it between his two. "He's continually without funds, and a bully to boot, so I suppose you're correct. He would indeed have forced himself upon you to achieve his aim."

She liked having Mr. Windberry hold her hand. She liked everything about him. "He's the kind of man who makes me wish my father would pick a truly old man to be my husband."

"Why so?"

"Because at least an old man would be unable to consummate the marriage."

Mr. Windberry lifted his brows and chuckled.

"Why are you so amused?" she asked.

"My dear, dear Lady Jessie. I'm sorry to disappoint you, but there isn't a man in England who wouldn't rise from his deathbed to consummate a marriage with you."

She didn't know what to say. She didn't know what to think. Most people, certainly most men, would never have responded to her frank observation about Jenour-Redmond. And although she had never made such an earthy comment about another human being—indeed, she could only blame her frankness on her upset—she doubted that anyone would ever reply in such a lustful manner. Although . . . although . . . "Was that a compliment?"

"It was the truth."

She couldn't restrain the smile that blossomed on her lips. "What did you have for breakfast?"

"Why?"

"Because I just kissed a man who tasted of sausage and kippers, and I don't want to kiss another one."

Three

It had happened at last. Some remnant of the lead bullet that had lodged in Harry's shoulder had migrated to his brain, for he was surely hallucinating. That was the only possible explanation for Lady Jessie. She smiled as she turned her fingers out of his grasp and slid them gradually . . . sensuously . . . up . . . his . . . arm, leaving a trail of desire that sank through his skin and into the depths of his soul. When her hand rested on his shoulder, she stepped closer. She leaned against him, her body warming his, her breasts crushed against his chest.

He stood immobile, frozen with shock . . . with unanticipated, bone-deep pleasure.

Rising on tiptoe, she twined her other hand in the hair at the nape of his neck and brushed her lips against his. For all her boldness, she seemed uncertain, bumping noses with him, twisting her face from side to side.

She smelled of cakes and soap and sweet, warm female, and if he were hallucinating, he might as well make this his favorite hallucination. Wrapping one arm around her waist, he pulled her tightly against him. He leaned her backward, letting the rail support her weight. She gasped and squirmed as he cupped his palm beneath her head. Smiling into her eyes, he commanded, "Relax. I won't drop you."

With a note of confidence that filled him with pride, she said softly, "No. I can't imagine you ever do anything you don't mean to."

"Remember that." With a firm, soft pressure he took control of the kiss.

He didn't completely close his eyes. A man who lived with the kind of danger he'd experienced never closed his eyes except in the deepest of slumber.

Her eyes, too, fluttered open, then closed, as if she didn't know what to do.

So he pressed his mouth over each eyelid. "Trust me," he whispered.

He molded her lips with his, discovering the contours. He alternated pressure to find her preference, and when he found the right combination, she rewarded him with a startled clutch of her fingers on his shoulder. Then he kissed her, close-mouthed, over and over, soft, pleasant, unthreatening kisses, until she relaxed in his arms. Until her mouth quivered beneath his. Until she sighed and he could sense feminine contentment and the faintest nudge of curiosity.

Lifting his head, he murmured, "Open your lips."

She tried to look at him, but he kissed her again. "Open them. Just a little," he coaxed. "Trust me."

"I do." And she opened to him.

He didn't wish to frighten her. She was young, untried. But the blood thrummed in his veins, urging him to thrust his tongue deep in her mouth, to set up a rhythm that drew her into the tangled world of sensuality where she had never before visited. Somehow he restrained himself, easing his tongue between her lips, tasting her with the expertise of a connoisseur.

She was unsure at first, startled by the intrusion, bewildered by the taste of a man. Of him. But as he continued his gentle assault, she relaxed again, and when she dared to meet his tongue, he could scarcely subdue his triumph.

Wrapping her arms around his neck, she clung and pressed herself to him in slow undulations.

What a woman. What a woman! How he wanted her. Fiercely, insistently. He wanted to lift her onto the railing, delve beneath her skirts, step between her legs, and take her. No whispers of devotion, none of the preliminary caresses he usually enjoyed, just a swift, definitive claiming that branded her as his. After that, he would make her happy . . . after that, he would know she was his.

In the air over the cottage, birds called and swooped. On the beach, the waves rolled in. Butterflies flitted among the wildflowers nearby. But in the shadow of the porch, two people stood, willing prisoners of unforeseen passion.

Unforeseen passion? When had he last allowed himself such license? There were reasons, good reasons, why he did not. He knew men who had done so, and died for their passions.

He had to rein himself in, for his sake—and for hers. He had taken control of this kiss. He had to honor her trust in him. He had shown her what a kiss could be. Now he had to let her go, and pretend it didn't matter that his balls ached and he, far too clearly, could imagine how Jessie would look stretched out on his bed.

Forcibly he subdued his instincts. Gradually he drew back.

She tried to clutch him closer. She murmured an objection.

Her ingenuous desire made him deepen the kiss again. He couldn't resist—but this would never do. Again he pulled away, gentling her new passion with slow caresses that calmed and soothed.

Intermittently she struggled against his restraint, trying inexpertly to lure him on, and that made him want her more.

The girl had driven him beyond sanity, and in less than an hour. He should flee from her now. Flee from her as he had never fled from an enemy or a fight. Abandon the cottage and the holiday and . . .

She watched him with an edge of wariness that proved her intelligence. "Why are you looking at me like that?"

"Like what?"

"Fiercely." She watched him with increasing caution. "Like you want to chase me away."

He almost laughed. Almost, but he couldn't, not when his body ached and yearned. "You're not good at reading faces."

"So my stepmother tells me." She pushed against his shoulders.

He resisted for one moment, then remembered—he was letting her go. Propping her against the post, he stepped away, and hoped she didn't observe his arousal. And if she did, he hoped she didn't know what it meant.

Putting her finger on her tongue, she rubbed it slowly back and forth. "Bacon and coffee."

"What?" He couldn't take his gaze off that pink little tongue.

"You had bacon and coffee for breakfast." She smiled and stroked her finger over her lower lip, dampening it.

She was teasing him. Deliberately enticing him, when only a few moments ago he'd taught her how to kiss! A man learned from experience, but a woman learned from her instincts. A man would do well to remember that. But . . . there were other lessons he could teach her.

Taking her wrist, he pulled her wet finger to his mouth and bit it. Gently—but he let her feel the edge of his teeth.

Closing her eyes, she leaned her head against the post.

He circled the bite with his tongue, then pressed a kiss on her palm, and closed her fingers over it.

Her eyes fluttered open. She gazed at him through passion-glazed eyes, and when he made no more move to seduce her, she straightened.

"Oh! You have that expression on your face again." Her eyelashes lowered. "I understand now. It's not that you want to chase me *away*. It's that you want to *chase* me."

He answered swiftly, without thought. "I would catch you."

Her gaze lifted. They stared into each other's eyes, the heat between them growing so intense it threatened to scorch away the veneer of civilization that barely held him in check.

Her bosom rapidly rose and fell. The color fluctuated on her tanned complexion. Her hand trembled in his, and deliberately—he had lost all reason—he reached out and cupped her breast. She didn't leap back or gasp; but her big eyes grew bigger and she stopped breathing. With his thumb, he sought the bead of her nipple, and when he found it, circled it, over and over. "You would be wise to kick me in the knee."

She paid no heed to his words. Instead she whimpered, a single, primitive sound of need, and pressed her hand over the top of his. "Is this what it's like to make love?" Her voice was low, vibrating with emotion, uncertain of her words. "This melting? This madness? If you and I decided to . . . to join ourselves together, would we survive the . . . the conflagration?"

"Survive, and live to love again." He tried to smile, but he feared his grin was savage. Turning his hand in hers, he caught her fingers and raised them to his lips. He kissed them once, then gave her back her hand. "But we're not going to make love. You've got a suitor to decide on, and I don't despoil young ladies who don't really understand what they're asking for."

She nodded, once, a jerky movement. Lifting her arms, she took the heavy tumble of hair from her shoulders and piled it atop her head. Taking the few hairpins she had remaining, she stabbed them into a careless pompadour.

He loved the way her upraised arms pushed her breasts against the low-cut neckline of her gown. He imagined their shape, soft, round, and heavy for their size, their color a cream contrast to the tan of her complexion. The nipples would be rosy—he examined the color of her lips—no, peach, and plush and sensitive to his touch. He indulged himself by imagining that, rather than putting her hair up, she was taking it down . . . for him.

Apparently she caught him, for she dipped her knees and leaned down until she caught his gaze. "I'm up here."

He staggered backward a step. He couldn't believe she had said such a thing. Never in all his life had a lady of quality noticed—or seemed to notice—his undying devotion to the glory of a woman's breasts. Now this girl chided him . . . nay, laughed at him from her glorious amber eyes. Hoarse with need, he said, "I will endeavor to remember the position of your face in reference to your body."

"Yes, do that." She finished her impromptu coiffure, and lowered her arms.

"You've only met one suitor. Perhaps the others will capture your attention." Damn them.

"No. I've met them all. One's old. One's not so old. Both are obnoxious in their own way."

He didn't want to be interested, but he couldn't help himself. "Will there be another one today?"

"Tomorrow." Gloomily she said, "Mr. Clyde Murray, arriving by post in the afternoon, if I know him."

"*Do* you know him?"

"For years. He's a hunting crony of my father's. He has five children from two wives, both of whom died from the pure drudgery of living with him. He just . . . rides over the top of every comment. He never listens to objections. He never permits a conversation. He tells everyone what to think, and he has such an air of . . ." She faltered.

"An air of what?"

"I rather think he's cruel. I suspect he strikes out when thwarted."

Her comments disturbed Harry in more ways than one. "Do you mean . . . he would beat you?"

Her smile wobbled alarmingly. "That sounds very dramatic, doesn't it? Maybe not. Probably not. But I don't relish our meeting tomorrow."

Before pity and lust drove him to do something absolutely contemptible, he had to send her away. "You should go now."

She gazed at him as if seeing the weakness in him, and targeted it with uncanny precision. "I have but one suitor a day, and I have most of the day in which to dread the next one. Won't you distract me?"

Distract her? God, yes, he would love to distract her. In bed, with her hair spread out on a pillow and her body tossing below his.

"We could walk through the garden. You could tell me about your life. We could take tea together . . ."

"Oh." Ridiculous to feel disappointed. Ridiculous to say yes. He was dangerous. It was dangerous to be around him.

True, he had been here for three days and there had been no sign of trouble, but that was no reason to take this female up on her not-so-innocent offer and possibly put her in harm's way.

On the other hand, how could he resist? "That sounds delightful." He offered his arm. "Let's walk."

Four

The next morning, Harry woke to a brilliant spill of sunshine across his bed and the illogical conviction that today would be both glorious and entertaining—and he hadn't undergone such a sensation for almost ten years. All his experience had taught him that life was grim, brutish, and short, filled with dishonorable people doing beastly things, usually for profit, sometimes for revenge, sometimes for ideology. Now, in one short day, a funny, rebellious, passionate girl had changed his mind.

For today, at least, he looked forward to every hour.

"Hurry, man," he urged Dehaan.

"Ya, ya." Dehaan laid out a costume of black trousers, a light green striped waistcoat, a crisp white shirt, and black boots.

Dehaan, an incurable romantic, had recognized the signs in his master and spent the evening before ironing and polishing. Now he insisted that Harry take the time to don each piece with the care of a dandy. And Harry, whose normal criterion for clothing was that it not bind, did just as Dehaan instructed.

Hurrying down the steps, he made his way up the sloped gravel path to the inn. To his surprise, Jessica wasn't dining on the porch with the other guests. For a moment, his breath caught in anguish. She hadn't left, had she? She hadn't fled in fear of the passion that coiled between them? Then, glancing into the dining room, he saw the back of a blond head, gracefully bent to her plate—and seated with her, a stocky gentleman of fifty years, using his knife and fork with an efficiency that fared ill for the food piled on his plate.

The second suitor, Mr. Clyde Murray. He wore a scowl on his broad forehead. His hands and neck were speckled with brown spots like those of a man who worked the fields and hunted without gloves. He spoke with a North country brogue, and even from a distance, Harry could hear the tone of his voice: querulous, condemning. As he watched, the last two guests vacated the dining room and hurried out, driven away by an unpleasant quarrel—except one person said nothing at all.

That left only the chaperone in the corner, placidly eating her meal without showing any sign of interfering.

Harry moved to a small, square table, and Jessica glanced up. She met his gaze, then shook her head slightly. *Don't meddle.*

Very well. He would not, but neither would he leave her alone. He seated himself close enough to heed every word spoken, and to observe Jessica as she listened. What he heard lifted the hairs on the back of his neck.

"My first wives did as they were told, and you will, too, miss. You'll trust me on this. I've got experience in marriage, where you do not." Mr. Murray stopped long enough to place a kipper in his mouth, chew, and swallow.

Jessica took the opportunity to answer, "No, I certainly don't, but—"

Mr. Murray interrupted. "I've got few requirements, and you'll fulfill them well." Lifting one finger, he said, "I need a woman to raise my children"—he lifted another finger—"to bring money to dower my daughters"—he lifted his third finger—"and to warm my bed."

"Mr. . . . Murray!" Jessica blanched.

"Ach, we'll have none of that missishness between us. I'm a plainspoken man, and you'd best get used to it." Picking up a crisp slice of bacon, he shook it at her. "Once you understand that, our marriage will do very well. You'll stay home and keep the house in a frugal manner. No running to London to party for you!"

Jessica shook her head.

Mr. Murray thought she shook her head in agreement with his strictures.

Harry knew better.

Mr. Murray continued, "I'll expect marital favors twice a week, on Tuesday and Saturday. Ten minutes should not trouble you too much. In return you'll be allowed three new gowns a year." He leaned forward. "I allowed my first two wives only two gowns, but you're a pretty thing, almost as old as my eldest daughter, and I'm growing indulgent in my dotage."

Jessica's fingers shook as she said, in a voice an octave too high, "Mr. Murray, as appealing as this all sounds, I must refuse your suit."

"What do you mean, refuse my suit? Are you daft?" Mr. Murray's blue eyes protruded in shock. "Your father has chosen me for your husband."

"But I don't want to marry you."

"You'll keep a civil tongue in your head, and do as you're told." Mr. Murray sighed heavily. "I suppose you're imagining you want to fall in love. Well, I assure you, my other wives have been well pleased with me, and you will be, too."

Again she shook her head.

Mr. Murray took her hand, the one holding her fork, and held it with enough force to bruise. "Yes, miss! You've got rank and a fortune, to be sure, but your father says you haven't a smidgen of sense, and your stepmother says you need only a firm hand, and I'm the man to give it to you."

The chaperone blotted her mouth, stood, and left Jessie alone with the beast.

Mr. Murray concluded, "Now, consider the betrothal done and we'll be on our way back to your home."

Harry couldn't stand it anymore. The bright girl he'd met yesterday was drooping under the weight of Mr. Murray and his bullying, and he had no doubt she could object all day to the betrothal and Mr. Murray would ignore and coerce her.

Standing, Harry approached the table.

Murray looked up in annoyance. "Can't you see, man, we're having a conversation here?"

"Yes, but I need to speak to Lady Jessica before I go off for the day."

"Who are you?" Murray demanded.

"One of Jessie's friends." Harry faced her. "I was in the village yesterday and the milliner asked that I tell you your new hats are ready. The bill is over eight pounds, which made me think they must be extraordinary hats."

Jessica's brow puckered in confusion. "Hats?"

"Eight pounds!" Murray sputtered. "What are you doing spending eight pounds on new hats you'll not need in the countryside?"

Jessie's lovely mouth puckered. "Ohh. Hats."

Harry straightened his cuffs. "The jeweler wishes to know when you'll pay him for the necklace. He seems rather anxious. Is it very expensive?"

"Necklace?" Murray slammed his fork down flat.

"It's not expensive at all." Jessica knew how to play the game now, and she smoothed her gown, calling attention to the fine pelisse of green poplin trimmed with cream-colored velvet. "Twenty pounds, and worth every penny."

"Twenty pounds." Murray's voice was rising. "Twenty—"

"Did the shoemaker say if my new slippers were ready?" Jessica's eyes sparkled with mischief as she looked back at Murray. "I would never have thought it, but I found a marvelous shoemaker in the village, and ordered twenty pairs of dancing shoes in every color. After all, one can scarcely expect to know the popular color next year, so I must be prepared." Putting her finger to her cheek, she looked thoughtful. "I wonder if I should order all new gowns, too."

Murray stood, leaned his fists on the table, and towered over Jessica. "I've arrived just in time, I see, before you fritter away your fortune on trinkets and baubles. The money should be spent on the land, on horses, on family, and I'm going to keep you on the straight and narrow from now on."

He crushed her with his condemnation, and the hopeful color faded from her cheeks.

Grabbing her wrist, Murray pulled her to her feet and glared at Harry. "Get out of my way, you dandy, I've a wedding to plan."

Harry couldn't stand to see the cheerful, bold girl reduced to a dutiful cipher. He stepped in front of her, trapping her between him and the chair, and stared into her eyes with all the anguish of a wounded lover. "What about me? Yesterday was wonderful, and now you go to be wed without a farewell?"

Murray bristled with suspicion. "Yesterday?"

"She taught me more about kissing than I've learned in all my thirty years." In a way, it was true. Harry had never enjoyed such a mixture of writhing passion and sheer exuberance.

Murray tossed her wrist back at her. "You kissed this man?"

"Well, yes, but that's all." For the second time in two days, she tossed her reputation to the wind. "I scarcely let him do any of the other things he wished to."

"Huh." Harry imbued that one syllable with a healthy dose of skepticism.

"I didn't," she insisted, knowing well her denial was an admission to the suspicious Murray.

Murray's voice grew guttural with rage. "Your father gave me to believe you a creature of virtue."

"I am."

Harry examined his nails as if he were possessed of the truth.

Murray's mouth worked as he looked from one to the other. "I've spent four pounds five to come on this wild goose chase, and for what? To find the female is unchaste? A spendthrift? I think not! I shall speak to your father about this, miss."

"But I am chaste!" she said.

"He'll reimburse me for the full amount of my expenditures." Murray started to storm away, then wheeled and returned. Picking up his half-full plate, he stomped out of the dining hall.

Jessie sank into her chair, her hands limp in her lap. "Thank you." Heartfelt gratitude quivered in her voice. "Thank you so much."

Pulling up a chair, Harry sat directly in front of her, shielding her from any onlookers. "Dreadful man. You know, his first wife died of eating poisoned mushrooms. And his second wife died of a fall."

Jessie stared at him, half believing. "Really? You know this?"

"She wouldn't eat her poisoned mushrooms."

He saw the moment she comprehended the jest. Her eyes lit up. She gave a crack of laughter. Covering her mouth, she chuckled, tears brimming in her eyes. As suddenly as the laughter had come, the tears turned to sorrow, and she put her elbow on the table, cradled her forehead in her hand, and cried, hard.

Dismayed at this display of genuine grief from such a sunny girl, he passed her his handkerchief and waited out the storm.

As quickly as she could, she choked back the weeping. "I'm sorry. That was uncalled for, especially after you've been so kind."

"It's not easy being the object of so many suitors' attentions, especially men such as those."

She peeked over the top of his handkerchief, and he could tell by her reddened eyes that she was trying to smile. "You've rescued me twice now, which is probably more than I deserve, and I must proclaim you my hero."

"I think not. I've rescued you both times by damaging your reputation, and I'm afraid the last time rather badly, for I couldn't threaten Mr. Murray as I did Jenour-Redmond."

Dropping the handkerchief, she groped for Harry's hand, grasped it, and raised it to her cheek. "You're modest as well as kind." She kissed his fingertips, then in imitation of his action the previous afternoon, she bit his fingertip.

His body jolted with the little shock of pain, and he watched with absolute astonishment as she swirled her tongue around the abused finger and briefly, with an innocent eroticism that brought him to immediate and desperate need, sucked the tip.

Grasping her shoulders, he swept her to her

feet and into his arms. In the broad light of day, in the middle of the dining hall, he kissed her. Not as he had done the day before, with care for her inexperience, but with all the desperate need of his hungry body and his benighted soul.

She didn't recoil. She didn't complain. She embraced him with all her strength and answered him, taking his tongue within her mouth, allowing him to thrust again and again in a froth of madness and desperation. The delicious scent of her intoxicated him. Her body pressed against his made him vibrate with a boy's eagerness. The way she answered him, with small moans and desperate writhings, gave him the strength of ten men. His manhood rose in reckless urgency, and it seemed as if he must have her, now, today, tonight . . . for always.

But he couldn't. Jessie deserved more than a man torn between his duty to his country and to his family. More than the danger that trailed his every movement. As suddenly as he'd clasped her, he set her away. "Get away from me. I'm not a hero. I'm not who you think I am. You deserve better than me."

She laughed, a clear peal of amusement that dismissed his warning. "Actions speak louder than words." Her cheeks were rosy with excitement. "I have only one suitor left, and he more repulsive than the rest. But I doubt he'll arrive until tomorrow. Will you spend the day with me, Mr. Windberry?"

"No. Absolutely not. We must never be alone together again."

* * *

"I thought I would faint from merriment when that rock gave way and you slipped halfway down the cliff toward the sea." Jessie grinned at Harry, taking the same delight in poking at his dignity as a boy stirring an anthill. "Your arms flailed like a fish's gills."

"Sophisticated of you." Harry crossed his arms over his chest. "The whole incident would never have happened if you hadn't been convinced that that fledgling would fall from its nest."

"It was dangling precariously. When the slope collapsed and the bird flew into your face . . ."

"So apparently the bird *could* take care of itself."

"If you hadn't landed on the path below, you would have skied all the way to the beach on a tide of dirt." She burbled with laughter.

Harry frowned. "You don't need to announce it to the whole inn."

She glanced around the long, candlelit veranda. Insects buzzed around the flames. Outside, the night was rich with stars, the kind of stars that bedazzled with their brilliance. They spangled the sky down to the unseen horizon, then dove below the inky ocean, extinguished by the depths. "There are only two other couples out here, and they don't care a fig what we say or what we do." They didn't, either. One was an old married couple who didn't have a speck of dignity and held hands between courses. The other couple, the maid had whispered, was on their honeymoon. The groom leaned across the table, speaking earnestly. The bride was blushing like a . . . well, like a bride, and she couldn't meet his eyes. "Harry, aren't they sweet?" Jessie had started calling him by his first name that day. One couldn't speak formally to a man whose bottom one had dusted and whose trouser knee one had mended.

Harry didn't even glance at the honeymooning couple. "Sublime." He looked only at her, so intent, she might have been the only woman in the world.

A footman stood by the door to the dining room, ready to serve the guests as needed. The innkeeper brought forth the courses, one by one, filling the night with the scents of rare beef, succulent vegetables, and fabulous desserts. Now they lingered over a cheeseboard and two glasses of wine, listening to the roar of the waves and never wanting this day to end. Or at least . . . Jessie didn't want it to end. She couldn't speak for Harry. As bedtime approached, he grew more and more quiet, more watchful, as he wished for things he could not have.

But he could. She had made up her mind. "I've never had such a lovely day. You don't really care that I laughed at you for falling down the slope, do you?"

"I wouldn't mind . . . if I knew I could get my revenge later."

In a voice as low and seductive as she could make it, she asked, "Is it revenge that you want? Really, Harry? Or is it something else entirely?"

She must not do *seductive* well, for he scowled. "Where's your chaperone?"

"Miss Hendrika? She's asleep."

Harry started to stand. "I'll see you to your room."

"No!" Jessie caught his hand. She'd been as bold with him today as any wanton, and he'd kissed her as if he wanted nothing so much as to take her. And on the cliffs today, she'd caught him watching her, a predatory expression in his marvelous eyes. But tonight . . . he was resisting. If only she could make him stay for a little longer . . . She searched her mind for a topic of conversation. "You never told me why you're here."

He hesitated, then slowly seated himself again. "My mother sent me."

"Your mother?" She knew how to do a conversational tone, and she put her heart into it now. She sounded interested, alert, fascinated.

"I went home to recuperate from an injury—"

"How were you injured?"

Again he hesitated. "It was nothing."

She didn't believe him, but she was not going to chase him off by calling him a liar. Nor would she betray her rather reckless need to comfort him. He didn't seem the type of man who wanted to be cared for, but since the first moment she'd seen him, she'd felt a loneliness about him, a wildness that defied taming, like the wild bird they'd tried to rescue. She thought if she reached out her hands, he would fly away with the same strong, serene soaring that that hawk had shown them. And while she couldn't deny—didn't want to deny—the passion, with him she experienced an affinity of being. They laughed at the same things, they spoke of the same matters, they kissed . . . with an ardent obsession.

"Rather than letting me recover at home, my mother rather forcefully suggested I needed a holiday and arranged for me to come here."

Feeling sorry for him, she said, "Your mother sounds just as eager to have you home as my step-mother is to have me."

"Actually, Mother's quite fond of me and complains I don't visit often enough or for long enough." He frowned as if his mother's behavior puzzled him.

"Perhaps you arrived at a bad moment."

"Perhaps . . ." His attention focused on Jessie once more, his blue eyes gray in the dusk of candlelight.

The illumination put part of his face in shadow, and that seemed right. He seemed a man of shadow to her, someone who, when she turned around, would disappear, never to be seen again. She had to snatch this time with him.

A smile played around his handsome lips. "So. Tomorrow we have our third and last suitor. Will you accept this one?"

"How can I? To marry a stranger, sans affection or desire." She didn't want to talk about the suitor. "If I were courageous, I'd run away."

"Run away? No, not you. You're young and soft."

"I am not soft."

"As butter left in the sun."

She gurgled with laughter. "Nor am I runny."

He smiled, a hard slash of amusement. "It's a hard, cold world out there."

"Hence the need for courage." Picking up a narrow slice of a pale, mild Swiss, she nibbled the edge. "But I know my father. If I ran away, he would never forgive me."

"How would you support yourself?

"Without my fortune, you mean? The usual way that impoverished gentlewomen support themselves. I would become a governess." She smiled woefully. "I wish I could find a way out of my circumscribed life, one that didn't involve a repulsive man, and one that wouldn't completely cut me off from the past."

Harry watched her lips, her teeth, her fingers, so closely, she could only imagine what he was thinking—and she knew what she was thinking. She was thinking that she would not waste herself and her body on a pathetic, unwanted bridegroom. Schooling herself to look and sound sensible, she said, "I do understand, you know. What's involved in mating."

She took his breath away with her combination of boldness and innocence. "It's not every young lady who would confess to that."

"That's because most young ladies *don't* know about mating. They live circumscribed lives, managed by a governess, two parents, and possibly older siblings. My governess left as soon as my father deemed my education finished, my mother is dead, I had no siblings until my stepmother delivered of a son two months ago, and I've done what I liked."

Harry lifted his eyebrows high.

"No, not *that*. I know better than *that*. What I mean is—I run Papa's farm when he's not there. Actually, I run it all the time, but I don't tell him. So I've observed the cows and the sheep." She scowled. "Although I suspect humans go at it differently, for sheep don't kiss."

He was almost faint between the desire to laugh and the desire to . . . just the desire. "No, they don't, and I can safely promise you they don't baa, either."

"Or butt each other." She ran her finger around the rim of her glass. "And from the conversations I've overheard among the servants, I believe mating among humans to be congenial."

He scarcely knew which part of that speech to address. Taking the coward's way out—although he preferred to call it the wise man's—he said, "Overheard?"

"I was hiding in the pantry, eating jellies." She waited as if he would scold her.

He was breathless, trying to keep his unruly body under control.

She straightened her shoulders and used a lecturing tone. "I suppose you'll say it's not right for me to give my maidenhead to a chance-met stranger when I'll be married before the summer's out, but I ask you—why is it right that I should never know the pleasure a man can give me? Never, in the whole of my life?"

He thought he understood her, but he had to ask. "What are you proposing?"

"You kiss very well." She looked him over with an air of mingled defiance and interest. "I presume you do other things well, too."

Wanting her, watching her, imagining her in her bed—that had been gut-wrenching. He had known he could never have her, yet at the same time he'd felt alive as he had not for too many years. Now she offered herself, and the primitive in him surged to the forefront, struggling against the feeble bonds of culture. "I may, but I don't debauch virgins."

"Think of what my life will be, married to someone like Lord Jenour-Redmond or Mr. Murray." She caught his hand.

The warmth of her palm, the clasp of her fingers weakened his resistance. "Perhaps the suitor tomorrow will turn out to be your true love."

"No, he won't. I haven't seen him since I was twelve, but a more self-conscious, righteous prig I never met."

Harry couldn't imagine a man like that with this creature. "Is he wealthy?"

"Very rich. And titled. And old. He is probably ten years older than I am."

Harry didn't like that little whiplash of scorn in her voice. Harry was almost ten years older than she was.

"He disapproved of my every frolic. He was hard, cold, and indifferent, and he grew a stupid little beard, like a goat's, only sparse and blond. I wager he dyed it, for his hair was quite black."

Harry stirred uneasily in his seat. "Where does he live?

"His largest estate is in Somerset. He's by far the worst of all my suitors, and he is . . . Edmund Kennard Henry Chamberlain, Earl of Granville."

Five

*H*arry choked on his drink, coughed. He stared at Jessie, feeling as if she'd buried an ax right between his eyes. His head throbbed, his jaw stood askew.

Jessie anxiously examined him. "Are you all right?"

Taking his first clear breath, he managed, "Edmund Kennard Henry Chamberlain, Earl of Granville?"

"Yes." She looked even more anxious. "Do you know him?"

"Know him? Know him?" He *was* him. But he didn't remember this young lady. He swore he did not.

She took his incoherent amazement as confirmation of her own beliefs. "You *do* know him, and think him as obnoxious as I do."

Obnoxious? Him? He was not . . . He had never

been . . . well, perhaps there was that brief period when he was young, but he didn't remember Jessie.

Yet it was no accident he was here. At the resort. Now. When she was also in residence. Slapping his palms on the table, he placed the blame squarely on the one woman who deserved it. "Damn you, Mother!"

Jessie inched her chair back just a little. "Excuse me?"

The other diners stared, examining him as if he'd quite lost his mind. The young groom looked nervous, as if he knew very well he was unable to fight Harry, yet equally unable, as a gentleman, to stand by when a lady was abused.

As if Harry would ever hurt a hair on Jessie's head. Harry shot the groom a killing glance, and lowered his voice. "You've *met* Lord Granville?"

"I said I had."

"Ten years ago. I doubt you'd recognize him after so long."

Jessie straightened indignantly. "I would so! I'll never forget that scowl. He always stroked his beard, like this"—she did a savage imitation of the younger, pompous Harry—"and he wore a stupid cap. He hadn't a care for his dress, and even came to the dinner table with mud on his boots!"

Harry made a weak clucking sound. Yes, there had been a time . . . but he still didn't remember this lush maiden with lambent passion in her eyes.

"Papa said the young lord had picked up stupid affectations while at school."

He had. "It happens."

Jessie didn't care. "But just last week, when Papa said that Lord Granville was one of my suitors and I reminded him of his disparagement, he claimed Lord Granville was undoubtedly older and wiser now. I don't want to destroy any illusions you may have about your gender, Mr. Windberry"—she called him "Mr. Windberry" again—"but in my experience men do not get wiser, they get more eccentric and spoiled as the years progress." She leaned forward with fire in her eyes. "Until by the time they are forty, they have raging gout and big bellies and false teeth and baseborn mistresses spread halfway across England."

"That's quite an expectation from a simple hat," Harry pointed out feebly. He wished he could somehow justify his early foibles, but they had been nothing but the posturings of a spoiled lad. Jessie had apparently received the brunt of them.

"Granville always hurried off as if he were too important to have anything to do with such a drab as me."

He tried to reply to that, but she was in full sail.

Resting her elbow on the table, she gestured grandly. "All I wanted was a little attention, just someone to think I was pretty instead of a short, pudgy, yellow-haired schoolgirl with spots. How was I supposed to know that that branch would break right when Lord Granville was standing beneath it, and how was I to know he was attempting a seduction of Miss Jones? It was just a broken nose, but the way he carried on you'd think I had ruined a classic countenance, which I assure he did not have!"

Harry stiffened. Now he remembered! At the house party at his estate, to celebrate his successes at Oxford. The little girl, Jessica, had come with her father, and she had mooned after him until he was ready to roar. She followed him everywhere—in the library, on the horses—and he just back from university and believing himself a man of the world. Then, just as he had finally lured the delectable Miss Jones into the apple orchard and taken her into his arms to press an ardent kiss on her luscious lips . . . Jessica had fallen out of the tree above, right between them, and broken his nose.

He took a long breath. He definitely remembered the ramshackle girl Jessie had been.

Looking across the table, he scrutinized the woman she had become. Once again, a little more softly, he said, "Damn you, Mother." For his mother knew him only too well. She had known he would be intrigued by the adult Jessie just as he had been annoyed by the adolescent Jessica. Mother had set the trap well.

Forcibly he brought his attention back to the young lady sitting across from him who confessed in quivering indignation, "He was bleeding into that stupid goatee, and I tried to help him, and he . . . he cursed me. He yelled at me! And told me I was a nasty girl who deserved a hiding. Then Miss Jones, who had been passing him handkerchiefs and cooing in a most nauseating way, got irked with him for talking to me so and escorted me to the house, and Papa took me away—"

"—And you have never seen Lord Granville again."

"No." Jessie shuddered. "Blessedly, I have not. He's always gallivanting about in foreign countries, seeking God knows what kind of dissipations and leaving his poor mother bound to care for his estates and fortune."

"Who told you that?" As if he didn't know.

"His mother."

"You're close?"

"She was so kind as to seek me out."

"Kind." It sounded like agreement. It was not.

"So you can imagine my distress at the thought . . . at the idea . . . at the mere mention of union with the despicable Lord Granville."

"Dreadful." Yet Jessie had kissed him easily enough, and with such fulsome enthusiasm he could scarcely bear not to tell her the truth. "I'm surprised you've borne up so well."

She smiled at him, but her lips were trembling. "I wouldn't have but for you, dearest Harry."

Staring at her grimly, he stroked the bump on his nose. The one he hadn't had until she broke it.

Oblivious, she confessed, "In fact, do you know I have never told anyone the complete story of that humiliating time? Cruel people remind me of it, of course, and Miss Jones is still a most dear friend—"

"That figures," he muttered. Only Jessie could make friends with the female he had so signally failed with.

"—but I've never been able to admit how much I loved Lord Granville and how dreadfully his indifference—indeed, his cruelty—hurt me."

"You really loved him?" Stupid to feel flattered.

"Of course. Why else would I have followed him?"

"Yet you described him as being absurd."

A smile softened her lips. "I like absurdity."

Now there was a compliment to treasure! If ever he had cherished the idea he had not been ridiculous, she had demolished it. When she had fallen, he *had* been a nasty blackguard. Nasty and supercilious and, yes, cruel. He'd had his reasons. His friends had already teased him mercilessly about Jessie's infatuation, and he knew they would give him no quarter about his broken nose. Because of Jessie, he had gone abroad, served his country, learned maturity and responsibility. He should thank her, not scowl at her.

But when he remembered that dreadful house party . . .

Yet when he looked at her now . . . oh, who gave a damn about old dignities trampled? She was beautiful, and engaging, and she offered herself to him. He could keep her safe from his past. He would keep her safe—and ignorant of all the things he had done in the name of patriotism. Taking her hand, he took a ridiculous pleasure in caressing the narrow fingers. "I'm glad you told me. I'm honored you told me."

She looked down at her napkin, then up at him. Her eyes looked damp—and he felt responsible. If he'd been asked yesterday about his own good sense, he would have said he was blessed with more than his share, and Jessie had been blessed with less. But apparently she'd infected him with her madness, for she was crying over a tragedy ten years gone, and he was feeling guilty over the same tragedy. She was a dangerous woman. A most dangerous woman.

"Really?" She clutched her napkin until it resembled a starched, wrinkled ball. "Most men want to run away when a woman reminisces or gets . . . emotional."

"That is the way I feel with most women, but not you. Not with you, my darling Jessie."

She audibly caught her breath. "Does this mean that you would like to . . . I mean, are you saying you would consent to . . . ?"

"There was never any doubt that I would like to . . ." he teased. "And I think your revelations have made it quite necessary that I consent to . . ."

"Good!" Her magnificent bosom swelled against the pink velvet gown. Then she shrank back against her chair. "That is . . . do you know, I have been wanting you to say just that, and now that you have, I'm nervous?"

She caught at his gut, at his heart. He had to have her, and tonight would be the night. Tonight, with no ghosts of the youthful, callous Harry or the childlike, impetuous Jessie. Tomorrow was soon enough for the truth. "Come with me." He helped her to her feet. "And I'll teach you never to be nervous of me."

The stranger stood in the shadows of the inn and watched them pass. He was a nobleman of Russia, welcome in every exalted household, and he had come a long way to wreak vengeance on Lord Granville. At first he had thought he would kidnap Granville's mother. But no. Granville's mother, in all innocence, had given him direction. She confided that she had recently arranged a betrothal for her son to a Lady Jessica Macmillian, and she cheerfully predicted great happiness for the couple.

The stranger could not allow Granville to obtain happiness, large or small. So he had discovered Lady Jessica's whereabouts and traveled to the Wildbriar Inn. There he had taken a single meal in the dining room, and at once heard the buzz of scandal about Lady Jessie—and the buzz of sympathy, too. She had met two of her suitors, dreadful men, and tomorrow the last of the suitors would arrive—the Earl of Granville.

But tonight Lady Jessie was with a man, a Mr. Windberry of Derbyshire. How amusing. Before the stranger killed Granville, he would happily report that Granville's intended bride had cheated on him—and that the charming young lady had painfully died for the sin of being betrothed to the Earl of Granville.

He *would* make Granville suffer.

Six

J essie shivered as they mounted the steps to Harry's cabin. She had irrevocably committed herself, and so he reminded her with the way he guided her, hand at the small of her back. She thought that, for all his usual watchfulness, tonight he scarcely took his gaze off her.

"Cold?" he asked, and his deep, velvet voice caressed her nerve endings and made her shiver again.

"No," she said, although the breeze off the ocean was chilly, and the porch was dark, lit only by candlelight through a window from some room at the back of the cottage. "I'm a little nervous of you."

"You have no reason to be." In the shadows of the porch, he turned her in his arms. "I will never hurt you, Jessie, I vow I will not."

Doubts assailed her. "You're bigger than I am,

lots bigger, and stronger, lots stronger, and in my experience, men have a tendency to use their strength to get their own way."

"You, my darling, have been keeping company with the wrong sort of man."

She peered through the darkness, trying to discern his features, needing the reassurance contained in his blue eyes, for although her heart insisted she could trust Harry, her mind told her to have caution. "I have the right to second thoughts. After all, I'm not only a virgin, but an old maid, too."

"Not so very old." His body shook slightly as if he were laughing at her.

She didn't care. His amusement contained nothing of viciousness or aggression, rather an indulgence that reassured her she had made the right decision. So while it wouldn't do to depend on a man like this, she had no grounds for maidenly trepidation. Tonight was her single chance to experience passion.

In the dim shadows of the porch, she grabbed his lapels, pulled at him—she moved toward him rather than the other way around—and opened her lips on his.

Wrapping his arm around her waist, he allowed her to buffet him with her need. His hand slid up her spine, gentling her. He cupped her head in his hand, his mouth slanted and opened, and he tasted her as if she were a succulent morsel. He held her as if she were precious and dear, and his tenderness drove away her fears and her doubts. This was right.

She didn't know everything about this man,

but she knew the important things. She knew his name, his home, that he hunted in the autumn and drove up to London in the spring. He was a gentleman, a man of her class, and that air of mystery that clung to his rough edges was nothing more than her own imagination. Yet for all the warmth of his embrace and her own self-assurances, when she drew back and looked up at him, she could see nothing but darkness and the gleam of two eyes. She caught her breath and pressed her hands against his chest.

His arms tightened around her. In a voice rough and gravelly, he said, "No, love. There's no turning back now." He kissed her again, his tongue thrust into her mouth, and his kiss possessed her, not gently, but backed by the full weight of his determination.

Her fingers dug into his coat. The darkness pressed against her closed eyelids. As his tongue plunged into her mouth, as his body compelled hers, they were melded into a single entity, one she feared and wanted in equal measure.

Breaking off the kiss, he leaned his forehead against hers. "Will you come with me willingly? Or do I have to carry you?"

Such a suggestion struck her as the perfect compromise. "How romantic! Would you carry me?"

He laughed aloud, the sound amazed. "Over my shoulder like a pirate, or in my arms like a bridegroom?"

Tapping her cheek, she thought about it and decided, "I would enjoy the pirate, but it seems as if that position would be uncomfortable. In your arms, I think."

"As you desire." Sweeping her up, he carried her across the threshold—a matter of some significance, in Jessie's mind—and through the sitting room, stopping every few feet to kiss her again, as if he couldn't bear to be without her for even a moment.

She liked that notion. She liked his kisses. She liked the way he held her, close against his chest. She would like him to be a part of her, for from him she would draw fierceness and courage, two virtues that seemed in short supply these days. Slowly, haltingly, they made their way toward the open door whence light spilled forth, and at last, after another passionate kiss, he bore her through the door of the bedchamber.

The room was plain, containing only a dressing table, a chair, a chest of drawers and a bed hung with netting. The old-fashioned furniture was painted white, and fat candles flickered on every surface, lending the atmosphere a warm and golden glow. Bouquets of purple, orange, and yellow wildflowers stood in vases, and their sweet, spicy scent permeated the air. The covers had been turned back, revealing lacy white sheets and mounds of soft pillows, and a silver tray rested on the tables beside the bed, with an open bottle of wine and two goblets.

Openmouthed with amazement, Jessie stared about her. "Harry, tell me—do you always sleep surrounded by flowers?"

"It's Dehaan's doing. He's a dreamer." Harry sounded resigned as he allowed her to slide to her feet. Removing his coat, he glanced about for somewhere to place it. At last, with a grimace, he tossed it on the floor. "I believe Dehaan had hopes I would bring you back here." Unknotting his cravat, he flung it after the coat, removed his collar and spread his shirt wide at the neck. At last he looked up, and noticed how she stared. Extending a hand to her, he said, "Don't be offended. I never dared imagine the evening would end this way. Dehaan acted completely on his own."

Mute, she nodded, but she didn't take Harry's hand. The candlelight didn't soften him. Instead it showed the edges of his mask, and beneath the mask she caught glimpses of the granite that formed his character. She didn't know this man. She didn't know him at all.

Misunderstanding her trepidation, Harry said, "I'm not the kind of man who makes his amours known."

"No," she whispered. "No, I didn't think you were." He wasn't the kind of man who made anything about himself known. He was an enigma, a puzzle which she didn't yet understand.

But he was handsome and strong. His chin was dark with the shadow of a beard. His neck was corded with muscle. In the vee of his shirt, she could see smooth, brown skin, and near the bottom the faintest hint of curling chest hair. She didn't understand why, but seeing him here, in privacy, with the secret of intimacy surrounding them, made her sure of her decision. Harry was a man in a world of spoiled lads. Harry could be battered by life and withstand its every hardship. In fact, she was sure he already had.

Standing very still, he watched her, hands open

and arms wide. "Have you changed your mind?"

"No. Oh, no."

In a world where all her choices had narrowed down to three, her heart had been captured by the one man she was never supposed to know. He laughed at her and with her, he rescued her from unwelcome suitors—and he obviously adored her breasts. He must; he kept sneaking peeks at them. Yes, he wanted her, yet now, when they were alone in the night with nothing between them except their clothes, he waited on her decision. Again. She didn't know him. She shouldn't trust him. But she loved him.

She loved him.

Her burst of joy couldn't be contained. She gave him a impish grin, a grin that startled him and make him wary in his turn.

The windows were open. The curtains fluttered in the breeze, and this part of the cottage was set high enough above the ground that no evening stroller could accidentally view the proceedings.

Taking a deep breath, she watched as his attention wavered between her face and her bosom. She sashayed toward him. "I haven't changed my mind."

He stood unmoving.

She flirted with her eyes, fluttering her lashes. When she stood close enough to feel his heat, she walked her fingers down his waistcoat, unbuttoning each button with the care of an accomplished valet. "I want this night with you to last me forever."

He cleared his throat. "That's a tall order."

She slid her hands under his shirt, and pressed

her palms against his abdomen. It was firm, and rippled with muscle, and naked. She'd never stroked a man's bare skin. Never experienced the contrast between smooth flesh and the rough growth of hair down his breastbone and along the center of his stomach.

Her lashes drooped as she pressed her palms against him. She savored the heat of his flesh, the rise and fall of his breath. The intent gleam of his blue eyes made her feel quite . . . well . . . aroused. Aroused as she had never been reading romantical novels by candlelight. Her breath hurried and tripped. Her breasts felt as they had when he caressed them. Overly warm and tingling. And between her legs, she was slightly aching. Slightly . . . damp.

"I realize you're new to this, and so I would offer a suggestion. You should remove my trousers."

She gurgled with laughter, then teased him with the honors she would grant him. "Yes, my lord."

His eyebrows winged upward; he stared at her as if she'd said something extraordinary. "What do you mean, calling me that?"

"Would you rather I called you sultan?" Beneath her hands, his taut muscles relaxed. "Or master?" One by one, she twitched the buttons of his trousers free.

"Master. That would fulfill a particular fantasy I've had about you."

Her fingers stopped their journey. "What?"

He smiled down at her breasts, then into her eyes. "I'll tell you some other night."

There wouldn't be another night. They both knew that . . . didn't they?

He watched her through slitted eyes, and she would have sworn the gleam burned as hot as blue coals. To have this man, with his aura of danger, look at her so intently was a lovemaking in itself. With him, she was beautiful and clever and desirable and wanted. Wanted for more than her fortune and her figure, but also for her humor, which most men did not understand, and her smile, which so many considered proved her frivolity. Harry made her feel perfect just the way she was.

As quickly as she could, she finished unbuttoning him.

"Do you have any idea what you're doing?" he demanded.

"Unbuttoning buttons. It's not so difficult."

"Saucy." He slid his arms out of his waistcoat and let it drop.

"I know how to untie a bow, too." She showed him the cord of his drawers. "Watch this." Leisurely, she pulled until his underwear loosened and slid down his hips. His shirt drooped down to his thighs, a sheer, white barrier that hid him and protected her—for the moment.

He placed his hands on her shoulders as if he feared she would run at the fearsome sight of him. "You're in grave danger," he said.

"Am I?" She skimmed her hands down his thighs, assisting the clothing on its fall to the ground. "Am I indeed? What danger is that?" The material tented over his groin in a most intriguing manner. "The danger of being impaled?"

"Yes."

"Of experiencing too much bliss?"

"So I pray."

"So do I, my dear sir, and probably twice as fervently as you." Curiosity and caution warred in her.

Curiosity won.

She urged him to abandon the puddle of his trousers, and when he had, she stepped back and viewed him, standing clad only in his shirt.

His calves were muscled, his thighs defined strength. Slowly she lifted the shirttails, teasing him by drawing out the tension. But her own nerves stretched taut, and she quietly moaned as his manhood came into view. He was large and beautifully formed, with blue veins beneath smooth, pale skin. A purple cap circled the top, and a drop of white liquid eased from the opening.

"You didn't run screaming. A good sign." Satisfaction eased through his voice.

She touched the sac that hung close to the base, using her thumb to seek out the rounded contents, which rolled away from her touch. Sliding one finger up the length of him, she marveled at the satiny skin.

His hands flexed on her shoulders, and when she gazed into his face, his eyes were closed, and he looked like a thirsty man savoring his first sip of water.

Again she was aware of the dampness between her legs, the full sensation in her womb, the desire, so new and yet so familiar. This sensation was more intense than she'd imagined, and with the intensity came a sense of worship, as if the two of them were indulging in some great, primitive rite of mating that united them forever.

Yet there would be no tomorrow.

She drew the shirt upward and over his head. He helped her, wincing when he lifted his arm and eased away his sleeve.

As she dropped the shirt, she swallowed a gasp. For his shoulder bore the scar of a terrible wound. "Harry," she breathed. "What happened?"

"I stood in the wrong place at the wrong time." His brow was lowered, his voice terse.

She caressed the scar, puckered and pink. "You're lucky to be alive." She traced the evidence of each purple stitch. "You must have been in agony."

"It's never agreeable."

An understatement, and one that indicated he had other experience with such agony. She kissed his scar. "Poor Harry, I might never have known you." Her voice thickened at the thought of such deprivation. "You must promise me never to—" A long, thin line across his belly caught her attention. "What did you do here?"

"I . . . fell."

At his odd tone, she glanced up at him and saw the lie. "A knife fight."

"It was a slight wound, done eight years ago."

"Slight? It cut through your clothing!"

"Perhaps I wasn't wearing any," he suggested, but he observed her far too closely.

"A lover? In that case, you would be more cautious with me." Exasperation made her brusque. "What have you been doing with your life, Mr. Windberry?"

"I hunt with a rough crowd."

Indeed he did. Had she thought him a gentleman farmer? She now suspected . . . She didn't know what she suspected, but she knew he needed more affection than any man she'd ever met, and she knew she was the woman to give it to him. Kissing his fingertips, she traced the line from one side of his belly to the other with her lightest touch.

He stroked her cheek with the backs of his fingers, and marveled at the satiny texture of her skin. "You're an extraordinary girl."

"Never forget that." She smiled and circled him, viewing him intently.

What did she think of this body, so battered by violence? Did she believe any of his tales? Did she care? Was she using him for just this one night and imagining she would move on without regrets or anguish . . . and why did the mere idea fill him with rage?

He was such a fool. He wanted her to love him. He was going to do everything in his power to make her love him—before she found out his true identity.

Her gaze warmed his back. The bullet had exited above his shoulder blade, and she found that place and kissed it. Her fingers traced his spine. She cupped the roundness of his buttocks. "You're the finest man I've ever had the pleasure of viewing." She praised him with a wanton's enthusiasm—and a virgin's ineptitude. "Of course, you're the only man I've had the pleasure of viewing naked."

He wanted to laugh, but he couldn't. He didn't dare move, could scarcely draw breath.

If she had experience, she would know enough to be frightened, for he was a man balanced on the sharp edge of control. The urge to take her *now* burned in him.

But he had so carefully cultivated her trust. If he scared her, if he hurt her, she would shy from him . . . and he couldn't bear that. She'd suffered bad experiences with the men in her life. By God, she would never compare him to her other suitors. She would always trust him. He was going to marry her.

And so he trembled in the novelty of having a woman view him from every angle, and stroke him as if touching his skin gave her delight. "Come here," he commanded.

He used his most coaxing tone, but something of his desperation must have sounded in his voice, for she skittered around and viewed him with some suspicion. "Why?"

He spread his hands wide at his side and injected innocence into his tone. "I want to help you discard your clothes."

She relaxed. "I'll wager you do. I'll wager I know why, too."

Now he circled her. The row of tiny pink buttons down her back challenged him as no fight ever had. He wanted to rip them open, tear her clothes away, get to the passion this instant. Instead he freed her one button at a time, and for each button he dropped a tiny kiss on her back. He kept his gaze fixed on the golden skin of her shoulders and spine, for he dared not lean over and watch as her breasts were freed from the constraint of her gown. That would strain his precarious control to the limit. It was difficult enough uncovering her and knowing soon he would have her.

Her head was bent, wisps of her blond hair brushed the tender skin of her neck. He pushed the cap sleeves down her arms, and for a moment, she caught the material and held it before her.

Charmed by her modesty, he murmured in her ear, "Please. Let me see."

She released her grip, and the gown slithered to the floor in a rich pool of velvet. He turned her to face him and saw the plain white chemise, free of all decoration yet made feminine by her form. He saw the color of her flesh beneath the material, the outline of her nipples, the faint mound of the curls between her legs. She was beautiful, a feast for his starving senses, and until he saw her, he hadn't even realized the truth—that he had been wasting away.

She was staring at him, too, staring at his erection as if the reality of her venture had finally hit her.

He bent down until his face was level with her gaze. Her eyes jerked to meet his, and he said, "I'm up here."

Her jaw dropped as she registered the quip that she had so recently used on him, then a lovely smile bloomed on her face, and she answered in his words. "I will endeavor to remember the position of your face in reference to your body."

Wrapping his arm around her waist, he kissed her lips softly, trying to beguile her into believing that he was poised and in control. He must have succeeded, for she sighed and relaxed into him, resting those magnificent breasts against his chest. Her nipples might as well have been red-hot pokers, branding his bare skin. And his erection hardened yet more, prodding at her belly in an inelegant declaration of lust. His patience, such as it was, was unraveling, and he led her toward the bed. "Your slippers are charming, but we can dispense with them."

"I did."

He glanced back to see she'd walked out of them. He took a breath. She was bold. She was shy. She was the epitome of woman to him, and he had her here, now, in his grasp. Lifting her by the waist, he placed her on the high mattress. She sat facing him, her feet dangling over the side. Her legs were long, the chemise rode up to the tops of her thighs. He couldn't resist touching the creamy skin on the inside of her knee and noting the sleek texture of her muscles. She was a strong woman, one who cared for her father's lands and duped unwanted suitors. He had no use for invalids or silly girls, so Jessie was perfect for him.

Perfect for too many men. All her suitors wanted her and not, as she imagined, just for her fortune. They wanted her for this. But she was his.

"Harry?" She sounded cautious. "You look so fierce."

He slid to his knees before her. "I'm feeling fierce." But he kept his voice mild and hoped that she didn't see the primitive force that clawed within him, demanding to be released. Fixing his gaze on her garters, he loosened first one, and then the other. Carefully he rolled the silk stockings down her legs and off the ends of her toes.

Her toes were pointed, and she moved restively. In an abashed voice, she said, "I don't think you ought to be down there because you might—"

He looked up at her. "See?" He *could* see. He could see the froth of her golden curls, and beneath them a hint, an actual hint, of the pink flesh he craved. He wanted to taste her, to see if she melted on his tongue like vanilla ice on a hot day.

"You look like a cannibal." Her heart thudded so hard she thought her chest would burst, but how could she help it? He wore his desire like a savage, with color painted high in his cheeks and muscles knotted across his broad chest.

"What a wonderful idea." He slid his palms up her legs, spreading them as he went.

She whimpered and tried to close them. She didn't understand him. What was he saying? The things she knew about mating did not include a man kissing her inner thigh and working his way up as if he wanted to . . . he desired to . . . be a cannibal. Pulling her bottom to the edge of the bed, he placed his mouth there, at the heart of her dampness.

"Stop!" She tried to push his head away. Then his tongue thrust inside her, and sensation sizzled along her nerve endings and straight to the center of her being. Flinging back her head, she gasped, and gasped again as his tongue lavished sensation inside her. Closing her eyes, she concentrated on each thrust as if only by concentration could she control this turmoil roiling inside her. Yet just when she thought she had achieved control, he withdrew. She still ached with need, but he was done. Thank heavens. Her heart fluttered, and she couldn't believe she had allowed such a thing—or rather, that he had dared to do such a thing.

Was this the way it was between a man and a woman? This wrenching madness that both enticed and demanded? This immodest intimacy, this glorious darkness?

Leaning back on her hands, she looked down at the intent expression on his face, one that pondered and planned—and realized he was *not* done. As he wrapped his arm around one of her legs and lifted it to allow him greater intimacy, she said, without a hope he would listen, "Harry, no."

He didn't listen. Instead he leaned into her and, using his teeth and lips and tongue, found her small, sensitive nub. Tenderly he eased his mouth around it and sucked on it, using his tongue to prod and stroke—and she lost control. She struggled to forbid him, and instead moaned aloud. No longer aware of modesty or propriety, she trembled and moaned. Yet she couldn't let go; it was too odd, too discomforting. Everything was too new. At last he gave a growl. Using the edge of his teeth, he scraped her lightly. So lightly.

As the world shook beneath her, her body took control. She couldn't breathe, she couldn't think, she could only accept the climax that overwhelmed her. Each spasm was mightier than the last, pulling her farther along the path of experience, until when Harry had stopped she was ready . . . for anything.

Dazed and enraptured, she looked at him as he stood between her legs, brown and muscled, magnificent in his nudity. She could scarcely speak, but she managed to say the words that popped into her mind. "I wish you would *hurry*."

His eyes blazed as he gazed down on her, gasping, satisfied, and yet still needy, and still clad in her chemise. "Wrap your legs around me."

She did.

He adjusted her so that their bodies matched. His penis pressed where his tongue had pressed before. He looked into her eyes. "Now. Watch while I make you mine."

She expected great pain. Instead, he moved inside eased by the moisture of her body. She found discomfort, heat, and a return of that odd, distracting, wonderful fullness that led, she now knew, to a grand and glorious release. "Harry," she breathed.

He observed her, as intent on her pleasure as on his own. Or was it possession that made him watch her so? She didn't know. No matter. It was too late. She loved this, the sweat, the effort, the pain, the pleasure. She loved *him*.

Her arms shook as she leaned on them, as she tilted her hips to accept him more easily. He moved forward until . . . he had to pause. To struggle. A sharper pain that made her clutch the sheets in clawed fists. Then he broke through and went on, and when he had sheathed himself to the hilt, she managed to smile up at him and pant, "Very . . . good."

His eyelids drooped, and he almost smiled back. Almost. But it appeared he couldn't quite move his lips in that manner. It appeared he clung to the last shreds of his restraint. "Are you ready?"

Ready for what? She didn't dare ask. She nodded.

Slowly he drew out, the long length of him slipping away. Then he pushed back inside her, filling her again. As he moved, the discomfort of his intrusion faded, to be replaced by another, more urgent discomfort. Her body was making demands.

"Can you feel it?" he whispered. "The pleasure's coming again. But this time it will be more."

"How much more?" Surely she'd experienced everything before. Surely . . . Her legs clutched him as he moved more quickly. Sensation built, filling her, stretching her capacity for control. She whimpered, and moaned, and finally, when she thought she couldn't bear the buffeting of pleasure anymore, another climax swept her away. And as he promised, this time it was more. Reaching up, she wrapped her arms around his shoulders. She muffled her screams in his chest. Her body demanded from him . . . and his body responded. He bent over her, his gaze fixed to hers as he thrust into her, burning her with his heat and his urgency. Lowering her onto the bed, he poured himself into her, and his shout of triumph told her everything she needed to know.

Although he might not realize it, she had given him love, and in that love he had found respite.

When they came to rest, she found she had to try and tell him a little of how she felt. She couldn't declare her love; he wouldn't want that. But she could slide her hands into his hair, bring his mouth to hers, and kiss him deeply, and say, "That was the most glorious moment of my life, from the past or in the future."

A slow smile quirked his lips. "From the past,

yes, but if I were you, I wouldn't be so confident about the future."

Her eyes widened.

He untied the bow at the neck of her chemise. "After all, I haven't yet seen your breasts."

$\mathcal{S}$*even*

$\mathcal{A}$t dawn, as Jessie slid out of the bed, Harry woke. He watched through half-closed eyes as she landed with a thump, and staggered as if her legs weren't functioning correctly. A satisfying notion for a man who had worked most of the midnight hours making sure she was dazed with love and overwhelmed with delight.

Pushing a lush blond curl off her forehead, she looked about. She gathered her gown and chemise off the floor. She found one stocking on the footboard, and after much searching found the other entwined with the bedclothes—and close by his side. Eyes wide, she reached for it. Drew back. Reached for it again. Gathered it in her hand and gradually, gently, drew it toward her.

So she wanted to leave before he could stop her. A notion he found he could not bear. Grasping her wrist, he asked, "Where are you going, love?"

She jumped violently and scattered clothes everywhere. Trying to hold her gown over her nakedness, she stooped to pick up her chemise again. "I . . . um . . . I need to go back to the inn before someone . . . um . . . sees me."

Releasing her, he stood.

She glanced at his nakedness. At his erection. And dropped the chemise again. "Oh, heavens." She carefully didn't look at him again, but he could see the fiery blush that lit her cheeks. "Oh . . . heavens."

Gathering the quilt, he wrapped it around her shoulders and trapped her in his embrace, holding her arms at her sides, cherishing the scent of her hair. "I don't want you to go."

She bent her head and whispered, "It would be best if I did."

"Best for whom?" He nuzzled the sweet, warm nape of her neck.

"I have a suitor arriving today, and my reputation is already well on its way to being destroyed by Mr. Murray." She struggled to sound stoutly brave. "So I should go back."

Harry hated this. To see all the warmth and openness of last night demolished by the advent of daylight. By the twin reminders of duty and fear. He ought to tell her the truth about himself now, but the sun was lightening the sky. Explanations would take time, and might include shouting—hers—when she discovered his identity. Besides, he rather cherished the notion of dressing in his best coat, gathering a bouquet of wildflowers, and coming to court her as the dreaded Edmund Kennard Henry Chamberlain, Earl of Granville.

She would either embrace him or plant him a facer.

He would take care to protect the nose she had already once broken.

So she was right. She needed to get back. Turning her to face him, he leaned down. At first she tried to avoid him, but when he caught her lips with his, she wavered, then answered him with a kiss both gratifying and passionate. Dropping her clothes on their feet, she slid her arms around his bare waist and caressed his backside with fingertips skilled for one so newly initiated. She stood on her tiptoes and pressed her breasts against his chest until all he could feel was the two points of her hard nipples, the soft touch of her lips, and the firm undulation of her hips.

Lifting his head, he gasped for air and grasped for wisdom. This wasn't a seduction. No. She stole his common sense without even trying.

"Harry." She rested her head on his shoulder. "Harry, if you would like—"

A mutual seduction, then. He pleased her as much as she pleased him. Before she could conclude her offer, he said, "You're correct."

She straightened. "I . . . am?"

"Yes." Picking up her chemise, he pulled it over her head. "It would be churlish to treat you with so little respect after you've allowed me to teach you the beginnings of passion."

When her face came through, her eyes were narrowed. "The beginnings of passion? You mean . . . there's more?"

He shook the worst of the wrinkles out of her gown, then lowered his voice to a whisper. "So much more, my darling."

"Oh. My." Her eyes grew wide again, and she considered him in a manner that both flattered and aroused. "When could we . . . ?"

As soon as we wed. But first he had to find that letter from his mother and read it. He expected that would explain everything. "Come on." He helped her into her gown and buttoned the back, then left her to put on her stockings and shoes as he threw on trousers, a shirt, and his boots. By habit, he slipped a knife into his sleeve, but nothing had aroused any suspicion here at tranquil Wildbriar Inn.

Such peace was enough to make a man of his calling very apprehensive, for in his experience that preceded chilling jeopardy.

He held her close to his side as they made their way across the lawn. The birds stirred, making sleepy chirps. From over the hill they could hear the occasional baa of a sheep, but nothing else was awake. Not even the insects buzzed. From habit, Harry scrutinized the windows at the inn. He saw nothing, yet . . . yet the hair lifted on the back of his head. Someone *was* watching them. Probably the chaperone, or a malicious gossip-monger, or even a romantic scullery maid. He could, and would, deal with any of them.

Yet in his experience, the explanation was usually more complex—and more deadly. He touched the knife in his sleeve.

When they arrived at the outer door, Jessie turned to him with a wobbly smile and prepared to dismiss him.

Reaching around her, he turned the knob. "I'll see you inside."

"That's not necessary."

"Yes, it is."

"If someone catches us—"

"They'll keep their mouths shut if they know what's good for them." He entered the inn ahead of her and looked up and down the length of the empty dining hall.

His vehemence seemed to startle her, and she followed him, plucking at his sleeve. "What do you mean?"

"I mean I am not a man to be trifled with." He heard her tiny gasp, swiftly swallowed, and turned on her. "Did you think I was?"

She held her hand over her heart, and she wore a solemn expression, one at odds with her usual merry demeanor. "No, I . . . no, I did suspect you could be a dangerous man."

"But not with you, love." Drawing her close, he tapped her nose. "I would never be a danger to you."

"Of course not." But she still looked troubled. "Are you really . . ." She swallowed. "Are you really a gentleman farmer from Derbyshire?"

"Well . . ." He did have a small estate in Derbyshire, and he could in all honesty assure her that was who he was. But he owed her at least part of the truth. "Let's just say that's not all that I am."

Harry's reassurance hadn't comforted Jessie, but she'd clung to him like a woman in love and fervently kissed him good-bye, and within a few hours she would know all the truth.

In the meantime . . . "Dehaan," he hollered as he entered the cottage overlooking the ocean. "Dehaan, come here!"

Dehaan bustled out of the small serving room at the back. He wasn't grinning; he was too urbane for such a jubilant exhibition, but his eyes gleamed. "Ah, master, after so many years! At last! You're looking happy this morning!"

"Yes, aren't I?" Harry replied dryly. "Where's my mother's letter?"

"Your mother's letter?" Dehaan pulled a long face. "The letter you told me you wished not to read?"

"That's the one. Where is it?"

"You told me not to give it to you. You told me to burn it."

Harry took a menacing step forward. "*Where* is it?"

Dehaan wisely scuttled away. "I will get it for you." He plunged into the dressing room, then plunged out again. "Here." He extended the folded, cream-colored sheets, sealed with wax and marked with the Countess of Granville's ring.

Harry took them with a sigh, and weighed them in his hand.

"Will you dress now, my lord?" Dehaan asked eagerly.

"Yes." Harry broke the seal.

"In your best." Dehaan raced around like a small black beetle on a mission. "Black suit, maroon-striped waistcoat, black boots, sparkling white shirt!"

"Yes, fine." Harry's gaze fell on the first line of the letter. *Dearest, most beloved of sons* . . . Closing his eyes, he groaned. He knew from experience that the more effusive the greeting, the more he was going to hate the contents.

"Let me help you remove your boots," Dehaan instructed, and pulled the scuffed boots from Harry's feet. "Now step out of your trousers."

Harry obeyed without paying a bit of attention. *I have done the thing I should have bestirred myself to do many years ago. I have betrothed you to a lovely young lady.*

"I'll just bet you have," he muttered.

"My lord?" Dehaan hesitated in the act of handing him the crisply pressed black pants.

"Give those to me." Harry impatiently snatched them and donned them without ever releasing his grip on the letter. *You met her once, she's lovely, she's demure and biddable*—so his mother didn't know Jessie at all—*and she has a fortune, all the necessary components of a good wife. She is Lady Jessica Macmillian.*

"Your shirt, my lord, if you please." Dehaan helped Harry ease the rumpled shirt over his injured shoulder and off.

Now you may ask, why did your mother do such a thing without your consent?

Because, my dearest lad, you're showing no signs of settling into the matrimonial harness.

"As if I were a horse to be bred," Harry complained.

This time, Dehaan ignored him and tossed the shirt over Harry's head.

I'm not getting any younger. I'm lonely, living without seeing my only close relative for years at a time—an exaggeration, he'd never been gone above eight months—*and I want grandchildren before I'm too old to dandle them on my knee.* His mother wasn't above playing the guilt card.

Harry allowed Dehaan to button his waistcoat, pin on his collar, and tie his cravat.

"Very elegant, my lord," Dehaan praised. "The young lady will look upon you most favorably."

Harry cast a cold gaze on his valet and wondered if Dehaan had been part of his mother's scheme. Better not to know. Harry was already torn between rage and, unfortunately, amusement. His mother had the gall of a street urchin picking pockets! *So I've sent you to Wildbriar Inn where you'll meet Lady Jessica and court her.*

"Inadvertently," Harry declared.

As he helped Harry into his boots, Dehaan looked worried, quite as if Harry had lost his mind.

Harry read the last, outrageous line of the letter. *So, darling boy, do make up your mind to like the match, for I've already ordered the vicar to call the banns and sent the announcement to the* Times. *You cannot, in all honor, do anything but wed Lady Jessica, on November 8, a mere six weeks from now.*

Resign yourself.

Harry stiffened. Resign himself? He would do no such thing.

Dehaan brushed at the stark, elegant, black jacket. "Let me help you with—"

Harry snatched his coat out of Dehaan's hands and stormed out of the door.

Dehaan hurried after him. "My lord! Don't forget your knife!"

Harry stopped on the top step of the porch. Quivering with impatience, he pointed at the post beside him. The blade whistled through the air and sank into the painted wood not two inches from his finger.

No one was better with a knife than Dehaan.

"Thank you." Freeing the knife, Harry stuck it up his sleeve and resumed his march toward the inn.

The morning light struck him full in the face, but off on the horizon he saw a bank of fog waiting to envelop the landscape. The weather had been almost too perfect for their idyll, but the good weather was over, and with it, any chance of romance.

For no matter what his mother demanded, he was not resigned. He was . . . oh, damn, admit it. He was eager. The night in Jessie's arms had whetted his appetite for a lifetime of passion and laughter and joy. It had been so long since he'd noted the pleasures of life. The sunlight, the flowers, the birds had all been hidden from him, masked by the grim duties of his trade. Jessie showed him a world he had thought he'd left behind, and her uninhibited joyfulness lit the dark corners of his soul.

Feeling like a fool, feeling like a lover, he gathered a single, late, wild rose, the exact color of her nipples, and entered the inn. Outside the dining room, he straightened his cuffs, touched the pin in the center of his cravat, prepared to propose— and confess the truth about who he was.

But when he stepped in the door, he stopped short.

Jessie sat at the same, two-person table she'd occupied the morning before. Just as before, she had her breakfast in front of her, and just as before, a gentleman sat with her. But today . . . today she observed the fellow with a bemused, amazed expression.

With no thought but to renew his claim on her, Harry strode forward and towered over the table. "What is the meaning of this?"

"Oh! Mr. Windberry." Jessie rose to meet him, a delightful young woman clad in the kind of frivolous gown she would wear to gratify her lover. *Him.* "I'm so pleased to see you. You'll never guess who this is."

He certainly wouldn't. The blackguard was a few years younger than Harry; handsome in an open, hale-fellow-well-met manner; well-dressed; and sporting a dark mustache that drooped over a repulsively smiling mouth. He came to his feet eagerly, with every appearance of respect and pleasure at Harry's appearance.

"I haven't the foggiest idea who he could be," Harry said with chilly precision.

As she dropped her linen napkin on the chair, Jessie smiled with blinding delight. "This is my third suitor." She reached a hand across the table to the obnoxiously open-faced knave. "This is Lord Granville."

Eight

*H*arry had the funniest expression on his face, like a skater right after he landed hard on his rump on the ice—but Jessie felt no inclination to laugh.

She couldn't allow Harry to influence her. He hadn't indicated any desire to make an honest woman out of her—well, why should he? she'd been free with her affections without expectation of return—and now Lord Granville had arrived. He had arrived, and he was so much better than she remembered. He was handsome and polite, making no mention of their previous acquaintance. He didn't stink, he didn't smirk, he didn't leer, he didn't bully, and he hadn't tried to kiss her. Yet. If she had to—and it appeared she had to—she could marry this man.

So she had to forget Harry and last night, and pretend an affection for Lord Granville and not shudder at his touch. Although with Harry looming over the top of them and glaring balefully, that could be difficult.

"_You're_ Lord Granville?" Harry peered at Lord Granville.

Although Harry hadn't offered it, Lord Granville grasped his hand and pumped it, a smile wreathing his face. "Yes, Mr. Windberry, I am, and I'm so pleased to meet you. Lady Jessica has been telling me how you defended her from the other, nefarious suitors who have been so crudely courting her."

"Did she?" Harry clipped off the words with a show of white teeth.

What did he mean by such rudeness? She couldn't contain the leap of hope in her bosom. Was he . . . did he feel some affection for her?

Granville began, "I would ask you to sit and dine with us, but—"

"Thank you. I'd be delighted." Harry snatched up a chair from another, unoccupied table and scooted it close. Seating himself, he crowded his knees between the table legs and snapped his fingers at the wide-eyed innkeeper. "I'll be taking breakfast with Lord Granville and Lady Jessica."

The innkeeper bowed and hurried off, and Jessie experienced a sinking feeling in the pit of her stomach.

Head forward, eyes fixed on Lord Granville, and mouth smiling savagely, Harry was the picture of aggression.

Lord Granville seemed oblivious. Casting Jessie a rueful glance, he indicated she should seat herself.

Harry noted and came halfway to his feet

again. "That's right! Ladies sit first! Always forget these niceties! Please, Lady Jessica, sit down."

She sat. She pulled her napkin into her lap. She wondered what in heaven's name had possessed Harry. He was behaving like a yeoman at the squire's table, forgetting his manners, speaking too loudly.

Lord Granville considered the rose Harry held in his hand. "Beautiful flower."

Harry looked down at it as if surprised to see it there. "Yes." He looked about as if needing somewhere to put it, then seated himself again and stuffed the stem into his buttonhole. "So, Granville, where's your country seat?"

Appalled at Harry's insolence, she said, "You know very well it's—"

Harry interrupted. "Let him answer."

Lord Granville seated himself also, and chuckled indulgently. He really was a pleasant-looking man. He had a little too much facial hair for Jessie's taste, but compared to Mr. Murray or Lord Jenour-Redmond, he was a wonderful suitor.

She sneaked a peek at Harry as the innkeeper set a filled plate before him. Compared to Harry . . . but she shouldn't compare Lord Granville to Harry. She should never again look at Harry, or desire would overcome good sense and she'd beg him to love her as she loved him. She had too much pride to beg . . . didn't she?

"My country seat is in Somerset," Lord Granville said. "After Lady Jessica and I have wed, Windberry, perhaps you'll do us the honor of paying us a visit?"

"No!" Jessie said. Both men looked at her. She

essayed a weak smile and pushed the points of toast about her plate with her finger. "I mean . . . we'll want to be alone, surely?" She cringed at Lord Granville's astonished expression.

"But, my dear, I thought that, during your visit at Wildbriar Inn, you and Mr. Windberry had grown to be very close friends."

Did she imagine it, or was there an edge to Lord Granville's voice?

Beneath the table, Harry bumped her knee with his—on purpose.

So he had noted Lord Granville's tone also. Oh, dear. Her impulsiveness had landed her in a terrible jam.

But the next moment, Lord Granville patted her hand. "Don't worry, little bride, we'll have our time alone."

With a grim set to his shoulders, Harry looked out the window. "It looks as if the fog will be closing in soon. The inn is so isolated, I hate to think how long we could be trapped here. Perhaps we should see if we can catch a ride inland."

How odd. From what she'd seen of Harry, very little frightened him, so why was he talking about the fog as if it brought evil in its wake? For all that she'd given her body and her heart into his keeping, she still knew very little about the man.

Heartily, Lord Granville said, "A little fog never hurt anyone, and if we have to stay here for a few extra days, well"—taking her hand, he kissed her fingers—"I can't imagine better company with whom to be trapped."

He really was a fine-looking fellow, with dimples he flashed on every suitable occasion and a charm that would make him easy to face across the breakfast table. She cast a glance at Harry. Harry wasn't nearly as likable, or as easy to get along with, or as handsome. In fact, right now he was looking querulous.

He said, "I hate to imagine what the atmosphere is like here when the fog blankets everything and one can't see his hand in front of his face."

Lord Granville shoved his chair back as if he could no longer bear Harry's timidity. "Lady Jessica, if you would give me a moment of your time?" He presented his hand.

Inwardly cringing, she placed hers in his keeping. Lord Granville had obviously had enough of Harry's irritability.

Drawing her to the corridor outside the dining hall, he looked into her eyes and said, "Pardon me, my dear, for my cheek, but as your future husband I might suggest that you be a little cautious with this fellow Mr. Windberry. He is a very fine fellow"—Lord Granville glanced into the dining hall at Mr. Windberry—"in the height of elegance this morning. Yet he seems to suffer an overabundance of familiarity."

"Yes. Yes, he does presume too much on a day's acquaintance." And a night's. But she kept that thought firmly in her mind and did not allow it to pass her lips.

"Good. We understand each other. You'll wait for me to escort you around the grounds."

"As you wish." She could be submissive when she tried.

"I'll be down in a few minutes. I haven't yet had a chance to unpack, and I wish to dress for the afternoon." Lord Granville's mouth took a scornful twist. "It takes time to achieve an elegance to match Mr. Windberry's."

"Yes." Modestly she lowered her eyes, yet she couldn't help but wonder if Mr. Windberry's newly acquired style was for her. To court her. To make his intentions clear.

Did he indeed have good intentions toward her person? Had last night been more than she dared hope?

"You're a good girl." In a proprietary manner, Lord Granville kissed the air above her forehead and started away.

Recalled to decorum, Jessie rushed into speech. "Perhaps, if you didn't bring your own valet, you could call on Mr. Windberry's valet instead. Dehaan is an artist."

Lord Granville halted in midstep. "Dehaan?"

What was wrong? Why did Lord Granville turn on her, nostrils flared, eyes narrowed? "Yes, Mr. Windberry is not always so cosmopolitan." Oh, dear, that wasn't the right thing to say, either.

A slow, broad smile stretched Lord Granville's lips. "I shall certainly think about using Dehaan. Thank you, my dear. I most certainly shall."

He left her standing in the corridor, staring after him. He was a very odd man.

Returning to the dining room, she found Harry eating his breakfast like a man taking his last meal. Glancing up at her, he said, "Good. You're back. Come on."

"Come on?"

Grasping her hand, he towed her, resisting, out the door.

"Where?"

"To your bedchamber." He towed her out the door and up the stairs. He seemed unafraid they would meet Lord Granville. In fact, he looked forbidding and intent. "I want you to stay there until I come for you."

"Why?"

Giving her a look that forcibly reminded her how little she knew of him, he said, "Because I tell you to."

She didn't care how forbidding he looked. "I do not do what you tell me to."

If her defiance impressed him, he hid it well. "Where's your key?"

"You will not—" Whirling her around, he pinned her, face first, against the wall. His hands groped her, but without passion. He did not take liberties with her body; he sought only her key, and that infuriated her even more. "Mr. Windberry, I seem to have given you the wrong impression. I chose you as a lover. I did not give you permission to command me in any way."

He delved into her pocket and found the key. Palming it, he pushed her irrevocably toward her door, opened it, and forced her inside. Following her in, he shut the door behind them.

"Big, mean, stupid man!" Infuriated by his bullying, she punched his chest hard enough to make him gasp. "Tell me why you're acting this way."

"I only have time for one thing, and an explanation isn't it." He took her head in his hands. He kissed her.

As kisses went, it wasn't his best. It was swift and direct. He opened her mouth to his and dominated her with the heat of his body and the thrust of his tongue. He kissed her cheeks, her eyelids, her neck. He acted as if . . . as if they might never kiss again, and for all that she was furious with him, she responded. How could she not? She loved the man, even if he was an mystery, even if he was arrogant, even if he treated her like a dithering idiot.

"Harry, please," she whispered, "please, tell me what's wrong."

Instead he glanced out the window at the wavering fog. "Stay until I come to get you."

"Get me? For what?"

"We're leaving. Don't pack anything"—his gaze swept her absolutely charming outfit without a fleck of interest—"just wear your traveling clothes. Before you open the door, be sure it's me. If someone comes begging for your help, deny them. If someone shouts the inn is on fire, climb out the window, but not before you see the smoke and feel the flames."

She stared at him, wondering if he'd run mad.

"Promise me." His voice was deep and vibrant with demand.

But no. He was the sanest man she'd ever met. Later she'd demand explanations and make demands. For now . . . "I promise."

He pressed the key into her hand. "Lock it behind me."

She did.

"He went out. He went out." Frank cleared the plates from the dining room and watched Mr. Windberry's advance. "Toward your cottage. Toward your cottage." He whispered the words under his breath, committing them to memory, trying to convince himself they were true.

Mr. Windberry leaned across the table at Frank, and his clear gaze looked different from Lord Granville's—and yet, somehow the same in intent. "Lord Granville is not in his room. It's imperative I speak to him. Do you know where he went?"

"He went out, sir." The crockery rattled in Frank's hands—a betrayal. A confession. "I believe he went out. Toward your cottage." He spoke too quickly. He had not been bred for lying.

"My cottage?" Mr. Windberry looked out the window at the fog. He glanced up the stairway. "*My* cottage?"

"Yes, sir. Your cottage. He left . . . he left ten minutes ago." There. Frank gasped with relief. He had said it all.

"Very well. Thank you." Mr. Windberry moved purposefully toward the door.

Frank put his hand in his pocket, pulled out the guineas, and recognized them for what they were. They were damned coins, and he was damned with them.

Knife in hand, Harry strode stealthily toward his cottage, listening for footsteps muffled by the damp fog, wondering if the supposed Lord Granville was lurking in the fog, waiting to attack. For there could be no doubt; it was Harry he sought. This villain must have tracked Jessie through the betrothal announcement in the *Times* to his mother, and from there to the resort. He planned to take Harry's fiancée captive and use her as bait, and neither Harry nor Jessie would survive such a scheme. Harry needed to get her out tonight.

Beneath the blackguard's British accent, Harry heard the faint meter of the Russian tongue. Harry had had a piece of luck when the fake Lord Granville hadn't recognized the real Lord Granville, and he'd thought he would be able to take the impostor unaware, find out who had sent him and why. But somehow Lord Granville must have discovered the truth. Why else would he have gone to Harry's cottage?

Harry hurried a little faster.

Dehaan was famous in the intelligence community. Dehaan could fight with a knife and advise his attacker on his wardrobe at the same time. He had an uncanny ability to sense trouble, and although many a spy had tried to obtain his services, he was dedicated to Harry. Dehaan always took precautions to warn of intruders, but one thing always distracted Dehaan—romance. And what had Harry been indulging in? Romance.

Blast it. He should have known his habit of evasiveness would catch up with him eventually. If only he'd told Jessie the truth about himself sooner . . . He glanced back at the inn. Jessie would obey him, he felt sure. Last night he had placed on her the bonds of the flesh. She was his. He had made her his.

Harry's lips curved bitterly. Had he imagined he could leave his past behind? Take up his life as before? Take a wife and live happily ever after? This proved that no matter what Harry did, he would be stalked. His past would always remain close at hand, waiting to pounce on all he held dear.

Yet for all his good sense, he didn't know if he could let Jessie go. Not after what they'd shared. His conscience warred with his desire. He adored her as he had never adored a woman before. He had thought he would marry her, for with her sweet love she'd brought him a joy he had never experienced. Now he had to give it up? No. No, it wasn't possible! He'd find a way to keep her.

Reaching the cottage, he circled the exterior. The windows were open, the curtains hung limp. Surely as the fog thickened, Dehaan would have shut them. This was a bad sign. A very bad sign. Harry had chosen this cottage because the ground fell away from the cottage, leaving the windows in the bedchamber high above the ground and relatively safe. Placing his knife in his teeth, Harry leaped up, caught the sill, and silently pulled himself up to peer inside.

The room looked normal. Like a snake, he slithered in, pausing, checking for movement, for ambush. Nothing moved. Once inside, he stood and took the knife in his right hand. Moving along the wall, he listened for the creak of a floorboard, looked for a sign of life. Nothing.

Where was Dehaan?

The door that entered the sitting room was ajar, and with a surge of power, Harry kicked it open. It hit the wall hard, rattling the windowpanes. Still nothing moved, but he saw a body. Dehaan's body, unmoving, stretched out across the table.

Blood covered his face and puddled beneath his cheek. His nose was broken, his eyes were blackened and shut. Dead? No, Harry saw the lift of his breath, and controlled the surge of his rage. The outer door stood open. This room showed the evidence of the fierce struggle. Chairs were overturned, vases shattered, the sofa cushions tossed aside.

Harry sidled across to the smaller bedchamber. No one. To the kitchen. No one. Going at last to his valet, his friend, Harry leaned down to turn him.

Dehaan's eyes sprang open, his hand shot out and he grasped Harry by the throat. Then recognition struck. His hand dropped away. His eyes, so swollen they scarcely opened, slid closed. "I'm sorry," Dehaan whispered. "I saw him too late."

"And I am a fool." *I thought only of protecting Jessie.*

Dehaan echoed Harry's thoughts. "Is Lady Jessica hurt?"

"She's secure." *But I can only protect one person at a time.*

"Good. Better I am harmed than her." Slowly, shaking, Dehaan sat up, touched his battered face, and winced. "He's good. I was careless." He glanced about at the wreck of the room. At the hiding place beneath the sofa cushions where the lockpick kit was visible, at the overturned chair where the knife had once been hidden. "Be wary. He knows who you are."

Harry helped him off the table. In the doorway of the bedchamber, Dehaan's knees collapsed, and Harry was forced to carry him. Because of Harry's past, his strong, annoying, romantic, vigilant valet had been attacked and brutalized.

Harry hoisted him on the bed. "Rest. I'll take care of matters."

Dehaan watched as Harry retrieved a loaded pistol from the dressing room and a small sword from the desk. "Lady Jessica," Dehaan said.

"I'll make sure she's safe." Harry tied a dark cloth around his throat to cover the white of his cravat, tied so precisely and with such hope just an hour ago.

"My lord . . ." Dehaan groaned, for he saw the harsh truth on Harry's face.

"Rest." Harry went swiftly into the fog. He couldn't bear for Jessie's joyous spirit to be exposed to the ugliness of the world. He was part of that ugliness.

After this was over, he would never see her again.

Nine

Jessie paced across to her closet. When Harry came back for her, she must be ready to go. When Harry came back for her . . .

She tried not to wonder where he had gone, how long he would be gone, why he was acting so mysteriously, who he really was . . .

No. No, she couldn't think of those things now. She needed to prepare for . . . for what? Travel, he said. Flight, she guessed. She stripped off the light blue lawn morning dress, and donned her dark wool traveling clothes. She removed her beribboned, satin slippers and laced on her black, ankle-high boots. She pulled on her plain dark bonnet and her sturdy black riding gloves.

After her flurry of activity, she had nothing to do. So she sank down on a chair, picked up her book, and stared blindly at the lines of black letters marching across the white page.

What had happened in the dining room this morning? She didn't understand. Harry hadn't liked Lord Granville, and surely that was good. After all—the letters grew blurry as she remembered—she'd just spent the night in Harry's arms. Which had not ended in a marriage proposal. Not that she wanted or expected one, but—she snapped her attention back to the present. Had she heard something outside the door? Yes, the rustle of petticoats.

Her chaperone rapped on the door. "Jessica, are you in there? Lord Granville is waiting for you on the veranda. He wishes to escort you for a walk."

Jessie remained still, frozen by the memory of Harry's warning.

"Jessica? Remember, your father wants you to get married, and the other two suitors are gone." Miss Hendrika knocked harder. "You must admit, Lord Granville is quite handsome." She thumped at the door. "He is your *last chance*."

Jessie put her hand over her mouth. Lord Granville *was* her last chance. What was she doing?

Miss Hendrika snuffled about, and Jessie imagined her looking in the keyhole, imagined opening the door and having her fall in, imagined her own satisfaction . . . and Harry's displeasure. Jessie hunched her shoulders and sat still, out of the line of sight.

"Where is that girl?" the old woman muttered, and shuffled away.

Jessie thought it was foolish for her heart to pound so hard at the sound of Miss Hendrika's voice. The woman meant her no harm, yet Harry had been so precise in his instructions. Perhaps the one she should be afraid of was Harry.

She rubbed her fingers over her forehead. She was so confused!

What could be wrong with Lord Granville? Her father had sent him as a suitor, and Harry was acting as if Lord Granville were a villain. She stood up. She ought to go down to the veranda right now, place her hand on Lord Granville's arm, and walk with him!

She sank back down. Except she'd promised Harry she would remain in her room, and she wouldn't break her promise.

A single, quiet knock sounded at the door. "Jessie? Come out." Harry's voice.

She rushed to the door, put her hand on the key. Yet he had spooked her. Or perhaps she sought a little revenge for her fright. "How do I know it's really you?" she asked softly.

He had the nerve to sound amused. "I know the location of the mole on your thigh."

Turning the key, she flung back the door. The corridor was empty except for her Harry, grim-faced and intent, yet still she had to say, "Shh!"

With a single glance, he encompassed her change of clothes, and warmed her with a nod of approval. "I won't tell anyone. Do you know how to shoot?"

"No."

"Can you use a knife?"

Irritated, she snapped, "No. But I know how to needlepoint!"

"Very useful if we needed chair covers. You can ride?"

"Like the wind."

"Then we'll ride. Go down the back stairs to the stable." Harry shut her door and locked it, then pocketed the key. "Quietly now."

She went, trusting him like the lovesick fool she was. "Lord Granville is waiting for me on the veranda."

"Good. He's out of the way. Lord Granville is an impostor."

She stopped short, then moved on with Harry's hand in her back. "An impostor? What do you mean, an impostor?"

"Quietly," he warned again as they hurried down the stairs. Before they reached the bottom, he moved in front of her. He looked both ways, then led her out of the stairwell and through the servants' quarters to the outer door. "I mean, I know Lord Granville, and that's not Lord Granville."

Jessie hurried after him, indignation bubbling over—but quietly, as he had instructed. "You know Lord Granville? And you let me discuss him in such a manner?"

Again Harry looked out before he allowed her to descend the stairs to the ground and into the foggy air. "I didn't say I liked him."

Harry sounded slightly ironic, and that infuriated her all the more. "That man on the veranda is *so* Lord Granville. He looks very like him!"

Taking her arm, Harry set a pace that was almost a run. "On Lord Granville's behalf, I am insulted."

She trotted at his side like a faithful dog and wondered if she hated him. "I have never heard anything so outrageous." The mist curled between them, and she could see nothing of the cottages. She could hear nothing but the waves, eternally grinding at the shore. For all she knew, the two of them were alone—and she was in peril. From whom, she didn't know. From Lord Granville, or from Harry? "Where, pray tell, is the real Lord Granville? Are you saying he is such a weasel he couldn't bear to come down to court me himself and so sent an emissary?" An idea that infuriated her.

"Shh," Harry hushed her soothingly. His own voice was deep and calm, pitched to reach her ears and no farther. "Nothing quite so bad. You see, the real Lord Granville didn't know that his mother—"

From inside the inn, she heard the report of a gun. She jumped violently, clutched at Harry. "Wha . . . ? What was that?"

He didn't pause, but pulled her along even more quickly. "It's not good."

Jessie tried to turn back. "Miss Hendrika?"

"She's not worth a bullet. Probably the lock on your door."

"Are you saying he wants to shoot me?"

"Just your door. He wants to take you hostage."

She assimilated that. "Why does Lord Granville—"

Harry shot her a glare.

"What would an impostor want with me?"

As the stable broke through the fog, Harry said, "Damn!"

The door stood open, the damp ground trampled by a dozen hooves. "The horses are gone," she whispered.

"Mischief, indeed." Harry's nostrils were white and pinched.

For the first time, a real chill struck her. This was not a distant gunshot. This was destruction and possibly harm, for the hostler would not have allowed the horses to go without resistance. "Did *he* do this?"

"Unless *he* has an accomplice. All right. We'll walk."

"Where?"

"Where *he* isn't." Harry urged her along the top of the cliffs.

Fear closed in on her. Truth to tell, she hated the fog, clinging so close around them. Yet Harry allowed her no pause. Silent now, he concentrated on their steps, glancing at each stone and bush, stopping and listening.

His silence deepened her dread. She wished she could see or hear *anything*. Then a faint gust of wind touched her cheek, and she breathed in, grateful for the fresh, salt-scented air.

Harry felt his gut tighten. "Damn it again. Our luck didn't hold."

"What luck?" Jessie asked, and she sounded truly puzzled.

The sea, which had so kindly gifted them with the blessed fog, was now whisking it away, tearing at their cover, gradually revealing Harry and Jessie to any watching eye. "What luck, indeed?" he repeated. For not a damned tree or a bit of cover was anywhere in sight. As he glanced up the hill, he saw the inn, then he saw it disappear in a puff of fog. No one had stood on the veranda; the inn might have been empty, but Harry knew the servants must be cowering in their hiding places, frightened by the gunshot. And the villain . . . ah, he was undoubtedly on their trail.

This morning, when Harry had dressed, he'd hoped to propose to her. Now he just wanted to keep her alive.

Turning toward the cliffs, he said, "Softly, now." Just yesterday, he had fallen down the cliff onto a narrow, winding path. It was not visible from above, and the rugged boulders along the way provided cover from any watching eyes on the beach. He would hide Jessie there, then go back and find the so-called Lord Granville.

The first step was long, waist-high on him, and he slid down, then turned and held up his hands.

She peered over and turned a pale green.

"Make haste. I won't let you fall."

"I know that," she said in a peevish tone. Then she took a breath and slithered over. Before them the vista opened up to the horizon. Wisps of fog smudged the ocean. Black boulders pocked the sandy beach below. She said, "This is not a reassuring sight for a gently bred young lady."

"Truth to tell, it's not a reassuring sight to me." If he were alone, he wouldn't think of the danger, but having to protect Jessie . . . yes, he'd made the right decision. He couldn't ever see her again—if they came out of this alive.

"Why are you looking at me like that?" Jessie asked.

He didn't answer. Pressing himself against the wall, he took her hand and led her along. Their feet dislodged bits of gravel, and she pressed herself against the rock as if she could meld with the stone.

"You never told me you were afraid of heights," he murmured.

"I'm not. I'm cautious."

She sounded snappish, and for some reason, that cheered him. "Very wise," he murmured.

"Where are we going?"

Yes, definitely snappish. "To hide you, then go after this Lord Granville." A movement on the beach caught his eye.

The impostor stood on the beach, scanning the cliff with a spyglass.

Harry pushed Jessie down so she was bent double, then pulled her toward the shelter of a large boulder along the path. When they were crouching behind it, he cautiously looked out.

The impostor still surveyed the cliff.

"He's rather casual, isn't he?" Jessie spoke in his ear.

Harry glanced around to see her peeking over his shoulder. "Get down!"

She ducked behind him, but seemed unrepentant. "Can you shoot him?"

"It's too far."

"Can he shoot us?"

"Only if he has a rifle, which he does not. Now, listen. I'm going to have to leave you here."

He was on his knees. She was on her knees. But she faced him without flinching. Her head was tilted, and her wide eyes watched him inquiringly. If she was frightened, she didn't show it, and his heart squeezed with the pain of knowing he must save her today and abandon her tomorrow.

She would face disgrace and ruin, he knew, but better that than death.

Somehow her chin had gotten smudged, and absently he licked his thumb and scrubbed at the mark. "I want you to stay put. No matter what happens, remain here until I come to get you."

She nodded.

"You do trust me to come and get you."

She nodded again.

He couldn't resist. One more time.

One last time.

Wrapping his hand around her neck, he pulled her toward him and kissed her. Her eyelids drooped. Her lips easily parted for him. He thrust his tongue into her mouth, and she sucked at it eagerly. Pulling her against him, he held her close, chest to chest, and the world faded away. For a brief, exultant moment, there was no crashing ocean, no lurking danger. There was only Jessie, and him, and love.

Love.

Tearing himself away from her, he stared into her exquisite face for one agonizing moment. He loved her, and his heart was breaking.

Her eyes widened as he gazed at her, and lifting her hand, she smoothed the hair off his forehead. "What? What is it?"

"Nothing." His voice rasped through a throat tight with anguish. "Stay here." He was off and running, staying low, dodging from boulder to boulder. He got off the path. He worked himself along the cliff into position above the impostor. The impostor still looked up on the cliff with his spyglass, and Harry realized he was searching the very top of the cliff, looking for the place where they had descended. The impostor was too sure of himself; he must have spotted them after the fog cleared. At last he seemed satisfied, and moved a little farther down the beach, closer to the place where Jessie was hidden—and closer to Harry.

Cupping his hand around his mouth, the wretch called, "Lady Jessica, I saw you go over the cliff. I know you're up there. You're frightened. Come, let me care for you."

Harry judged the distance between them. He smiled. He was now close enough to shoot. Kneeling behind a rock, he pulled his pistol free.

"Listen to me. The man you're with . . . he's an impostor."

Harry froze.

"He's not who he says he is. He has a dark past."

True, but not true, and Harry had never wanted to kill someone as much as he wanted to kill this bastard.

The man had a smooth voice that soothed and charmed. "He's a criminal, wanted by the law. A murderer. I fear he'll harm you. Come to me. I'm Lord Granville. You can trust the man your father wants you to marry. I'll protect you."

She wouldn't listen, would she? She didn't have any doubts about Harry, did she? Not since last night. Surely she didn't think he would injure her.

He steadied on the boulder and took aim right at the bastard's heart. He pulled the trigger . . . and nothing happened.

Damn it! He almost flung the pistol on the ground. Damp powder, probably. The mists of England were notorious for ruining shots.

"He let the horses go so you couldn't get away. Think of the poor horses, running free, falling in holes, breaking their legs . . ."

Harry glanced over at Jessie. She watched him, her face solemn. She didn't believe that bastard, did she?

"He's a dangerous man, a villain of stunning treachery. He has a gunshot wound in his shoulder. He's trying to kidnap you so he can threaten me. Come down, darling, I'll protect you."

She stared at Harry for one more moment, then she stood.

"No!" Harry was far enough away and the ground was precarious. He couldn't reach her in time to stop her. "Please. Jessie, no."

She ignored him, fixing her gaze on the faker below, and scooted down the path as quickly as possible. The impostor shouted encouragement.

Grimly, Harry descended with less stealth and more purpose, allowing the impostor to see him.

The blackguard smiled, a repulsive uplift of the lips. "Hurry, darling, so I can protect you." He moved to intercept Jessie.

No matter how much Harry rushed, Jessie had the easier descent. He wanted to shout at her to remember last night, to believe in him, but what was the use? She either trusted him or she didn't. Apparently she didn't. If only he'd been frank with her . . . but he'd learned the habit of secretiveness in a hard school. He'd never imagined it could work against him. And now, right before his eyes, the woman he loved would be killed.

It would be his fault.

As she reached the lower slope, she glanced at

him and seemed to slow. She wound out of sight behind the jagged boulders, and the impostor must have lost sight of her, too, for he dropped the open, earnest mask and donned an expression of fierce intent. He whipped out a pistol and pointed it at Harry. "Don't come any closer," he shouted. "Or you know what I'll do."

Harry loosened the knife in his sleeve and kept coming. It was a race now. Each man moving to catch Jessie and seal his victory over the other. The stranger moved to the place where she should come out.

She didn't.

Instead she appeared from around the edge of the cliff, walking on the sand right toward the impostor.

"No!" Harry shouted, and raised his knife. But he was far away and had no chance of an accurate throw. He might hit Jessie. He slid, landing hard on his rear, rising to hurry again.

The blackguard grinned and strolled toward her, pointing the pistol at her head.

Still walking, she stooped to the ground, rose to her full height, and as he reached out to grasp her, she threw two handfuls of sand in his eyes.

He staggered back, clutching his face and cursing.

Harry made a last, suicidal leap onto the beach and stumbled on the soft ground.

Baring her boot, Jessie kicked the impostor in the knee.

Harry heard the bone and ligaments crack.

The impostor dropped the pistol. He screamed. Clutching his leg, he fell and rolled in agony.

Picking up the gun, she skipped back, looked at Harry, and in that sweet, pleased tone of hers, she said, "You were right. Kicking him in the knee worked awfully well."

Harry wanted to shake her, to shout at her, to make it clear she was never to endanger herself again. Instead he stalked toward her and stripped off his black cravat, then his white one.

"Here?" She lavished a flattering look on the vee of his chest, then glanced around. "Now? Don't you think you ought to tie him up first?"

With a blow of the elbow, Harry knocked the fellow unconscious. "I'm going to tie him up first." He knelt on the villain's spine. "Then I'm going to load you on the first coach and send you home to your father with a note to keep you there until you're no longer a menace to society, which will be never."

She seated herself on a boulder and watched him truss the bastard like a Christmas goose. "Don't be silly. I'm not going."

"Yes, you are."

"No, I'm not. Why should I do what you tell me? You're not my husband. You're only my lover."

Harry's head shot up, and he glared at her.

"And a very exciting lover, too." She placed the pistol on the flat surface beside her. "Give me one reason for me to leave you."

"If you stay with me, you'll be in danger." Standing, he poked at the stranger's body with the toe of his now-scuffed best boot. "From people like this."

"Yes." She gave the body a thoughtful look. "I

can see that would be a problem for a farmer from Derbyshire to be chased by blackguards like this one."

Harry crossed his arms over his chest and did his best to look forbidding.

Apparently Jessie was not impressed. "In fact, when Lord Granville was shouting that you weren't who you said you were, I decided he was telling the truth."

She made him want to snarl—and he did. "If that's what you believe, why didn't you go with him?"

"When two men are telling lies, a woman has to make a decision whom to trust, and for me there was never a doubt. I trust you." The wind tossed tendrils of hair about her delightful face. "I just don't know who you are."

She managed to make him feel foolish, and there weren't very many people who could do that. Taking a breath, he plunged into confession. "I'm the real . . . I'm your real suitor." He held his breath, waiting for her reaction.

Covering her chest with her hand, she gasped, "The real Lord Granville!" Then she dropped the pretense of surprise. "On the path, I wondered if that wasn't the case. The nose looks familiar, like one I might have broken."

He grunted. She had to bring *that* up.

"Lord Granville. Sent by my father and your mother to be my fiancé." Her delectable lips curled derisively. "I wonder why they thought I would have you."

"You've got a wicked tongue."

"So you said last night." She chuckled. "Well,

my Lord Granville, what have you been doing all these years while your poor mother tended your lands?"

He poked morosely at the body on the sand. "Attracting trouble, it seems."

"Making enemies. Getting shot at and stabbed. Watching every word, learning every exit, knowing far too much about escaping a villain. Do you know what *I* think? I think you're a famous thief."

"Of all the ridiculous . . . I am not a famous thief! I'm a spy." And he had never blurted that out in his entire life.

She didn't seem particularly surprised. "On which side?"

"England's."

"Yet a girl has to wonder why you didn't tell me last night."

"I keep secrets well."

She considered him narrowly.

Apparently she wanted more than that. "I was an idiot."

She hopped off the rock and strolled toward him, hips rolling, chin jutted out. "You're still an idiot if you think you're going off on your dangerous adventures without me. You're wearing that faraway, noble expression that says you're going to abandon me."

"Not abandon you."

"Pardon me. Go away and never see me again so I won't be in harm's way." She poked him in the chest with her finger. "Your sense of honor makes me sick. And it's not going to work, because wherever you go, I'll go, too, and if you think I'm in danger in England, wait until you travel to India or Egypt or America. I'll wager there are hundreds of men there who would kidnap me for their love slave."

He broke into a sweat at the very thought. "You are not going to do that."

"You can't stop me. There's only one thing that can stop me."

"Let me hazard a guess. A ring around your finger?"

"More to the point, one around yours. A good, tight one. After all, a wedding ring is supposed to cut off your circulation."

"Assassins," he said incoherently.

"We'll face them together. Surely your other spy friends sometimes marry."

He thought of Throckmorton and Celeste. Of MacLean and Enid. Of their love. Of their devotion. Grudgingly, he admitted, "Sometimes."

"I know you, Harry. You'll protect me. You're my chosen mate."

The way Jessie talked about Harry, the way she looked at him . . . she made him feel impregnable. "I'm leaving the spy business."

"So eventually the assassins will stop. In the meantime, for our honeymoon, you can take me shooting in Scotland. I need to learn how to hit a target."

A honeymoon. She was planning a honeymoon. "This is blackmail."

"Poor Harry," she mocked. "Blackmailed into marriage. Do you mind so much?"

"Perhaps." Taking her by the waist, he looked down into her warm, amber eyes. "Did you choose me because I'm the best of your three suitors?"

She dimpled. "That's not saying much."

Silently, Harry insisted on an answer.

Touching his lips with her fingertips, she said softly, "No, silly. I choose you because I love you. I slept with you because I love you. I want your children . . . because I love you."

Flinging back his head, he laughed the hearty laugh that she had taught him. Picking her up, he swung her in a joyous circle. She shrieked with mirth, and when he set her on her feet again, he wrapped her in his arms and held her, as he would hold her for the rest of her life, and said the words he never thought he could say. "My darling Jessie, I love you, too."

"I need a hero!"

Imagine that you are the heroine
of your favorite romance. You are
resilient; strong; intrepid.
You rule a country, own a business,
or, perhaps, run a drafty country house
on a shoestring budget. You *can* do it *all* . . .
and, usually, you do.

But every now and then a gal needs
some help—someone to vanquish
the enemy soldiers,
keep your business afloat . . .
or just plain offer to keep
the servants in line.

Sometimes you need a hero.

Now, in three spectacular new romances by
Kinley MacGregor, Samantha James and
Christie Ridgway—
and one delicious anthology
by Stephanie Laurens, Christina Dodd
and Elizabeth Boyle—
we meet heroines who can
do it all . . . and the sexy,
irresistible heroes who stand
by their side every step
of the way.

May 2005
Experience the passion of
Kinley MacGregor's

Return of the Warrior

The unforgettable second installment
of the "Brotherhood of the Sword"

Queen Adara has one mission: to find her wayward husband and save their throne! But handsome warrior Christian of Acre doesn't seem to care much about ruling his kingdom; he clearly doesn't even consider himself married! All he wants to do is travel the countryside, helping the poor and downtrodden. But it's Adara who needs his help right now, and she'll do anything—even appear in his bedroom naked and alluring—to get him to rule with her . . . forever.

"Well?" Queen Adara asked in nervous anticipation as her senior advisor drew near her throne.

Xerus had been her father's most trusted man. At almost three score years in age, he still held the sharpness of a man in the prime of his life. His once-black hair was now streaked with gray and his beard was whiter than the stone walls that surrounded their capital city, Garzi.

Since her father's death two years past, Adara had turned

to Xerus for everything. There was no one alive she trusted more, which didn't say much, since, as a queen, her first lesson had been that spies and traitors abounded in her court. Most thought that a woman had no business as the leader of their small kingdom.

Adara had other thoughts on that matter. As her father's only surviving child, she refused to see anyone not of their royal bloodline on this throne. Her family had held the royal seat since before the time of Moses.

No one would take her precious Taagaria from her. Not so long as she breathed.

Xerus shook his head and sighed wearily. "Nay, my queen, they refused to allow you to divorce their king. In their minds you are married and should you try to sever ties to their throne by divorce or annulment they will attack with the sanction of the Church. After all, in their eyes they already own our kingdom. In fact, Selwyn thinks it best that you move into his custody for your own welfare so that they can protect you . . . as their queen."

Adara clenched her fists in frustration.

Xerus glanced over his shoulder toward her two guards who flanked her door before he drew closer to her throne so that he could whisper privately into her ear.

Lutian, her fool, crept nearer to them as well and angled his head so that he wouldn't miss a single word. He even cupped his ear forward.

Xerus glared at the fool.

Dropping his hand, Lutian glared back. A short, lean man, Lutian had straight brown hair and wore a well-trimmed beard. Possessed of average looks, his face was pleasant enough, but it was his kind brown eyes that endeared him to her.

"Speak openly," she said to her advisor. "There is no one I trust more than Lutian."

"He's a half-wit, my queen."

Lutian snorted. "Half-wit, whole-wit, I have enough of them to know to keep silent. So speak, good counselor, and let the queen judge which of the two of us is the greater fool present."

Adara pressed her lips together to keep from smiling at Lutian. Two years younger than she, Lutian had been seriously injured as a youth when he'd tumbled from their walls and landed on his head. Ever since that day, she had watched over him and kept him close lest anyone make his life even more difficult.

She placed a hand on his shoulder to silence him. Xerus couldn't abide being made fun of. Unlike her, he didn't value Lutian's friendship and service.

With a warning glare to the fool, Xerus finally spoke. "Their prince-regent said that if you would finally like to declare Prince Christian dead, then he might be persuaded toward your cause . . . at a price."

Closing her eyes, she ground her teeth furiously. The Elgederion regent had made his position on that matter more than clear. Selwyn wanted her in his son's bed as his bride to secure their tenuous claim to the throne, and the devil would freeze solid before she ever gave herself over to him and allowed those soulless men to rule her people.

How she wished she commanded a larger nation with enough soldiers to pound the arrogant prince-regent into nothing more than a bad memory. Unfortunately, a war would be far too costly to her people and her kingdom. They couldn't fight the Elgederions alone and none of their other allies would help, since to them it was a family squabble between her and her husband's kingdom.

If only her husband would return home and claim his throne, but every time they had sent a man for him, the messenger was slain. To her knowledge none of them had ever reached Christian and she was tired of sending men to their deaths.

Nay, 'twas time to see this matter closed once and for all.

"Send for Thera," she whispered to Xerus.

He scowled at her. "For what purpose?"

"I intend to take a lengthy trip and I can't afford to let anyone know that I am not here to guard my throne."

"Your cousin is not you, Your Grace. Should anyone learn—"

"I trust you alone to keep her and my crown safe until I return. Have her confined to my quarters and tell everyone that I am ill."

Xerus looked even more confused by her orders. "Where are you going?"

"To find my wayward husband and to bring him home."

June 2005
It's a special treat

Hero, Come Back

Three unforgettable original tales
Three amazing storytellers:
Stephanie Laurens, Christina Dodd, Elizabeth Boyle

Imagine, the return of three of the characters you love best—Reggie from Stephanie Laurens's *On a Wild Night* (and *On a Wicked Dawn*)! Jemmy Finch from Elizabeth Boyle's *Once Tempted* (and *It Takes a Hero*)! And Harry Chamberlain, the Earl of Granville, from Christina Dodd's *Lost in Your Arms*!

Now you get to meet them all over again in this delicious anthology of heroes who were just too good *not* to have stories of their own.

Lost and Found
Stephanie Laurens

Releasing Benjamin, Reggie looked at Anne. He'd recognized her soft voice and all notion of politely retreating had vanished. Anne was Amelia's sister-in-law, Luc Ashford's second sister, known to all family and close friends as highly nervous in crowds.

They hadn't met for some years; he suspected she avoided tonnish gatherings. Rapid calculation revealed she must be twenty-six. She seemed . . . perhaps an inch taller, more assured, more definite, certainly more striking than he recalled, but then she wasn't shrinking against any wall at the moment. She was elegantly turned out in a dark green walking dress. Her expression was open, decided, her face framed by lustrous brown hair caught up in a top knot, then allowed to cascade about her head in lush waves. Her eyes were light brown, the color of caramel, large and set under delicately arched brows. Her lips were blush rose, sensuously curved, decidedly vulnerable.

Intensely feminine.

As were the curves of breast and waist revealed by the tightly-fitting bodice . . .

Jerking his mind from the unexpected track, he frowned. "Now cut line—what is this about?"

A frown lit her eyes, a warning one. "I'll explain once we've returned Benjy to the house." Retaking Benjy's hand, she turned back along the path.

Reggie pivoted and fell in beside her. "Which house? Is Luc in town?"

"No. Not Calverton House." Anne hesitated, then added, more softly, "The Foundling House."

Pieces of the puzzle fell, jigsawlike, into place, but the picture in his mind was incomplete. His long strides relaxed, he retook her arm, wound it with his, forcing her to slow. "Much better to stroll without a care, rather than rush off so purposefully. No need for the ignorant to wonder what your purpose is."

The Matchmaker's Bargain
Elizabeth Boyle

"Oh, this cannot be!" Esme said, bounding up from her chair. "I can't get married."

"Whyever not? You aren't already engaged, are you?" Jemmy didn't know why, but for some reason he didn't like the idea of her being another man's betrothed. Besides, what the devil was the fellow thinking, letting such a pretty little chit wander lost about the countryside?

But his concerns about another man in her life were for naught, for she told him very tartly, "I'm not engaged, sir, and I assure you, I'm not destined for marriage."

"I don't see that there is anything is wrong with you," he said without thinking. Demmit, this is what came of living the life of a recluse—he'd forgotten every bit of his town bronze. "I mean to say, it's not like you couldn't be here seeking a husband."

The disbelief on her face struck him to the core.

Was she really so unaware of the pretty picture she presented? That her green eyes, bright and full of sparkles, and soft brown hair, still tumbled from her slumbers and hanging in long tangled curls, was an enticing picture—one that might persuade many a man to get fitted for a pair of leg-shackles.

Even Jemmy found himself susceptible to her charms—she had an air of familiarity about her that whispered of strength and warmth and sensibility, capable of drawing a man toward her like a beggar to a warm hearth.

Not to mention the parts, that as a gentleman, he shouldn't know she possessed, but in their short, albeit rather noteworthy acquaintance, had discovered with the familiarity that one usually had only with a mistress . . . or a hastily gained betrothed.

He shook that idea right out of his head. Whatever was he thinking? She wasn't interested in marriage, and neither was he. Not than any lady *would* have him . . . lame and scarred as he was.

"I hardly see that any of this is your concern," she was saying, once again bustling about the room, gathering up her belongings. She plucked her stockings—gauzy, French sort of things—from the line by the fire.

He could imagine what they would look like on her, and more importantly what it would feel like sliding them off her long, elegant legs.

When she saw him staring at her unmentionables, she blushed and shoved them into her valise. "I really must be away."

The Third Suitor
Christina Dodd

Leaning over the high porch railing, Harry Chamberlain looked down into the flowering shrubbery surrounding his ocean front cottage and asked, "Young woman, what are you doing down there?"

The girl flinched, stopped crawling through the collection of moss, dirt and faded pink blossoms, and turned a smudged face up to his. "Shh." She glanced behind her, as if someone were creeping after her. "I'm trying to avoid one of my suitors."

Harry glanced behind her, too. No one was there.

"Can you see him?" she asked.

"There's not a soul in sight." A smart man would have let her go on her way. Harry was on holiday, a holiday he desperately needed, and he had vowed to avoid trouble at all costs. Now a girl of perhaps eighteen years, dressed in a modish blue flowered gown, came crawling through the bushes, armed with nothing more than a ridiculous tale, and he was tempted to help. Tempted because of a thin, tanned face, wide brown eyes, a kissable mouth, a crooked blue bonnet and, from this angle, the finest pair of breasts he'd ever had the good fortune to gaze upon.

Such unruliness in his own character surprised him. He was, in truth, Edmund Kennard Henry Chamberlain, earl of Granville, the owner of a great estate in Somerset, and because of the weight of his responsibilities there, and the additional responsibilities he had taken on, he tended to do his duty without capriciousness. Indeed, it was that trait which had set him, eight years ago, to serve England in various countries and capacities. Now he gazed at a female intent on some silliness and discovered in himself the urge to find out more about her. Perhaps he had at last relaxed from the tension of his last job. Or perhaps she *was* the relaxation he sought.

In a trembling voice, she pleaded, "Please, sir, if he appears, don't tell him I'm here."

"I wouldn't dream of interfering."

"Oh, thank you!" A smile transformed that quivering mouth into one that was naturally merry, with soft peach lips and a dimple. "Because I thought that's what you were doing."

July 2005
Be swept away by the
passion of Samantha James's

A Perfect Hero

The third in her Sterling Family trilogy

When Lady Julianna Sterling is left standing at the altar, she heaves a sigh and reminds herself that the Sterlings never had much luck. But one fateful night, Julianna's luck changes in a most unexpected way, and her staid, steady life is turned upside down. Her coach is attacked by the Magpie—a mysterious and enticing highwayman who audaciously kidnaps her, plunging Julianna into a life of seductive excitement.

Julianna felt herself tumbling to the floor. Jarred into wakefulness, she opened her eyes, rubbing her shoulder where she'd landed. What the deuce . . . ? Panic enveloped her; it was pitch black inside the coach.

And outside as well.

She was just about to heave herself back onto the cushions when the sound of male voices punctuated the air outside. The coachman . . . and someone else.

"Put it down, I s-say!" the coachman stuttered. "There's nothing of value aboard, I swear! Mercy," the man blubbered. "I beg of you, have mercy!"

Even as a decidedly prickly unease slid down her spine, the door was wrenched open. She found herself staring at the gleaming barrel of a pistol. In terror she lifted her gaze to the man who possessed it.

Garbed in black he was, from the enveloping folds of his cloak to the kerchief that obscured the lower half of his face. A silk mask was tied around his eyes; they were all that was visible of his features. Even in the dark, there was no mistaking their color. They glimmered like clear golden fire, pale and unearthly.

The devil's eyes.

"Nothing of value aboard, eh?"

A gust of chill night air funneled in. Yet it was like nothing compared to the chill she felt in hearing that voice . . . So softly querulous, like steel tearing through tightly stretched silk, she decided dazedly.

She had always despised silly, weak, helpless females. Yet when his gaze raked over her—*through* her, bold and ever so irreverent!—she felt stripped to the bone.

Goose bumps rose on her flesh. She couldn't move. She most certainly couldn't speak. She could not even swallow past the knot lodged deep in her throat. Fear numbed her mind. Her mouth was dry with a sickly dread such as she had never experienced. All she could think was that if Mrs. Chadwick were here, she might take great delight in knowing she'd been right to be so fearful. For somehow Julianna knew with a mind-chilling certainty that it was he . . .

The Magpie.

Dane Quincy Granville did not count on the coachman's reaction—nor his rashness. There was a crack of the whip, a frenzied shout. The horses bolted. Instinctively, Dane leaped back, very nearly knocked to the ground. The vehicle jolted forward, speeding toward a bend in the road.

The stupid fool! Christ, the coachman would never make the turn. The bend was too sharp. He was going too fast—

The night exploded. There was an excruciating crash, the sound of wood splintering and cracking . . . the high-pitched neighs of the horses.

Then there was nothing.

Galvanized into action, Dane sprang for Percival. Leaping from the stallion's back, he hurtled himself down the steep embankment where the coach had disappeared. Scrambling over the brush, he spied it. It was overturned, resting against the trunk of an ancient tree.

One wheel was still spinning as he reached it.

The horses were already gone. So was the driver. His neck was broken, twisted at an odd angle from his body. Dane had seen enough of death to know there was nothing he could do to help him.

Miraculously, the door to the main compartment had remained on its hinges. In fury and fear, Dane tore it off and lunged into the compartment.

The girl was still inside, coiled in a heap on the roof. His heart in his throat, he reached for her, easing her into his arms and outside.

His heart pounding, he knelt in the damp earth and stared down at her. "Wake up!" he commanded. As if because he willed it, as if it would be so . . . He gritted his teeth, as if to instill his very will—his very life—inside her.

Her head fell limply over his arm.

"Dammit, girl, wake up!"

He was sick in the pit of his belly, in his very soul. If only the driver hadn't been so blasted skittish. So hasty! He wouldn't have harmed them, either of them. On a field near Brussels, he'd seen enough death and dying to last a lifetime. God knew it had changed him. Shaped him for all eternity. And for now, all he wanted was—

She moaned.

An odd little laugh broke from his chest, the sound almost brittle. After all his careful planning that *this* should occur . . . But he couldn't ascertain her injuries. Not here. Not in the dark. He must leave. Now. He couldn't afford to linger, else all might be for naught.

The girl did not wake as he rifled through the boot, retrieving a bulging sack and a valise. Seconds later, he whistled for Percival. Cradling the girl carefully against his chest, he lifted the reins and rode into the night.

As suddenly as he had appeared, the Magpie was gone.

August 2005
We're going to make you
an offer you can't refuse in
Christie Ridgway's

An Offer He Can't Refuse

The first in her delicious new Wisegirls series

Téa Caruso knows what everyone thinks about her
family . . . her very large, very powerful family. After
all, she grew up in the shadow of her grandfather—
The Sun Dried Tomato King—and her uncles, with
their mysterious "business." And, of course, there
are her aunts, who don't ask too many questions.
She's spent a lifetime going legit, and now her past
comes back to haunt her when she falls for John
Magee. He's a professional gambler, the worse kind
of man, one who'd make the family proud . . . or
is he?

Téa Caruso had once been very, very bad and she wondered
if today was the day she started paying for it. After spending the morning closeted in the perfume-saturated powder
room of Mr. and Mrs. William Duncan's Spanish-Italian-
Renaissance-inspired Palm Springs home, discussing baby
Jesus and the Holy Mother, she emerged from the clouds—
both heavenly and olfactory—with a Chanel No. 5 hangover

and fingernail creases in her palms as deep as the Duncan's quarter-mile lap pool.

Standing on the pillowed limestone terrace outside, she allowed herself a sixty-second pause for fresh air, but multitasked the moment by completing a quick appearance check as well. Even someone with less artistic training than Téa would know that her Mediterranean coloring and generous curves were made for low necklines and sassy flounces in gypsy shades, but her Mandarin-collared, dove gray linen dress was devised to button up, smooth out, and tuck away. Though she could never feel innocent, she preferred to at least look that way.

The reflection in her hand mirror presented no jarring surprises. The sun lent an apricot cast to her olive skin. Tilted brown eyes, a slightly patrician nose, cheekbones and jawline now defined after years of counting calories instead of chowing down on cookies. Assured that her buttons were tight, her mascara unsmudged, and her hair still controlled in its long, dark sweep, she snapped the compact shut. Then, hurrying in the direction of her car, she swapped mirror for cell phone and speed dialed her interior design firm.

"She's still insisting on Him," she told her assistant when she answered. "Find out who can hand paint a Rembrandt-styled infant Jesus in the bottom of a porcelain sink."

Glancing over at the Madonna blue water of the pool, Téa was reminded of the morning's single success. "The good news is I talked her out of the Virgin Mary in the bidet bowl." Surely the Mother of God would appreciate that fact.

Still on forward march, she checked her watch. "Quick, any messages? I have lunch with my sisters up next."

"Nikki O'Neal phoned and mentioned a redo of her dining room," her assistant replied. "Something about a mural depicting the Ascension."

The Ascension?

Téa's steps faltered, slowed. "No," she groaned. "That means Mrs. D. has spilled her plans. Now we'll be hearing from every one of her group at Our Lady of Mink."

A segment of Téa's client list—members of the St. Brigit's Guild at the posh Our Lady of Mercy Catholic Church—cultivated their competitive spirits as well as their Holy Spirit during their weekly meetings. One woman would share a new idea for home decor, prompting the next to take the same theme to even greater—more ostentatious—heights.

Three years before it had been everything vineyard, then after that sea life turned all the rage, and now . . . good God.

"The *Ascension*?" Téa muttered. "These women must be out of their minds."

But could she really blame them? Palm Springs had a grand tradition of the grandiose, after all. Walt Disney had owned a home here. Elvis. Liberace.

It was just that when she'd opened her business, filled with high artistic aspirations and a zealous determination to make over the notorious Caruso name, she hadn't foreseen the pitfalls. Like how the ceaseless influx of rent and utility bills and the unsteady trickle and occasional torrent that was her cash flow meant she couldn't be picky when it came to choosing design jobs.

Like how *that* could result in gaining woeful renown as designer of all things overdone. She groaned again.

"Oh, and Téa . . ." Her assistant's voice rose in an expectant lilt. "His Huskiness called."

Her stomach lurched, pity party forgotten. "What? *Who*?"

"Johnny Magee."

Of course, Johnny Magee. Her assistant referred to the man they'd never met by an ever-expanding lexicon of nicknames that ranged from the overrated to the out-and-out ridiculous. To Téa, he was simply her One Chance, her Answered Prayers, her Belief in Miracles.